A Magical

Jennifer Joyce lives in Manchester with her daughters. She's been scribbling down stories for as long as she can remember, graduating from a pen to a typewriter and then an electronic typewriter. And she felt like the bee's knees typing on THAT. She now writes her books on a laptop (which has a proper delete button and everything).

Also by Jennifer Joyce

The Grown Up To-Do List
A Magical New Year's Kiss

JENNIFER JOYCE

A Magical New Year's Kiss

hera

First published in the United Kingdom in 2025 by

Hera Books, an imprint of
Canelo Digital Publishing Limited,
20 Vauxhall Bridge Road,
London SW1V 2SA
United Kingdom

A Penguin Random House Company
The authorised representative in the EEA is Dorling Kindersley Verlag GmbH.
Arnulfstr. 124, 80636 Munich, Germany

A CIP catalogue record for this book is available from the British Library.

Print ISBN 978 1 80436 855 8
Ebook ISBN 978 1 80436 857 2

Printed and bound in Great Britain by Clays Ltd, Elcograf S.p.A.

Look for more great books at
www.herabooks.com | www.dk.com

I

For Luna.

How could I love you more?

Chapter One

I've had some terrible dates lately. Like, cringe-so-hard-you-turn-yourself-inside-out-three-months-later terrible. But this one is hands down the most terrible of them all. I will still be cringing over this date in years to come, even when I'm in a nursing home, sitting in a winged-back chair in the communal lounge while we all stare at ancient repeats of *Homes Under the Hammer* on a wall-mounted TV. This date really is that bad. I should have walked out when my date greeted me by pressing his lips to the back of my hand with a 'it's so nice to meet you, Gabriella'. Which isn't *that* bad, I guess, except my name isn't Gabriella. Not even close.

'It's Daisy.' I'd laughed, to show that I wasn't uptight. That I understood people make mistakes. And it was an easy mistake to make if you were on the dating treadmill. This was my third date this week (if you counted the first, who didn't show up and had blocked me on the *Love Today* app by the time I skulked home) so I wasn't too put off by the blunder.

'It's nice to meet you too, Dean.' Dean was definitely his name. I was confident of the fact because my best friend had pointed out how cute 'Daisy and Dean' sounded while she was giving me a pep talk half an hour earlier, but my date was giving me an odd look, his eyebrows pinched together and his lips scrunched up on one side. Perhaps he wasn't called Dean after all.

'You look… different… from your profile pic.'

'Do I?' I laughed again. It was an involuntary sound. More of a nervous splutter than a reaction to amusement.

'It's a bit misleading, the pic on the app.'

'Is it?' Okay, so the photo had been taken on a good day, when the sun was shining and I was sun-kissed and glowing from the inside as well as the outside, and maybe it was cheating a little bit as I'd had my make-up done by a professional, but there'd been no tinkering with the photo after it had been taken. It was me, one hundred per cent. Just the best version of me that was humanly possible.

'But it's fine.' Dean's face relaxed, his eyebrows returning to their natural position. 'It's no big deal, honestly. I'm not saying you're hideous in real life. Or fat. Not at all. Just… different. You really do look stunning in your profile pic.'

I should have walked away then. But I didn't. I allowed myself to be led to a table towards the back of the restaurant, where the exit was too far away for my liking, and I sat and listened to Dean as he talked at me, telling me about his job as an estate agent and his plans to get into property development and retire before he hit forty. I hadn't managed to get a word in all through the starter, not even when Dean asked if I was *absolutely sure* I wanted a starter, even though he'd just ordered salt and pepper squid for himself. But finally, as our main course was placed in front of us, Dean finally shut up going on about himself.

'So, Gabriella.' He picked up his knife and fork and attacked his steak. 'How's your day been?'

'It's Daisy.'

2

He paused the hacking of his steak to look over each shoulder in turn. 'Who's Daisy?'

'I am.'

'Eh?' His eyebrows pinched together again.

'I'm Daisy. Not Gabriella.'

He pulled his chin back. He rummaged in his trouser pocket and pulled out his phone. He tapped on the screen a few times and then his eyebrows lifted.

'So you are! Why didn't you say so before?' He shook his head and tutted. 'You've made me look like a right tool. So, *Daisy*.' He resumed his sawing of his steak but eyed me across the table with slightly narrowed eyes. 'You're not very chatty, are you? You were much more responsive on the app. I didn't think I'd be dating a mouse. Come on, tell me about yourself. What do you do?' He shoved a chunk of steak in his mouth and chewed with his mouth open.

'I work in a factory. We make biscuits.'

'A factory?' A fleck of steak catapulted from Dean's mouth and pinged against my wine glass. 'But you don't work on the shop floor? You're, like, in accounts or HR or something?'

I'd speared a prawn on my fork, but I didn't pop it into my mouth. I wouldn't talk and chew like my dinner date. 'No, I'm right there on the production line, hand-finishing the biscuits.'

Dean scrunched up his nose. 'Like tossing sprinkles on top?'

'Like delicate piping work. All freehand. Very artistic. They're high-end, luxury biscuits, not your bog-standard packet of digestives. They're beautiful, actually, and presented in decorative tins or gift boxes and hampers.'

'And you're happy making biscuits in a factory? You don't want an actual career?'

I looked down at the prawn still speared on my fork and wished it was Dean's eyeball stuck on there instead.

'I do have plans to progress actually. I had an interview this morning for a promotion.' It had gone almost as badly as this date was going, but Dean didn't need to know that I'd accidentally knocked my boss's water over his interview notes or that I'd had a complete mind block midway through and simply stared at him with my mouth goldfishing away.

Dean snorted. 'What's the promotion for? Boxing up the biscuits? Driving the delivery lorry?'

Dean, I concluded, was an absolute wanker and I didn't want to spend another second more than necessary with him. Spearing as many prawns onto my fork as possible to create a mini kebab, I dispatched them into my mouth and, cheeks bulging, rose from my seat, snatched up my jacket and handbag from the back of my chair, threw enough cash down to cover my share of the disastrous dinner, and snaked my way through the other tables to the exit.

'That's it. I'm done with dating.'

It's still light outside but it's chilly and I wish I hadn't been so quick to put away my big coat as spring approached. The flimsy jacket I've shoved my arms through is doing nothing to ward off the bite in the air as I march away from the restaurant. My phone is pressed against my ear as I turn to glance backwards. Thankfully, Dean hasn't given chase.

'Oh, babe. What happened? Do you need me to come down there and karate chop his nuts off?'

I smile, despite the churning disappointment in my stomach. Jesy can always cheer me up, even when I've reached my limit of dating dickheads.

'No nut removal necessary. I've walked out. Left him shovelling steak in his stupid gob.' I twist to double check he hasn't followed, but the only other person on this side of the street is a woman laden down with carrier bags. 'This was a bad one, Jesy. Really bad.'

'It can't have been as bad as the fireman who accident-ally flashed you a photo of his trouser hose while trying to show you a pic of his kitten.'

'True, that wasn't what I was expecting on a first date. We only met up for coffee.' I stop at the kerb, checking for traffic before crossing. 'But this was worse. He basically said I looked like a fat troll compared to my profile picture, talked non-stop about himself for ages, scoffed at my job and called me Gabriella even after I'd corrected him. *And* he chews with his mouth open.'

'Gross.'

'Very. He is not for me.' I turn the corner and head for the bus stop. I could get a taxi home – it'd be much quicker and quieter – but I don't want to throw any more money at this date. 'I don't think anyone is, to be honest.'

'Rubbish.' Jesy sounds almost cross. Almost, because she just doesn't have it in her to be anything but the upbeat, joy-filled angel that she is. Even when she's offering to detach my date's testicles from his body, she sounds cheery. 'The right man is out there for you. You just haven't found him yet.'

'But I'm tired of looking.' I heave in a breath and puff it out. 'You're so lucky to have found Ant, to have found the man you're going to marry. You don't have to go through these endless rounds of dating. You don't have to gear yourself up to meet another guy. To fill yourself up with hope only to have disappointment dumped on you as soon as you've said hello.'

'Don't give up. He's out there, Daisy. I promise.'

I reach the bus stop and lean against the shelter, eyes trained on the road ahead. 'I wish I believed that, but I don't. I can't see me ever finding The One. I'm destined to be alone.'

'No.' Jesy's tone is firm. 'You are not. You *are* going to meet The One. Maybe not tonight, though. Tonight, you're going to meet me and Callum at Clementine's and we're going to get very drunk even though it's a school night.'

I smile again, because getting drunk with my two best friends in our favourite bar sounds like the most marvellous plan, the perfect antidote to my disastrous date with Dean.

'I'm on my way.' I push myself away from the shelter's wall as the bus comes into view. 'I'll be there in twenty.'

—

Jesy, Callum and I claimed Clementine's as our favourite bar back when we were at college for three very important reasons: it was a short walk from where we lived, meaning no wasted money on buses or taxis, they served cheap cocktails from seven until nine p.m. and they never asked for ID. Being in our mid-twenties now, we no longer require ID, but Clementine's is still a massive part of our lives. It's where we go to celebrate or commiserate or to simply get blind drunk on those cheap cocktails, and I feel a little jolt of pure happiness when I spot the neon-yellow sign above the door. My step quickens in my eagerness to get inside to meet up with my friends and sink a Raspberry Beret cocktail. Clementine's is a riot of colour, with a bar painted a vibrant mustard-yellow taking up the left-hand wall of the vast space and vintage posters and neon lights decorating the walls. The seating is a mix of comfy sofas in shades of pinks, blues and greens, and American diner-style rows of booths. It's usually pretty quiet on a Wednesday so I'm taken aback by the blast of noise as I push the door open. And it isn't just the music that rushes at me, which is unusual as live acts aren't normally a midweek thing at Clementine's, but the general vibe of the place. Clementine's is *alive*, with chatter and laughter and a riotous energy pulsing through the building. Instead of a few customers dotted around the bar as I'd expected, the place is *heaving*.

My eye is drawn to the right-hand corner of the bar, towards the stage, where there's a man dressed in a sequinned jacket and huge star-shaped sunglasses sat in front of a piano as he belts out Elton John's 'Crocodile Rock'. Above him is a string of glittery red-and-gold bunting, spelling out 'Happy New Year!' and the people singing and dancing along in front of him are wearing party hats and waving balloons in the air.

My eyes flick to the bar, where I spot Jesy perched on a high stool. Jesy raises a hand and clambers off the stool, and I notice her stomach. Her very large, very round, very *pregnant* stomach.

What. The. Heck.

Jesy isn't pregnant. At least she wasn't the last time I saw her *a couple of hours ago*. But she looks as though she's about to pop, her dress straining over the newly formed bump. But that isn't even the strangest thing. The strangest thing is beside me, holding my hand. I haven't entered Clementine's alone. I am holding the hand of a tall man. A super-handsome tall man with brown hair and stubble across his jaw, and when he looks down at me and offers a smile, I almost melt into a puddle on Clementine's tiled floor.

Who are you, I'm dying to ask but the words won't come out. *Where did you come from?*

I look across at Jesy again, to see if she's clocked the hot bloke I've bagged out of nowhere. Jesy is waving her hand above her head now and I realise I'm playing with the pendant of my necklace with the hand that isn't clutching hold of the hot guy. I drop the pendant so I can wave back at Jesy, who starts to make her way towards us. I sneak a peek at the hot guy again, to make sure he's still there, and he's looking down at his watch. Weird. I don't know anyone who wears an actual watch these days – what's the point when you can check the time on your phone? – and this one is even more strange because it's old and broken, with a crack across its face.

'It's almost midnight.' His voice is muffled against the roar of the party playing out in front of us. 'Nearly a new year.' He says something else, but I don't quite catch it as 'Crocodile Rock' has reached the chorus and the crowd goes wild. I spot Callum across the room, but I'm distracted when the hot guy stoops to kiss my cheek and I feel an intense rush of love that makes my knees turn to jelly and it takes all my effort to remain upright. I don't know who this man is, but I know with every single cell in my body that I am utterly, head-over-heels in love with him. The realisation tips me over the edge and I stumble to the side, and when I manage to right myself, the party scene before me has disappeared. The stage is empty. The glittery banner is gone, along with the performer and the revellers. And the hot guy. I'm standing in an almost empty, almost silent Clementine's, as Jesy and Callum make their way towards me.

'Daisy? Are you okay?' Jesy – with no hint of a bump whatsoever – reaches out to touch my arm. 'You spaced out for a moment then.'

'Was the date really that bad?' Callum slings his arm around my shoulders and gives me a squeeze. 'Come on, let's get you drunk.'

'That was so weird.' My steps are careful as I let my friends lead me to the bar.

'Jesy told me all about him.' Callum gives me another squeeze. 'He sounds like a right tosser.'

'No.' I shake my head. 'He wasn't a tosser. I think he's The One. I really, truly do.'

'You think Dean's The One?' Jesy guides me to a stool and practically lifts me up onto it by the armpits as I'm still too dazed to function properly. 'The guy who insulted you? And couldn't even get your name right? And who eats like a pig?'

I shake my head again. 'Not him. The other guy.'

'There was another guy?' Jesy hops up onto the stool next to mine and I remember how ungainly she'd slipped down off it only a few moments ago with a humongous baby bump.

'He wasn't real.'

My friends share a look: eyebrows raised, wide eyes flicking to me before meeting again.

'It was so weird. When I opened the door just now, this place was packed. It was all set up like New Year's Eve. You guys were here and so was he.'

'He?' Jesy's talking to me, but her eyes are on Callum. They think I'm mad. I probably am.

'This really, *really* handsome bloke. I was holding his hand. He kissed me on the cheek and I felt it. I was in love.' I shake my head to get rid of the image. 'But it wasn't real. Obviously.'

'Obviously.' Callum places a hand on my shoulder, his skin barely making contact in case he breaks me.

'But it *felt* real. Like when you get deja-vu. Except it wasn't something I'd experienced before. It was new. Like I was glimpsing the future.'

Callum nudges me, but ever so gently. 'Deja-*new*.'

'Yeah.' My shoulders slump. It *felt* so real, but it *wasn't*. It isn't fair. I've never felt like that before, never knew that was what real love feels like, but it's like a drug and I'm hooked and hungry for more.

Jesy reaches out and takes my hands in hers. 'Maybe this is a sign that your dream man is about to walk into your life and sweep you off your feet.'

'Or maybe it's a sign that serial dating is sending me crazy.' I'm already coming down from the love drug and having to face up to bleak reality. 'Maybe it's a sign that I should stop dating and accept the fact that I'm destined to end up alone.'

Chapter Two

It was never in my life plan to work on the production line of a biscuit factory forever. I took a summer job packing at Brinkley's Biscuits while I was at college and I've never left, instead moving over to the hand-finishing line, where we create intricate designs to elevate the biscuits into premium products. Dean may have had snobby feelings about it but I like my job. I've always been creative, always sketched and painted, and piping bags and fondant modelling tools have become my pencils and paints.

I also love my work family, from Marvin and Richie on security, to Johanna and the guys in the canteen and, best of all, the rest of my team on the line. Maybe not Kath, the team manager whose role I covet, but she's working her notice and will be off within days with a thank you card, a bunch of flowers and however much is in the collection tin once Melanie's finished doing the rounds. She shakes the tin at me now, encouraging me to write my 'best of luck! xxx' message in the card quicker so she can move on to the next person. It isn't that Melanie is eager to fill the card and tin for Kath – she's worked for the tyrant nearly as long as I have – but the sooner she gets everyone to scrawl their names and dig out the cash, the sooner she can sneak outside for a puff on her e-cig.

'A quid?'

Melanie tuts as the coin drops into the tin with a clang. I shrug and shove my purse back into my handbag.

'It's the only change I've got and she's not having a tenner. That woman has slated me daily for years. She's never off my back. Or yours, for that matter. How much did you put in?'

Melanie looks down at the tin in her hands and lifts one shoulder in a shrug. 'Three pounds twenty-eight. But that's literally all I had in my purse. I haven't even got enough to buy a new vape until we get paid.'

'But we've only just been paid.' I check my phone for any messages before switching it off and shoving it in my locker.

'I know. It's going to be a tough few weeks. You couldn't lend me that tenner, could you?'

I close my locker and push the padlock until it clicks into place. 'Absolutely not. You still owe me thirty quid from our Christmas night out.'

Melanie pulls a sheepish face.

'But I will buy you a brew at break. Might even stretch to a biscuit.'

'Oh, ha ha. A biscuit? Like I'm not surrounded by them all day.' Melanie rolls her eyes. 'But seriously, this is why you're my best work sister.' The money rattles in the tin as Melanie pulls me into a hug, but we're interrupted by a cough from Kath, who's standing in the doorway. The money rattles again as Melanie thrusts the tin behind her back.

'Hey, Kath. Fancy seeing you here.' She snatches the card from the table, and it joins the tin behind her back. 'I'm not skiving. Jack sent me on an errand.'

Kath purses her lips. 'You do look very busy.' She holds Melanie's gaze until my friend can't bear it any longer and aims her eyes down at the floor, while Kath focuses on me instead. 'Daisy, Jack would like to see you in his office.' The corners of Kath's lips start to creep upwards, but it isn't a gesture of goodwill. It's a sly, you're-in-trouble-now-girlie and she's happy to bear witness to it.

'I'm not skiving either. I'm not even clocked in yet.' I twist and look up at the clock on the staffroom wall. I have two minutes to go.

'Don't you think you should run along and clock in then, instead of gossiping in here?' Kath tilts her head to one side, one eyebrow inching up her forehead. 'Quick as you can. Don't leave Jack waiting, girlie.'

I hold my hand out once Kath has left and I can no longer hear her squeaky-shoe footsteps in the corridor. 'Can I have that pound back?'

'Nope. Even narky old cows deserve a leaving pressie.' Melanie shrugs and heads for the staffroom door with the tin and card.

'You can forget about that biscuit with your tea then.'

Melanie doesn't even bother to turn around when she replies. 'You wouldn't do that to me, Daisy Grant.' She's right, I wouldn't. Melanie can be a bit flaky, but she makes the long hours on the production line fun and I'd be lost without her here at Brinkley's. 'Clock in and I'll walk over to the office block with you.' She jiggles the tin and disappears.

I place a hand on my stomach as a wave of nausea hits me. *Jack.* The HR manager wants to see me and as I'm pretty sure I haven't done anything wrong, it must be about the promotion. The interview was only yesterday so is it a good thing or a bad thing that he wants to talk to me so soon? Is he desperate to pass on the good news that I'm being promoted to supervisor? Or is he ripping

13

off the plaster and letting me down before my hopes can reach giddy heights?

Think positive. I've been a loyal, competent employee at Brinkley's for years and I filled in for Kath that time she collapsed in the canteen and had to be rushed to hospital. It was appendicitis and not food poisoning, as the rumours claimed until Kath returned and flashed her scar as evidence. I can do this job. I'm capable. I'm ready. And the pay rise would be more than welcome. I could move out of Mum and Dad's into my own flat, where I can blast my music in the shower as loud as I'd like and where I'd never have to sit through an ITV crime drama again or have my precious lie-ins disturbed by the whirlwind that is my twin nieces as they crash through the house whenever my brother pops round.

Don't get me wrong, living with my parents has its upsides, like the pretty cheap rent I pay each month, only having to cook a couple of times a week and having the household chores split between the three of us, but I'm twenty-five. None of my friends still live at home, apart from Melanie who'd end up on a park bench within a month if she depended on her wages to provide a roof over her head, so I'm getting quite desperate to fly the nest. This promotion – and its pay rise – would make that more feasible.

The door to Jack's office is open, so I tap on the glass before stepping inside. The sickly feeling washes over me again, but I push a smile onto my face. *Think positive.* This is it. I'm finally climbing up the career ladder. In your face, Dean-the-Gobshite-Dater.

'Daisy.' Jack smiles and nods at the chair on the opposite side of his desk. 'How are you?'

'I'm good, thank you.' Nervous as heck. About to throw up or do a little wee. I somehow manage to keep my bodily fluids inside and sit down. 'How are you?'

'I'm not too bad. Looking forward to the weekend.'

I would be too if I had a Monday to Friday office job, but shift work means there's no such thing as a weekend. I don't point this out, obviously.

'I'm going to get straight to the point, Daisy.' Jack places the palms of his hands down on his desk with his fingers splayed. I focus on them instead of his face. 'Unfortunately, your application for team manager wasn't successful this time.'

Has a hole opened up below me? Because I feel like I'm falling, very fast. I place the tips of my fingers onto the desk to tether myself.

'I know this isn't the news you were hoping for, but I wanted to let you know as soon as possible. It wouldn't be fair to keep you in limbo any longer than necessary.'

I nod, still looking at Jack's hands instead of his face.

'You are a very valued member of the Brinkley's team, and we appreciate the work you put in, it's just that we've gone with an external candidate with more experience.'

More experience? I've been at Brinkley's for seven years. How much more experience do they want me to have? Twenty years? Thirty? Why not wait until I'm about to retire before deeming me ready?

'I really am sorry to be giving you this news today, but I hope it won't deter you from applying for similar roles should they arise.'

I take that as my cue to leave and push myself up out of the chair. I shuffle towards the door, my feet leaden with disappointment.

'Thank you for the opportunity.' I'm shocked I manage to choke the words out. Shocked that I don't tag 'Sir Alan' on the end as I sound like a candidate on *The Apprentice*. Even more shocked that the words aren't accompanied by snotty tears, because I am devastated. I'd really thought that this was it, that I was finally back on track. That I'd be doing something with my life other than coasting. That I could go home and tell Mum and Dad the news that I'd been promoted and they'd be proud. Now I have to tell them that I've been rejected because I'm not good enough.

—

'You *are* good enough, babe.'

Jesy places a Raspberry Beret cocktail on the table and slides into the booth next to me, bumping her arm against mine.

'Then why didn't I get the job?' I clutch hold of the martini glass, my grip so tight I wouldn't be surprised if the stem shattered. 'God, my life is shit.' I snatch the glass up off the table and tip the deep pink liquid into my mouth, almost draining the cocktail in one. Raspberry Berets aren't my day-to-day drink of choice; I'd usually have a glass of wine, maybe a gin and tonic, but there are days when you need to indulge, especially between seven and nine when Clementine's practically give their cocktails away. Days when you've had a particularly bad date, or you haven't bagged the promotion you'd set your heart on.

'Your life isn't shit.' Callum reaches across the table and flicks me on the arm, his own special form of affection.

'It definitely is.' I lift my hand so I can count out all the ways my life is shit on my fingers. 'I'm in a crappy dead-end job with no hope of promotion.' Thumb up. 'I still live at home with my mum and dad.' Index finger. 'And despite going on date after date, I haven't had an actual relationship since Harvey, and that was over a year ago.' This one really does deserve the middle finger. 'My longest love affair has been with Vinted, which is very, very sad. You know whose fault this is, don't you?' I look from Callum to Jesy but from the blank looks on their faces, they have no idea where my run of bad luck with men stems from. I roll my eyes and slam my hand down on the table. 'It's Rhys, obviously.'

Callum twists around in his seat, so he can look across towards the bar. 'Rhys the barman?'

'No, you idiot.' I roll my eyes again, so aggressively they ache. 'Rhys my ex-boyfriend.'

'Ah, *that* Rhys.' Callum is nodding, but he stops and frowns at me. 'How exactly is this Rhys's fault? You haven't seen him since the day we got our A-level results.'

'*The day he dumped me.*'

Callum nods. 'I remember. He nearly messed up his exams, didn't he? Blamed you for it too.'

I fold my arms across my chest. 'All his mum's words. She never liked me.' Unfortunately, spending so much time together distracted us from our coursework and while Rhys scraped the passes he needed for uni, I failed two of my exams and only passed the third by the skin of my teeth.

'I still don't understand how you dating all these losers years later has anything to do with Rhys though.'

I eye my friend across the table. Is he serious? Rhys was the first in a long line of disappointing men, each seemingly worse than the last.

'Rhys was the one who sparked my bad luck with men and now I'm going to end up on my own forever.'

Callum flicks me on the hand. 'You won't end up on your own forever, you idiot.'

'You're still young.' Jesy rests her head on my shoulder. 'You've got loads of time to meet somebody.'

'That's easy for you to say. You've both found the loves of your life and are marrying them this year.' I clutch hold of my cocktail glass again. Two weddings in one year is a bit of a kick in the teeth. 'Everyone's getting married. Or already are married. Even my little brother! *And* he's got two kids already.'

'They're twins though.'

I've lifted my drink but I pause, the glass almost touching my lips. 'So?'

Jesy shrugs. 'I was just trying to help. To make you feel better. Clearly, I'm failing, big time. Maybe a shopping trip will help? Are you working on Saturday?'

'I'm on the early shift, until three.'

'Great. We'll meet up afterwards for a bit of retail therapy.' Jesy beams at me. I do not share her joy. It'll take more than a trip into town to make me feel better about my failure of a life.

Chapter Three

There's something familiar about the dress on the rack in front of me and I can't help feeling drawn to it, like to a bowl of crisps among platters of salad. Jesy's telling me about the exhibition she and the kids she works with are putting on, her arms flying about and her face lit up like a Christmas tree as she describes the talents of one particular kid. Jesy's a community arts worker and it's clear for anyone to see how passionate she is about her job. I envy her because as much as I enjoy a biscuit, I can't get *that* enthusiastic about piping tiny roses on a jam and vanilla shortbread sandwich.

Jesy's words fade as I take a step towards the dress. It's a long-sleeved silver sequinned wrap dress with a V neck and high waist, and I feel a little jolt in my stomach as my fingertips touch the fabric, as though the sequins are filled with low voltage electricity.

I know this dress. I've worn this dress. Except this is the first time I've seen it.

An image bursts into my head. An Elton John lookalike. Glittery New Year's Eve bunting. A handsome man beside me, holding my hand. I was wearing this dress in the weird dream-like state I was in the other day as I stepped into Clementine's. I can almost feel the nipped-in waist under my bust. Almost see the disco ball effect of the sequins as I walk. I wore this dress on New Year's Eve. Or I *will* wear this dress on New Year's Eve.

'Honestly, Daisy, she's amazing. And she's only twelve! Imagine having that much talent at twelve years old. She's going to be famous one day, I promise you. She's the next Jennifer Louise Martin.'

'This dress.' I snatch the dress off the rack and practically shove it under my friend's nose. 'This is the dress.'

'Ooh, sparkly.' Jesy holds the fabric delicately between finger and thumb. 'And it's on sale. Seventy per cent off. Wow, what a bargain. You should definitely buy it.' She switches her focus from the New Year's Eve dress to the others on the rack. 'There are loads more in the sale. This one's pretty.' She plucks a green-and-black velvet dress from the rack and holds it out to me. 'You'd look amazing in this.'

I shake my head. 'You don't understand. This is the dress I was wearing in the deja-new.'

'The what?' Jesy is rifling through more dresses: burgundy high-necked, spaghetti-strapped midnight blue, shimmery gold.

'The deja-new. That dream thing I had in Clementine's.'

'Ah.' Jesy pulls a fringed red-and-gold dress from the rack and holds it against her body. 'Your little episode.'

'Maybe it wasn't an episode.' I take the fringed dress from Jesy and hook it back on the rack. It's hideous, even with seventy per cent off. Even if it had one hundred per cent off. 'Maybe it was a premonition and this…' I waggle the dress at her, 'is a sign that it's coming true. Because I was definitely wearing this dress and I've never seen it before today, other than in the dream.'

'Or maybe it isn't a premonition and you've simply seen Fearne Cotton wearing it on the cover of *Grazia*?'

It does sound more plausible that I caught a glimpse of the dress on the cover of a magazine a few months ago and conjured it up during my *episode*. 'Maybe you're right.' I reluctantly place the silver sequinned dress back on the rack. 'I mean, you're not pregnant so it can't be real.'

'What?'

I've started to walk away from the sales rack but Jesy has remained in the same spot, so I have to twist around to explain. 'You were pregnant in the dream. Like, really, *really* pregnant. About to pop pregnant.' I hold my hands out to demonstrate the vastness of the bump. 'You'd probably have to be up the duff now to be *that* pregnant by New Year's Eve.' I snort at the ridiculousness of believing – if only for a minute or two – that my episode was an actual flash forward of my future with The One. 'Shall we go and get a coffee? I've been on my feet since seven this morning. I seriously need a sit down.'

We head out of the shop and up the escalator to the coffee shop, choosing our favourite spot by the window where we can watch people go by. A man wearing red corduroy trousers two inches too short wanders by and I realise Jesy has been unusually quiet when she fails to ask, as she normally would, whether he grew two inches during the night and hasn't realised, or he wants his ankles to turn blue from the chill to make a snazzy contrast with his red trousers.

'Everything okay?' I wait for a response, but none is forthcoming. My friend is staring down at her coffee as though it holds all the answers to life's questions. I wonder if Jesy's coffee can tell me if I'll get the happily ever after everyone around me is enjoying.

'Hello? Earth to Jesy. Can you hear me?'

'What?' Jesy blinks in a dazed fashion as she looks up at me. 'Sorry. Miles away.'

'Everything okay?'

Jesy nods but her face doesn't match up with her answer. Jesy is usually all bright-eyed and toothy smiles, but her eyebrows are pulled down low and her mouth is pressed into a thin line.

'Are you sure?'

The corners of Jesy's lips flick upwards and there's a flash of her teeth, but we both know the smile is fake as heck and Jesy drops it almost immediately. 'Actually, no.'

'What is it?' Fear makes my pulse quicken. Because this isn't my Jesy sitting across from me. Jesy Wilson-Jones is joy personified. She is chirpy and animated, not frowny and shoulder-slumpy.

'It's about what you said before.'

I think back over our shopping trip. I'd driven into town straight after work and hadn't been in the best of moods, to be honest. 'About wanting to shove Kath head-first into a vat of cookie dough? Because I was joking. I'd never be able to drag her that high up for a start.' I grin at Jesy but she doesn't return the gesture. 'Honestly, I'm fine. I was just letting off steam because Kath's been doing my head in all day. But I never have to put up with her again. It's her last shift tomorrow and I'm not even working, so yay.' I hold my fists up and give them a little jiggle.

'It's not about Kath.' Jesy directs her gaze down at her coffee again. 'It's about what you said about me being pregnant.'

My eyes widen and I tilt forwards towards Jesy. 'You *are* pregnant?'

Jesy pulls her chin back and huffs out a laugh. 'No. I don't know. Maybe?' She shrugs and fiddles with her mug, twisting it to the left and right on its saucer by the handle. 'I guess I am a teeny bit late, but we haven't been trying. I've got a beautiful wedding dress to fit into. Having a baby now isn't the plan. Get married first. Move out of our flat into a house. Grow up a bit more. *Then* babies. Maybe.'

Jesy stops twisting her mug and reaches across the table to grasp my hand. Quite hard. 'If you saw me on New Year's Eve this big…' She makes a semicircle motion with her free hand in front of her. 'Then that means I'll be ginormous on my wedding day. I'm getting married four days before Christmas. Less than two weeks before New Year's Eve. Oh, god.' She places a hand over her mouth. 'I'm going to have to get married in a sack. No, no, no. This can't be happening. This isn't how my big day is supposed to be. I'm supposed to get married in the most beautiful, most perfect dress. You've seen it, Daisy. You've seen how perfect it is.'

Jesy's dress is stunning. It's a figure-hugging Art Deco-style silver-and-rose-gold mermaid dress with a deep V neckline and a slit to the side; there definitely isn't enough room to fit another small human in there. Jesy had looked at what felt like a million and one dresses before she found this one and she'd fallen in love with it almost as hard as she'd fallen in love with her fiancé, Ant. Her eyes are starting to well up at the prospect of kissing goodbye to it.

'You will get married in that dress. I'm just being silly about this dream thing. It isn't real. It can't be.' But even as I say the words, I'm wondering… What if this dream thing is real? Because if Jesy *is* pregnant, my dream man could be out there waiting for me to find him – and soon.

Chapter Four

Callum stoops down to pick up the worn tennis ball while Frankenstein, his black and sandy brown rescue dog tap dances his front paws on the damp grass in anticipation. Callum swings his arm back before launching the ball across the field, with Frankenstein galloping after it. It is Sunday morning and we're in the park at the back of my house, strolling along and throwing the ball for Frankenstein.

This is my favourite kind of Sunday. The kind where I'm not at work and I have the whole day stretching ahead of me, starting with our walk in Boyd Mill Park. Soon, we'll drop Frankenstein off at Callum's and pick up Jesy so we can go to Clementine's for brunch. Jesy doesn't do early mornings if she can help it so it's usually just the two of us (three, including Frankenstein) on our walks. I lift my camera as Frankenstein bounds back towards us with the tennis ball clamped between his teeth, capturing several shots that I'll sift through later. It's a good day for taking photos with the clouds softening the shadows, meaning I can rely on natural light.

'Oi.' Callum nudges me. He's thrown the ball again and Frankenstein is tearing after it. 'Are you listening to me?'

'Sorry. What did you say?' I push the lens cap on my camera and let it dangle from its strap around my neck.

'Nothing.' Callum nudges me with his shoulder. 'Doesn't matter. Let me see.' He nods at the camera, and I show him the image of Frankenstein bounding towards us on the display. 'You're amazing. You really should go back to college and do a photography course. You might even pass this time.' He nudges me when I don't respond to his jibe. 'Hey, everything okay?'

'Sorry.' I let the camera dangle and shove my hands in my pockets. 'Bit distracted today.'

'I've noticed.' Frankenstein drops the ball at Callum's feet, and he reaches down to scoop it up. 'Anything you want to talk about?'

I shake my head. 'You'll think I'm silly.'

'I've had that thought since the day I met you, Daisy Grant. Do you remember that day?'

'Obviously.' It was a few days after I'd enrolled at Woodgate Sixth Form, and I hadn't made any friends yet. And then Jesy entered my life, bursting into the photography class late because she'd been distracted by a bee collecting pollen from one of the massive planters outside.

'Is this seat taken?' She hadn't waited for an answer before she'd flopped down next to me. 'I'm Jesy, by the way. That's Jesy with one S and a Y. What's your name?'

'I'm Daisy. Also with one S and a Y.'

Jesy had tipped her head back and laughed. 'You're funny. I like you.' She continued to chatter, even after she'd been shushed multiple times by the tutor, and once the class was over and we were packing up, she'd asked if I was going to the canteen in a way that was an invitation rather than an enquiry. 'Hey, Callum. Meet my new best friend, Daisy.'

The boy sitting at the table we'd stopped at had looked up, eyes narrowed at Jesy. He had wild, ginger curls that seemed to complement Jesy's kooky personality. 'You've replaced me as your best friend already?'

'I'm only your bestie because of your massive, hugely embarrassing crush on my sister anyway.'

Callum rolled his eyes. They were slate blue and framed by long lashes. 'I do not, for the millionth time, fancy Anna.'

Jesy snorted. 'Yeah, right. Next, you'll be telling me you don't have dainty teenage-girl's knees either.'

Callum's mouth gaped open. 'I do *not* have dainty teenage-girl's knees. My knees are extremely masculine.' He'd scraped back his chair and rolled up his jeans so he could display his knee, which he lifted in triumph. 'See? What do you think, Daisy?'

I was taken aback for a moment as I hadn't been expecting to be included in the knee debate and had simply been enjoying observing the dynamic between the two.

'I don't think they're particularly dainty.'

Callum had twisted his lips and scrunched up his nose at Jesy in an odd display of triumph.

'For a teenage girl.'

Jesy's mouth had dropped open, frozen like that for a moment before she tipped her head back and roared with laughter, slinging her arm around my shoulders.

'And that is why you're my new best friend.'

–

'You said I had dainty teenage-girl knees.' Callum pouts as he recalls the same memory. 'I thought that was *very* silly so whatever's on your mind now can't top that.'

'I wouldn't be too sure about that.' I fiddle with the strap of my camera. I haven't stopped thinking about the dress I found in the shop yesterday and what it might mean.

'Try me.' Callum tosses the ball for Frankenstein. 'What's the worst that can happen? I could fall about laughing and call you a knobhead, but you'll survive.' He nudges me with his elbow. 'I've called you much worse over the years. Sometimes to your face.'

I jab him playfully with my elbow. 'You will definitely call me a knobhead because that's exactly what I'm being.'

'You need to tell me what's going on. Don't make me ask Jesy, because I know she'll be clued up about this, she always is. And you know what a blabbermouth she is. So come on.' Callum flicks me on the end of my nose. He can be an annoying flicker sometimes. 'Tell me what it is.'

'Fine.' I sigh, because Callum is also right about Jesy being a blabbermouth. I'm surprised she hasn't spilled about it already. 'It's about that dream I had at Clementine's.'

'Your funny turn?'

'Yes. Except maybe it wasn't a funny turn. Maybe it was a premonition.'

Callum grabs the ball and chucks it across the field. 'Like a flash forward? You think you saw your future?'

I hold my hands up. 'It's silly, I know, but I saw the dress I was wearing in the dream in a shop yesterday and I swear I've never seen it before.' I don't tell him about the possibility of Jesy being pregnant because that isn't for me to gossip about. She hasn't taken a test or even discussed it with anyone else, not even her fiancé. 'And if it's true, then my dream guy is out there waiting for me.'

'Then I'll need to find him quick, before you do.'

'Why?'

'To warn him that you're completely fucking cuckoo and to run as fast as he can.'

'Oi.' I lunge at Callum but he's already set off. My camera bumps against my chest as I give chase, with Frankenstein bounding after us with the tennis ball in his mouth. By the time we reach the park gate, Callum and I are bent double and I'm in no fit state to go on the attack.

'You are a massive knobhead, Daisy Grant.' Callum attaches the lead to Frankenstein's harness, and we head out onto the pavement. 'But I love you for it.'

'So you don't think the dream was a glimpse of my future?'

'Do *you* seriously think it was a glimpse of your future?'

I dig my hands in my pockets. It's still early on in spring and nippy. 'I suppose not.' It would be nice though, to know that my dream guy was close by. To know that I'm not going to be left on my own while my best friends get married and live happily ever after.

It's a ten-minute walk to Callum's flat. We drop Frankenstein off and I say a quick hello/goodbye to Callum's fiancée, Zara, and then we continue up the road to pick up Jesy. More often than not it's just the three of us for brunch at Clementine's. Zara and Jesy's fiancé occasionally join us, but Zara is about to leave for a bridal make-up test run and Ant usually plays rugby on a Sunday afternoon so it's just the three of us today. Clementine's is reasonably busy, but we find an empty booth and place our order. I go for my usual buck's fizz and pancakes with mixed berry compote, which is usually Jesy's brunch of choice too, but she opts for a plain old orange juice instead of its boozy cousin.

'I had a really heavy night last night. You know what Ant's rugby mates are like. I'm surprised they can stand up today, never mind run around a field.'

Jesy's excuse for the orange juice switch is swift and unprompted and she hasn't made eye contact with me since she gave her order, so I know she's lying. But I can't probe her in front of Callum, so it has to wait until he heads off for the loo, which takes ages.

'Well?'

Jesy doesn't need any further inquisitions. She knows what I'm asking with that one word.

'I did a test last night.' Her eyes flick towards the toilets, to make sure Callum isn't on his way back. 'And it was positive. Your dream was right. I'm going to be the size of a house by New Year's Eve.'

Chapter Five

I haven't been able to stop thinking about the dream. The premonition. The deja-new. About the fact that Jesy is pregnant. I had no idea she was pregnant when I conjured up my dream man, but I saw it. I saw my actual future. How else could I have known about Jesy's pregnancy when she didn't even know herself? And now the most important question is, how do I find my dream man?

Not at Brinkley's, that's for sure. I've been working at the factory for ages, and I've never had a sniff of romance. Not even a harmless crush. Which isn't surprising; it's quite difficult to get heart-eyed over men in bright blue hairnets.

I park as close to the factory as I can without straying into the reserved spots – another perk I'll miss out on after losing that promotion – and head inside to the staffroom. I check my phone for any updates from Jesy – how is she feeling about the pregnancy, both emotionally and physically? Has she had any morning sickness yet? Any cravings for weird stuff? My sister-in-law couldn't cram salmon paste on digestive biscuits into her mouth fast enough when she was pregnant with the twins.

Melanie bursts through the staffroom door, marching into the middle of the room and extending her arm like a circus ringmaster. 'And this is Daisy. She's amazing. The best piper we have. Show him how steady your hands are, Daisy.' Melanie holds her hand out and nods at me, encouraging me to do the same. I don't. Instead, I look at the man behind her. He's wearing the usual Brinkley's shop floor uniform of white coveralls, shoe coverings and hairnet.

'Hi.' He steps forward and offers me a hand. His fingers are long, with clipped, clean nails. 'I'm Joshua Michaels.'

Oh crap. I forgot we were going to be meeting Kath's replacement today.

'I'm showing Joshua around and introducing him to everyone.' Melanie leans in close so she can whisper to me. 'Isn't he fit?'

Fit? He's wearing a hairnet (not sexy in the slightest) and *he stole my promotion. I* should be starting today as the new team manager for our line, not this dude. I wouldn't even need to waste time being given a tour or need any introductions. Obviously, I despise him and will pick fault with him, no matter how petty. His fingers, for example, are skeletal (holding hands with Joshua Michaels would be like holding hands with Skeletor), and his low, heavy eyebrows make him look far too serious, as though he's already thinking about telling us off for making jokes and injecting too much joy into our working day. He'll probably make Kath seem delightful and cheeky, like a female Stephen Mulhern in protective clothing. I miss Kath already.

'It was nice meeting you, Daisy.' Joshua's eyebrows lift slightly, and he gives me a curt nod. 'But I think it's time we got on with some work.'

See? Less than thirty seconds in and he's already on a power trip. It seems there's no time for harmless chitchat when Joshua Michaels is around, it's all work, work, work with the New Kath 2.0. Who needs pleasantries and camaraderie when you can simply work your fingers to the bone like a robot?

Melanie's face falls. If her bottom lip protrudes any further, it'll become a trip hazard. 'But we haven't even gone over to packing yet. You haven't met Dougie. You *have* to meet Dougie. He can walk the entire length of the loading bay on his hands.'

'That does sound impressive.' Joshua's low-down eyebrows say otherwise. 'And I'm sure I'll witness Dougie's talent one day soon, but right now I need to get back out on the floor. You do too.'

Melanie's shoulders are slumped as she shuffles out of the staffroom. It seems the new supervisor is as much of a whip-cracker as Kath. More so maybe. Melanie's days of getting away with doing as little as possible may be over.

–

Joshua Michaels is a stickler for the rules. Aka an annoying jobsworth bellend. He stalks around the shopfloor with his clipboard, barking out orders and pointing out the most minor errors and telling us off for giggling too much. He is a major killjoy, and it becomes my mission to act as defiantly as possible without getting into trouble. So I giggle louder with Melanie, and I 'accidentally' smudge my piping on a biscuit or two so they have to be rejected, and when Joshua says no, I can't go to the toilet since my break is coming up in less than an hour, I clutch my stomach and claim I have cramps and that I suspect I might be leaking, which isn't very hygienic, especially in a food production setting, and Joshua shoos me off with a barely suppressed sigh.

Phones are banned from shift but I grab mine from my locker on the way, opening up the 'Friends Without

Benefits' group chat with Jesy and Callum as I plonk myself down on the closed lid of the toilet.

> **Daisy:**
> You guys are so lucky you don't have to work with Joshua Michaels

> **Callum:**
> Who is Joshua Michaels?

> **Daisy:**
> He's a smug-looking idiot who thinks he can tell us what to do

> **Callum:**
> He's the guy who got your promotion then?
> Isn't it his job to tell you what to do?

> **Jesy:**
> Is he fit?

I'm about to reply that no, Joshua Michaels is not fit, that he looks like an old toilet brush (which isn't true, but it would make me feel better) when there's a knock at the door. Anxiety makes my skin prickle. Would Joshua come to find me, even in the ladies? I want to act defiantly but I don't want there to be any consequences. I may be peeved about being stuck in this job, but I don't want to lose it.

'Daisy? You okay in there?'

I puff out a breath, the built-up tension leaving my body. It's only Melanie.

'Joshua sent me to check on you. How sweet is that?'

Sweet? More like controlling. Afraid he'll lose two minutes of production.

'Do you need paracetamol? I've got some in my bag.'

'I'm not actually on my period.' I close the chat and slip my phone down my bra. 'I just needed a breather. If he stalks past me with that clipboard one more time, I'll shove it up his arse. Who knew there was someone out there worse than Kath?' I flush the loo, even though I haven't used it, and join Melanie out by the sinks.

'I like him.'

I eye Melanie's reflection in the mirror as I roll up my sleeves. 'Seriously?'

'What?' Melanie's reflection shrugs. 'He's cute.'

I snort as I bash the tap down and shove my hands under the stream of water. 'As cute as haemorrhoids.' I squirt three blobs of soap onto my palm, each push against the dispenser more aggressive than the last. 'I can't find any man in a hairnet attractive.'

Melanie leans against the neighbouring sink as I lather up. 'Then imagine him without the hairnet. Imagine him without anything on at all.' She pulls in a breath, a smile lighting up her face. She closes her eyes and releases it slowly. 'It's a delicious image, Daisy. Try it.'

'No thank you.' I rinse off my hands and drag three sheets of paper towel from the dispenser on the wall.

'Suit yourself.' Melanie pushes herself away from the sink and opens the door, holding it open to let me out once I've dumped the paper towels in the bin.

'I'll be back out on the floor in a minute. I just need to go to my locker.' I can feel my phone slipping from its position in my bra. The last thing I need is for it to slip out in front of Mr Clipboard. I head for the staffroom, wriggling my hand down my top to pull out my phone once I reach my locker. I'm typing out a reply to Jesy (No, he is NOT fit. Far from it) when the staffroom door opens and Mr Clipboard himself catches me, thumbs mid-tap on the screen of my phone. His head tilts to one side and I hear the murmur of a sigh. I close the app, message unsent, and slip it into my locker.

'I don't want us to get off on the wrong foot on my first day, Daisy.'

Too late for that, I think, but I have the sense to keep it zipped.

'So I won't give you a warning about the phone. I'll let it slide, but just this once. Okay?'

I nod, turning to click the padlock on my locker shut. God, he's annoying, pretending to be Mr Reasonable while still looking down on me, holding the fact he's caught me on my phone over me. *I'll let it slide, but just this once. Okay?* Joshua's voice is irritatingly nasal as I repeat his words in my head.

'Shall we?' Joshua opens the door, holding it back and allowing me to step through first. I roll my eyes as I oblige. You know you've taken against someone when even an act of politeness gets under your skin. But he's just so annoying! Look at him, marching along the corridor with that stupid clipboard tucked under his arm! And oh my god, the way he sighs as he looks back and sees me several paces behind as he swings the door to the shopfloor open makes my skin prickle with irritation.

'Come on.' He nods towards the cavernous area beyond the corridor, his voice barely audible over the din of the machinery. 'You don't want to miss your target.' He consults his clipboard and shakes his head, even though there's no way I'm behind. I always hit my targets. Always. 'You'll need to work through your break to make up the lost time.'

And that is the first final straw of the day.

⸻

Callum presses his lips together. He's been listening to me vent about Joshua Michaels ever since I plonked myself on Jesy's sofa and let rip about my new supervisor. He's kept quiet as I bemoaned the fact I was rejected in favour of a smug-looking dictator who thinks he runs the whole factory after being there for five minutes, letting me spew it all out in one go.

'He does sound like a bit of a knob.'

I look at Jesy, to see if she agrees with Callum's assessment, and am pleased when she nods. 'Bit heavy-handed, if you ask me. He hasn't even got to know you yet.'

'Exactly!' I throw my hands up and shoot Jesy a look of pure gratitude. 'I said as much to Melanie but all she kept banging on about is how fit he is.'

'And is he?' Jesy leans towards me, eyebrows raised. Beside her, her fiancé clears his throat and raises his own eyebrows. 'Obviously I wasn't asking for *me*. I'm happily engaged.' She waggles her left hand at Ant, the diamond of her engagement ring glinting. She catches my eye and silently adds *and about to have a baby!* She hasn't told Ant the news yet because she isn't sure how to break it to him. Babies were not on the cards right now.

'Hmm.' Ant nods in a not-convinced-in-the-slightest way, but he can't quite pull it off. There's amusement flickering at his lips and I know if he catches Jesy's eye he'll crack into a full-on grin. Ant doesn't do jealousy or acting proprietarily. He's secure in the knowledge that infidelity would never even occur to Jesy, that no matter how teasing and flirty she can be, she would never cross any lines. Because Jesy adores Ant. She is all-in on the relationship, and so is Ant. They're very different as people – Jesy is tiny in stature but loud in character, while Ant is seriously huge yet much more laid-back and calm off the rugby pitch – but they work so well together, their personalities finding the perfect gaps to slot into seamlessly.

'It's really rubbish that you didn't get that promotion, Daisy.' Ant pulls the corners of his mouth down before clamping his hands down on his thighs and turning to Jesy. 'Right. Better go. I said I'd meet the lads at the Farthing for a quick pint. Won't be long, babe.' He pecks a kiss on the top of Jesy's head and holds his hand up in farewell to me and Callum before heading out of the flat.

'Right.' Jesy claps her hands together as soon as she hears the click of the front door. 'We've got more important things to think about than your new boss.'

My head snaps up and I glare at Jesy. 'He isn't my boss. He's my *supervisor*. There's a difference.'

'Supervisor. Boss. Whatever.' Jesy waves her hand and leans in towards me. 'We've got a mission to work on.'

'What mission?' Callum groans. 'We're not going to stalk this Joshua dude on Instagram and set up fake profiles to send him rude messages, are we? Because I thought we'd grown out of all that.'

'We're not Insta stalking anyone.' Jesy grabs a notepad from the coffee table and sets it down on her lap. 'Not until we find out who he is, at least.'

Callum's gaze darts from Jesy to me. 'Who are we looking for? And why?'

Jesy reaches for the pen on the table and removes its lid. 'That's our mission. Daisy's dream guy.'

Callum shifts, so he's facing me full-on. 'You're dating again? I thought you were having a rest?' He turns to Jesy. 'And why do you have a pad and pen? What are you writing? It isn't a lonely hearts ad, is it? Do they still do those? Isn't it all online now?'

'We're looking for Daisy's *dream guy*.' Jesy emphasises the last two words, but they're met with a blank look and a one-shouldered shrug from Callum. 'The guy from her dream.'

Callum sniggers. 'Yeah, right. We're seriously going to look for some dude she imagined during a funny turn.' He looks at Jesy. He looks at me. 'Seriously, we're doing this? We're actually going to try to find the bloke Daisy dreamed up?'

'Yep, except maybe it wasn't a dream.' Jesy jots something down at the top of the notepaper.

'It was definitely a dream.' Callum gives me a hard stare. 'You know it was a dream, right? It wasn't real.'

I shrug. 'Maybe it was.'

'You can't actually believe that.' Deep lines crevice Callum's forehead. 'Jesy, you don't believe it's real, do you?'

Jesy nods. 'I do.'

'But how? Why? People don't see flashes of their future. Have you both gone mad? Without me?'

Jesy hasn't told Callum about the pregnancy. She will, but she needs to share the news with Ant first.

'You're just going to have to trust us.' Jesy looks at me, pen poised above the notepad. 'Right. What can you remember about your dream guy?'

I don't remember much about him. He was taller than me (but then I'm only 5'1 so most people are), he was handsome as heck (though his actual face is too hazy to pick out any specific features) and he had darkish hair. Brown? Or maybe dark blond? The only detail I can clearly recall was the watch. It had a conker-brown leather strap with gold edging to the face, which had a crack through the middle. The clock hands and winder were also gold, while the only numbers – 12 and 6 – were black, with thin, long black lines marking out the other digits.

'It isn't much to go on.' Jesy waves her list at me. 'Tall, handsome, darkish hair with a broken watch. What else do you remember about the dream?'

I close my eyes to bring the image back into my mind. 'It was New Year's Eve and there was an Elton John tribute act performing. I was wearing the dress I saw on Saturday and a necklace.' I squeeze my eyes tighter, to beckon the necklace to the forefront of my memory. I remember the feel of it between my fingers. It was squarish, with pointed corners, and maybe a jewel on the front protruding. 'I can't actually *see* the necklace, and it didn't feel like anything I own.' I open my eyes. Jesy is scribbling the details down on her list. 'Sorry. It isn't much to go on.'

Jesy studies the list, her lips pursed in concentration. 'It isn't, but we can't give up.'

'Can't we?' Callum mutters the question, but we hear it and both turn to glare at him. Callum clears his throat and examines the freckle on his left wrist.

'I think our most solid lead is the dress.' Jesy prods the item on her list. 'We need to go back to the shop and buy that dress ASAP. We also need to hang out at Clementine's as much as possible.'

Callum stops examining the freckle. 'Not that I'm complaining about that, but why?'

'Because maybe that's where they meet? It makes sense; we're there a lot anyway and that's the place the dream showed her.'

'And if not, we get to eat good food and get drunk. I'm in.' Callum holds up a finger. 'But I want it on record that I think you're both completely nuts.'

Are we nuts? Probably. We are looking for my one true love based on a five-second vision and a very flimsy plan, but it's all we've got. It's the beginning of May now, which means we have less than eight months to find him.

Chapter Six

'Have you told Ant yet?'

Jesy has barely got a bum cheek on the passenger seat of my car when I ask the question.

'No. Not yet.' She's been putting off telling her fiancé that they're going to be parents for days now. I know she's nervous about telling him but, speaking as someone who has never been even remotely close to being in this predicament, surely it's better to get it over and done with, like ripping the plaster off in one swift move. I offer this unsolicited advice and earn myself a look of contempt.

'Ripping the plaster off hurts like hell.'

'Okay, bad analogy, because telling Ant won't be painful. You've talked about having kids. He *wants* to have kids with you. So why the nerves?'

Jesy drags the door shut and pulls on her seatbelt. 'We've talked about having kids way, *way* in the future. Not now, when we're living in a little flat with no garden. We wanted to travel more, and Ant wants to start up his own landscaping business instead of working his arse off for someone else to take the profits. And he's never been around babies. He's an only child and none of his mates have kids yet. Remember how overwhelming he found my family when he first met them?' To be fair to Ant, Jesy has four sisters, and they can be... a bit much. 'Was

41

Ant there? At the New Year's Eve party at Clementine's? You know, in your deja-new thingy?'

I pretend to have a good look for traffic before pulling out, even though the road is empty of moving vehicles. 'I didn't notice him, but that doesn't mean he wasn't there. It was only a brief flash. I was back in the present in the blink of an eye.'

'You were there long enough to get a good look at that watch and the dress.'

Both our phones ping, saving me from responding as Jesy's focus is transferred to ferreting in her handbag. I turn the radio on while she reads the message, hoping music will be enough of a distraction so we don't return to the Ant convo because maybe he *wasn't* there at all and maybe it has something to do with the unplanned pregnancy. I'm afraid to delve into it and I'd kick myself for bringing him up but I'm driving.

'It's Callum in the group chat. He's asking if you're sure you want to go ahead with this, and I quote, *mad as a box of frogs scheme*?'

'Why wouldn't I? I'm literally looking for the man of my dreams.'

Jesy taps out a quick reply before dropping her phone back into her bag. 'Ignore him. He's being a grump because he's jealous. He's stuck at boring old work and we're going on an adventure.' Jesy claps her hands together and does a little squeal. 'I'm so excited for you, Daisy. This is it. You're going to find The One.'

Finding The One had better be easier than finding The Dress, because although the sales rack is still set up in the shop and the dress I was wearing in the dream is on there, there are none in my size. I rifle through the dresses several times but they're all so small: six, six, eight, eight, eight, ten. Nothing bigger. Damn.

'I need my size.' I wade through the dresses again, more slowly this time, checking the sizes on both the hanger and the label. My shoulders slump when I come to the same conclusion. 'They don't have my size.'

'They must have.' Jesy elbows me out of the way so she can conduct her own search. 'You were wearing this dress in the dream so it must be here. Oh. Are you sure it was *this* dress? This one's similar.' She grabs a sleeveless pale grey belted dress and holds it up to my body. It's nothing like the dream dress. The length is wrong. The neckline is scooped. It doesn't sparkle.

'It was definitely this dress.' I hold out the silver sequinned dress. 'But bigger. Shall I buy this one and diet myself into it?' It's two sizes too small and I've never had much success with dieting, but there are nearly eight months to go until New Year's Eve.

'Absolutely not. You are gorgeous and sexy as you are. You are not changing yourself for any man, not even the man of your dreams. *Especially* not the man of your dreams, because he's going to love you exactly as you are.' Jesy shoves the inferior grey dress onto the rack and grabs my hand, towing me to the tills, where she asks the assistant if they have my dream dress in a bigger size. Hope flares in my chest. It fizzles out when the sales assistant shakes his head.

'It's an end of line product, I'm afraid. All we have is whatever's out. You could try online?'

Online! *Of course*. Everything is done online these days. I don't even wait until we're out of the shop before I load up the website and search for the dress. But while the belted grey dress is on there, my dream dress is not. The plan is not going very well at all. No man. No watch. Not even the dress.

'We'll work it out. Don't worry, babe.' Jesy threads her arm through mine and guides me towards the doors. I try really hard to take comfort from her words, but I can't seem to manage it. Because how can we work it out when we don't have the dress? If the dream is a glimpse of the future rather than a weird episode, surely all the pieces have to be there?

I step aside when we reach the doors, to allow a new customer to step inside, but his carrier bag catches on the zip of my handbag. I give a little tug and untangle our bags, but it comes with consequences. Because the carrier bag is made of paper, and it now has a rip down the side.

'I am so sorry.' I am so stupid. A pack of socks pokes out of the gap and I place a hand over my mouth, mortified at what I've done.

'Don't worry about it.' He prods the pack of socks back into the bag, but they slip straight out again. 'The perils of trying to save the planet.' He looks up and smiles and my stomach does a little flutter. He is gorgeous. Tall, slicked-back dark hair, green eyes alight despite the fact I've wrecked his shopping vessel. And the smile! Full lips, white teeth (without being fake, brighter-than-the-sun, Turkey-teeth white) and it creates a dimple in both cheeks. Excuse me while I crumble to the floor in a heap.

'Why don't we buy you coffee, to apologise for our clumsiness?' Jesy says 'we' and 'our' as though she was part of my ineptness. 'In a reusable cup, obviously.'

'Obviously. Gotta save the planet, one bag and one cup at a time.' His smile widens. The dimples deepen. My legs really are going to give way. 'Lead the way.' He steps back and holds his arm out so we can leave the shop. We usually go to the Costa on the top floor of the shopping mall, but Jesy steers us to the right, where there's an independent coffee shop on the corner. Clever girl. With its single use plastic-free policy and its mismatched reclaimed decor, it's the ideal choice for our new eco-conscious friend.

'Oh no.' Jesy pauses at the door of the coffee shop and releases my arm. 'I said I'd meet Callum to help pick out your birthday present.' Callum, who's currently at work? And my birthday that's three months away? 'What a shame. But never mind.' Jesy turns to our new friend and grins at him. 'Daisy will buy you your coffee.' She backs off, winking at me before she turns and scuttles away. Smooth, Jesy Wilson-Jones. Very smooth.

'Shall we?' He indicates the door, holding it open when I nod. 'What can I get you?'

'I'm buying, remember?' I nod at his shopping bag, where the socks are still peeking out.

'I insist. Why don't you grab that free table over there?'

I'm impressed. He cares about the planet, and he seems like such a gentleman. Jesy is obviously impressed by him too and I see she's messaged me when I check my phone while I wait at the table.

> **Jesy:**
> It's him! He's The One!!!

My stomach does another little flutter, ignoring the fact that his hair is darker than I remember. My memory of the dream guy's features are hazy, so maybe his hair *was* darker, or perhaps the product he's used to slick it back is making it appear darker than its natural brown? I look across to the queue at the counter, where he's talking to the barista. Could it be him? My stomach tenses, but it isn't a pleasant feeling this time. It feels heavy. He's still busy placing our order so I tap out a reply.

Daisy:
How do I know it's him?

Callum:
Who is The One?

Jesy:
Some guy D's just met. They're having coffee

Daisy:
But how do I know he's the guy from the dream?

Jesy:
The dress led you to him. That can't be a coincidence!

Callum:
It absolutely can be a coincidence

I glance up in time to see the shopping bag guy heading towards me with two coffees in hand. I close WhatsApp and drop my phone into my bag as he places the mismatched mugs down on the table. *Could* he be the guy from my dream? It can't be a coincidence that I meet-cute a guy (the first movie-worthy moment I've ever had) while searching for the dream dress, no matter what Callum says. Maybe it *was* the dress that led me to him?

'Thank you.' I pull my mug closer and wrap my hands around it. The mug is too hot for this, and I snatch them away. 'I really should have been the one buying the drinks after I wrecked your bag.'

'It's hardly wrecked.' He sits down opposite me and nudges the bag under the table. 'Minor damage. No big deal.' He smiles and his cheeks dimple again. It *has* to be him. I don't go for coffee with random guys I meet in shops. I don't go for coffee with guys this utterly gorgeous, to be honest. The dimples alone are enough to make my palms sweat, and I have to wipe them down my thighs under the table.

As well as being gorgeous and having lovely manners, Oliver is also an easy person to chat to. He doesn't tell me that I look much fatter than my profile pic. It helps that there is no profile pic involved, but I get the impression Oliver wouldn't be a dipshit and say it even if there was. He doesn't chew with his mouth open (we aren't eating, but again, he doesn't give the impression that he would) or any of the other off-putting stuff my dates usually do. Not that this is a date. But it could maybe lead to one? The chat is flowing, and I've made Oliver laugh three times; the third time he almost expelled coffee out of his nose. I'm starting to think that maybe Jesy was right. Oliver could be the man of my dreams. This could be the beginning of something special. The beginning of falling in love.

'It was lovely meeting you, Daisy, but I'm afraid I should be getting on with my shopping.' With the coffees long gone, Oliver pushes back his chair and stoops to pick up his carrier bag. The paper audibly rips a little bit more, but he has the good grace not to mention it.

'It was lovely meeting you too.' I watch as Oliver stands, and my heart starts to pound as I await the moment he asks if he can see me again. Because surely he will. We've had such a good time (I don't think I've ever made anyone snort coffee with my humour, not even Callum or Jesy) and I'd love to do this again, to see if this spark can ignite into a declaration of love on New Year's Eve.

But Oliver hasn't said anything as he starts to back away. He lifts his hand in farewell and then he turns to leave without setting up another date. Didn't he feel that spark? Was he faking the coffee-snort? I don't want this – whatever *this* is – to end so abruptly. I've never asked a man out before – have never had the balls to do it – but I can't let Oliver leave without at least exchanging numbers.

'Would you like to meet up again?' My voice is an anxiety-laced squeak, the words pushed out as quickly as possible. I want to shut my eyes as soon as they're out there, to block out Oliver and the coffee shop and pretend I never suggested it.

'I'd love to.' Oliver turns back around again, and I see the dimples in his cheeks as he smiles.

'Oh.' I swallow. Hard. 'Great. Do you know Clementine's Café Bar? We could go for a drink?'

'I do know Clementine's. I live just up the road from there.'

This is definitely it. The dress led me to a lovely, gorgeous man who knows the setting of our dream New Year's Eve and he seems to find me charming enough to go on an actual date. I can't quite believe this is happening and my hands are trembling slightly as I tap Oliver's details into my phone. Callum won't be so dismissive of the plan when I update the group chat, and I can practically hear Jesy's squeal of delight.

Chapter Seven

My date with Oliver is on my mind for the next few days. I think about it as I brush my teeth in the morning – what will we talk about? Will I make him laugh again? – and I wonder what I will wear as I flick through my wardrobe in search of a t-shirt to wear to work. I could go with my old faithful monochrome floral V-neck dress, which is casual and comfortable but also a little bit flirty, in a cute rather than sexy way, or I have a jumpsuit I bought from Vinted a few weeks ago but haven't been brave enough to wear yet. It's black with a rhinestone halterneck and matching belt and I'm still not convinced I don't look like the Teletubbies' goth cousin while wearing it. Maybe the jumpsuit is a bit OTT for first date drinks at Clementine's?

> **Jesy:**
> You'll look amazing whatever you wear.
> And if you compare yourself to a Teletubby
> one more time, I'll kick your arse. Okay?

Jesy's message makes me smile. I *will* look amazing whatever I wear, because I'm an amazing person, who happens to have amazing friends. I send a smiley face reply before shoving my phone in my locker.

'Ah, Daisy. I was hoping to run into you.'

Funny, because I was hoping *not* to run into Joshua.

'What can I do for you?' I make sure my locker is secure before turning to Joshua. Not many people can pull off a hairnet, and Joshua is definitely *not* one of those people. I don't know how Melanie can fancy him.

'It's about your shift tomorrow.'

My eyes start to narrow. 'What about it?'

'You're on an early.'

I am. Seven a.m. (ugh) until three, when I get to go home and prepare for my date with Oliver. This date has to go well so I'm thinking the works: exfoliate until I have barely any skin left on my frame at all, shave my legs (I hadn't really kept up with my leg hair removal over winter and I've still yet to brave skirts without tights so there's been little point), moisturise from head to toe until my whole body is a slip hazard, and use every tip Zara has ever given me while applying my make-up. Your best friend marrying a make-up artist really is a bonus.

'I need you to switch to the mid-shift.'

I observe Joshua with care, looking for the tiniest hint of humour: a twinkling of the eye, a twitching of the lips, anything to suggest he is joking. Because he must be joking.

'I can't do the mid-shift.' The mid-shift is three until eleven p.m. I'm meeting Oliver at eight. This is not possible.

'I need you to switch.' Joshua holds his hands out at his sides in a what-are-you-gonna-do kind of way. What I'm going to do is say no.

'I can't do the mid-shift.'

'But I need you to do it. Sabina's phoned in sick. She can't come in for forty-eight hours. Health and safety. I've asked Jeremy to cover but he can only do an early, so you're going to have to switch.'

'But I can't. I have plans tomorrow night.'

'So does Jeremy. It's his kid's parents' evening.'

'I have a date.'

Joshua quirks an eyebrow. He is silently asking what is more important: your child's parents' evening or a date. Quite frankly, this date is the most important thing that has happened to me in a long, long time. My future happiness depends on it.

'I'm scheduled to work the early shift and that's what I'm going to do.' I tilt my chin in the air, challenging Joshua to make me do otherwise. We stare at each other for a moment, me chin-up, Joshua still with that eyebrow quirked. Perhaps it's stuck.

'You've requested a few days off next month.'

My chin dips, ever so slightly. It's Callum's stag weekend next month. He kept flip-flopping over what he wanted to do so it's only just been booked, and I've only just put my request for leave through.

'Are you blackmailing me? You'll deny my time off request if I don't do the mid-shift tomorrow? The schedule isn't even your job. You can't deny my request.'

Joshua shrugs. His eyebrow finally drops back into its natural place. 'I'm not blackmailing you. Like you said, the schedule isn't down to me. But I really would appreciate it if you'd switch your shift tomorrow.'

And I'd really appreciate it if Joshua Michaels would crawl away, back to where he came from before he stole my job. Because he may be saying he isn't blackmailing me, but it very much feels as though he is and I can't miss Callum's stag weekend, not even for Oliver. My hands clench themselves into fists.

'Fine. I'll do the shift.'

'Thank you, Daisy.'

I stalk past Joshua, yanking the door to the staffroom so hard I wouldn't be surprised if it came off its hinges.

–

Oliver and I rearrange our date for Monday, which is my next day off, and the only thing that gets me through the Friday mid-shift is the hatred I feel for Joshua Michaels. I feed on it. Thrive off it. And the hatred becomes a full-on buffet when, on Sunday evening, after a shift that leaves me on my knees with gratitude that I have the next day off (a *whole day* to prepare for my date with Oliver), I receive a text while having a comfort-scroll through Vinted while Mum watches a *Vera* repeat.

My initial reaction to seeing a message from Oliver is joy. It ignites in me like a pop of warmth in my chest and I'm grinning as I close the Vinted app and tap on my messages. But the pop of warmth is cooled when I read Oliver's words and, rather than reply to him, I head straight to the 'Friends Without Benefits' group chat.

Daisy:
Guys! O has cancelled our date! Saddest face

Jesy:
You're rearranging again?

Daisy:
Nope. Full cancel. He's 'getting back together with his ex'. How many times have I heard that before? Why not just say he finds me hideous and doesn't want to go out with me?

Jesy:
He does not find you hideous

Callum:
Maybe he really is getting back together with his ex. It happens!

Daisy:
It's an excuse. It's always an excuse

Callum:
Then he's an idiot. You should count yourself lucky that you don't have to endure a whole date with him to find that out

Daisy:
This is all JM's fault

Callum:
JM?

Daisy:
Joshua Michaels. My stupid supervisor
with his stupid face and his stupid
I'm-the-King-of-Brinkley's attitude

Callum:
How is this his fault? OMG is he the ex?

Daisy:
THERE IS NO EX

Callum:
I'm confused

Daisy:
This is JM's fault because if I hadn't
cancelled our date for Friday, we would
have met up and fallen in love by now

Callum:
But why would you want to fall in love with
an idiot?

I close the group chat. Sometimes, there's no arguing with stupid.

'Everything okay, love?' Mum turns away from the TV as the adverts start. I could tell her about Oliver and Joshua 'Stupid Face' Michaels, but I don't think she'd get it. Veronica Grant is not at all clued up on the world of dating. She met my dad when she was sixteen, married him when she was eighteen, and had me and then my brother an orderly two years apart. She hasn't experienced the trauma of being dumped. The limbo of will-he-call? She hasn't had her date cancelled with a pathetically lame excuse. By the time Mum was my age, she had a husband, her own home, and an eight- and six-year-old.

'Everything's fine.' I push my phone away as a notification for the group chat lights up the screen. I resist it for almost thirty seconds before I snatch it back up again.

> **Jesy:**
> So Oliver isn't our dream guy. We need to regroup. Clementine's?

I'm exhausted, both physically and now emotionally, but a girl needs her friends when she's been dumped. Does it count as being dumped if you've never actually made it to the first date?

'I'm going out.'

Mum frowns at me and nods towards the telly. 'But don't you want to know who killed that poor girl?'

'I know who killed that poor girl.' I drag myself off the sofa and look down at my outfit. Jeans and a slightly scruffy t-shirt will do for Clementine's on a Sunday evening, especially as I haven't done my washing yet this week.

'This is the third time you've seen this episode. I don't know why you waste your time with repeats. That's why I pay for Netflix and Amazon Prime, so there's always something for us to watch.'

'With my memory, it's like watching it new again.' Mum reaches for her mug and finds it empty. 'You have fun, love. I'm putting the kettle on.'

–

I'm the first to arrive at Clementine's, even though I live the furthest away. I order my drink and have a little chat with the barmaid while I wait for the others as it's pretty dead. Brunch has been and gone and it's a bit early for the night-time crowd, so Christina is hardly rushed off her feet. I tell her about Oliver (who she brands 'a complete knob' and I can't disagree, no matter how charming he'd been during coffee the other day) and Christina recounts some of her horror stories of dating, which makes me feel less alone. Less of a loser. Because it seems like everyone around me has got their love lives sorted: Mum and Dad, my baby brother, Jesy and Ant, Callum and Zara. It's tough being the only singleton but Christina gets it. She is a loser without love too.

'Hey, you.' Jesy finally arrives and places a hand on my back, making little soothing circles. 'How are you doing?'

'I'm feeling bitter. Rejection smarts.'

'I know, babe.'

Jesy does know, because once upon a time she was a loser without love too. Before Ant, Jesy had experienced the lot: first-date butterflies, rejection, intoxicating first flushes of lust, ghosting, floating-on-a-cloud of love, being dumped-by-text. But that's what I find so inspiring about her relationship with Ant. She's been through the hell of dating and not only survived; she's found that one person she wants to spend the rest of her life with. The man she wants to marry. To have babies with, even unexpected ones.

'Shall we get very, very drunk?'

I lean my head against Jesy's shoulder. 'You can't.'

'But you can. I'm eating for two, you can drink for two.'

'That sounds like a very good plan.' Smiling, I peck a kiss on my friend's cheek. 'Have you told Ant yet?'

'I have.'

'And?'

Jesy bites her lip and fiddles with the button on her cardi. 'And he's so excited about it. We both are. Obviously, he was shocked at first – we really weren't trying, quite the opposite – but we've been talking and getting our heads around it all and actually I can't wait. I'm going to be a mum!'

'You're going to be an amazing mum.' I throw my arms around my friend and give her an enormous squish. Despite the rejection from Oliver still stinging, my heart feels full for my best friend.

'Shall we go and grab a booth before I start crying? Hormones are all over the place.'

I release Jesy and hop down from my stool. We choose a booth towards the back, where we can spot Callum when he arrives. We order more drinks and a plate of chips to share, which have all been gobbled up by the time Callum appears.

'So, before we discuss Daisy's dream guy plan, I have news to share.' Jesy waits until Callum has slid into the booth and removed his jacket before she continues. 'Don't be offended that Daisy already knows. It doesn't mean she's a better friend than you. Even though she is.' Jesy smirks at Callum. 'It was Daisy's dream that prompted me to take the test in the first place.'

'Test?' Callum's head tilts almost imperceptibly to the side. 'As in a…'

Jesy nods. 'A pregnancy test. I'm pregnant!' Jesy's face is alight, her eyes burning brightly and her smile doing its best to stretch from ear to ear. Any doubts she'd had about the pregnancy have clearly been drop-kicked into oblivion because she could not look more thrilled right now.

'Congratulations.' Callum reaches across the table as best as he can and envelops Jesy in a hug as she rises to meet him.

'It'll be you and Zara next.'

Callum plops back down into his seat. 'I don't know about that.'

'You don't want kids?'

Callum shrugs. 'Maybe. One day. But not any time soon.'

Jesy places a hand on her stomach, even though it's as flat as the pancakes on Clementine's brunch menu. 'I thought that. Sometimes life surprises you. Anyway.' She reaches into the pocket of her cardi and produces a slip of paper, which she unfolds. 'Let's get on with Daisy's dream guy plan.'

I snort. 'What plan? It's gone completely tits up. Oliver clearly isn't my guy, and we don't have the dress.'

'So what?'

I pull back my chin and look at my friend in a way that I hope conveys how ridiculous I think she is. 'So we have nothing.'

'Not yet, no.' Jesy smooths out the slip of paper. 'But we *will* have the dress. I've emailed the shop's head office to see if they can help locate it.'

Bubbles of hope fill up my chest. 'And?'

'And they haven't got back to me yet.'

Pop, pop, pop.

'But it's the weekend. I'm sure they will, because your dream is going to come true. We're going to find the dress and you're going to find your dream guy.'

'How?'

Jesy taps the paper in front of her and I notice there are a few amendments to the notes she initially jotted in her flat. 'You're not going to leave it up to fate. You're going to be proactive. You're going to get back on that app and start dating again. Because he's out there, Daisy, and you won't find him sitting here in Clementine's.'

I groan. 'Do I have to go back on the app? Because I've been there, done that and got a million tear-soaked t-shirts.'

'But this time it's going to be successful. We have the proof right here.' She places a hand on her pancake-flat stomach again. 'You're destined to find The One.'

Chapter Eight

I've had some terrible dates lately, but this one isn't so bad. He didn't cancel to get back with his ex, which is always a good start, and he arrived on time, early in fact, and was waiting at a table beside the community bookshelf when I arrived at the coffee shop. He'd plucked a crime novel from the shelf and was reading the blurb when I approached.

Jesy's revised plan says I have to date as many men as possible to stand the best chance of finding my dream guy so I'm opting for the more casual (and less costly) coffee date and have chosen the independent coffee shop where Oliver and I had our pre-date (pre-non-date?) coffees. Callum says it's like returning to the scene of a crime but I had a good vibe while I was there and a tiny, petty part of me is hoping to run into Oliver so he'll see I'm absolutely fine with him snubbing me.

My date today is Jordan, a plumber from Bolton who likes action films, his cats and baking. I've gleaned this information from his profile on the *Love Today* app because, as per Jesy's plan, I'm not to get too invested in messaging potential dates. If they're not interested in meeting up within a handful of messages, it's time to move on and find someone who is. It feels a bit cold and clinical but, as Jesy pointed out, we're on a clock here and time is running out.

Jordan offers to buy the coffees, which is a nice touch and although I could be super feminist and insist on paying for my own, I graciously accept. I'm further impressed when Jordan not only returns with coffee but with cakes too.

'You choose.' Jordan slides the plates towards me and, after careful consideration, I opt for the cheesecake.

'Your profile says you like to bake.' I pick up the fork from the side of the plate and slice off a dainty piece.

'I love it. I find it really relaxing to switch off from the world and simply focus on creating something delicious for my friends and family to enjoy.'

Jordan's face is lit up like the midnight New Year sky. Baking is clearly his passion, and it reminds me of how I used to feel about photography back in college, where capturing the perfect shot gave me such a buzz.

'What's your favourite thing to bake?'

Jordan wriggles the pretzel free from his cupcake. 'Apple crumble. It's my gran's recipe and even the smell of cinnamon and apple brings back memories of being in her kitchen with my sleeves rolled up and my pinny dragging on the floor.'

I find myself leaning in towards Jordan as he tells me more about baking in his gran's kitchen. His delight is infectious and I can almost smell the cakes fresh from the oven. He seems like the perfect date. He isn't setting my heart racing but he's attractive and he's down to earth and there have been no awkward silences as we chat, moving on from baking to films and then our bucket lists. My bucket list isn't nearly as packed as Jordan's, but I'd like to see the Northern Lights and getting the promotion to team manager and moving out of Mum and Dad's was definitely on there.

We're two coffees down and there's nothing but crumbs left on the plates when Jordan lifts his sleeve to check the time on his watch. 'I've had such a great afternoon but I'm afraid I'm going to have to get going. I said I'd pop round to take a look at my mum's kitchen sink. I'd like to meet up again though. Do you like bowling? Or maybe we could watch a film?'

Jordan's waiting for an answer but all I can focus on is his wrist. Or rather, the watch that's wrapped around it. It's steel grey with a black face and silver hands. It isn't the watch I saw in the dream. Not even close.

'Do you have another watch? One with a broken face?'

Jordan straightens, a frown lining his forehead as he processes my out-of-the-blue question. 'No.' He covers his watch with his sleeve. 'This is my only one.'

I can picture that second date with Jordan. We'll go bowling. We'll laugh at how terrible I am, and Jordan will tease me every time the ball drops into the gutter. I'll nudge him and pout and pretend to be offended and he'll say sorry while still grinning, because I really am that bad. Maybe we'll kiss that night. Maybe it'll be on the third date. Maybe we'd go on a fourth date, a fifth. Maybe we'd become a cute couple who dunk our biscuits as we watch films. That sounds like a damn good relationship, but it isn't the relationship I'm searching for. Jordan, unfortunately, is not my dream guy. So, we won't go bowling because I have to find my dream guy, because I have never felt the way I did when I was with him. I need to find the guy from my dream so I can feel it all over again.

–

'So let me get this straight.' Callum has his most serious look on his face as he processes what I've just told him and

Jesy about my date with Jordan. It's about an hour after the date and I'm sitting on Jesy's sofa for a post-mortem. 'You had a really nice date but you're blowing him off because he doesn't have a broken watch?'

'The watch is important. Without the watch, he isn't my guy.'

'Maybe he is your guy but he hasn't bought the watch yet and you've just ballsed the whole plan up.' Callum purses his lips and raises his eyebrows as he awaits my response.

'Who buys a broken watch?'

Callum's eyebrows drop back into place and his lips un-purse. 'Good point. But now you're still back at square one.'

Square one sucks. Square one means chatting to random blokes on the app while trying to dodge dick pics.

'Please don't make me go back on the app.' I drop my face in my hands and groan. 'My poor phone has seen enough knobs, thank you very much.'

'You don't have to.'

I move my hands down so I can peek at Jesy. 'Really?'

'Really.' Jesy opens her phone, taps the screen and slides it across the table towards me. 'You're going speed dating. No, don't look at me like that, Daisy Grant. I know we did the whole speed dating thing yonks ago and it was awful.' It truly was. I still have flashbacks about it. 'But this time it'll be different.'

'How?' Will dickheads and weirdos be ejected upon arrival? Because, from my experience, there won't be many dates to speed through if that's the case.

'This one has cake.'

Okay, now I'm intrigued.

Speed dating with cake? Five dates. Five mini desserts. Five chances to meet my dream guy. Plus, *five mini desserts*. I'd be a fool to turn down the opportunity.

The speed dating event is being held in a café tucked down a side street on the outskirts of the town centre. It's a cute little place with quirky mismatched furniture in bright colours and prints, and I'm hit with the scent of vanilla and freshly baked cakes as I step inside. I didn't think anyone did speed dating any more but any scepticism I'd felt about the event fizzles away and is replaced with joy and hope as I'm enveloped into the warmth and cheeriness of the place. With its whimsical décor and promise of sugary treats, this café feels like the kind of place where magic really can happen and perfect guys from dreams can appear in the flesh, ready to live happily ever after.

I'm given a sticky name tag, which I press down onto my chest. I've gone for my old faithful monochrome floral dress and Zara, who is top-notch at hair as well as make-up, has loosely French braided my hair, gathering it into a messy bun at the nape of my neck. I feel fabulously flirty and ready to meet my dream guy as I sit down at the table with the yellow rubber duck pattern. Nerves are jumbling around my tummy, but I do my best to push them away, to make room for the cake I've been promised. I look across at the next table, where there's a girl who can't be a minute older than eighteen but who appears to be a million per cent more confident than me as she sits with her back straight and her chin high, a smile playing at her lips as she observes the line of dates approaching us. I'm so busy watching her watching them, I don't notice my date sitting across the table from me until he clears his throat.

'Hello, Daisy.'

My eyes snatch away from the girl as she reaches out to touch the arm of her first date, telling him how great it is to meet him. I take in the height of my date, because he's towering over me even when we're sitting down, and the grimace on his face, as though he'd rather be sitting across the table from Agatha Trunchbull than me. To be fair, *I'd* rather face the chokey than date this guy, even if it's only for a matter of minutes.

I slump back in my seat and cross my arms with a sigh. 'Hello, Joshua.'

Chapter Nine

While moments ago my stomach had felt light with the flutter of nerves, it now feels heavy, as if there's a boulder lodged in there. I'd quite like to slump down further in my seat, to keep slumping until I'm under the table and no longer have to face Joshua.

It's a shock to see my supervisor sitting across the table from me, and not just because he's hijacked my speed dating event. I've never actually seen Joshua without the protective garb of the Brinkley's shopfloor and it's a jolt to see him without the heavy white coveralls and the hairnet that makes him look like an old woman gossiping over the garden fence with her rollers in. Joshua has rather nice hair and he's obviously made an effort tonight as the product he's used is giving his hair a glossy, sculpted look that still somehow appears soft. He's wearing a white shirt with a navy tie and an open cardigan, which should make him look ancient and school-teachery, but it somehow works in a hot nerd-boy sort of way.

I shake my head. Not a hot nerd-boy. Joshua Michaels is not hot. He is an uber knobhead who stole my promotion and made me miss out on my date with Oliver, potentially thwarting my chance to live happily ever after with my dream guy.

'I didn't expect to see you here.' Joshua pulls at the collar of his shirt. 'This is a bit…' He drums his abnormally long fingers on the table as he struggles to pinpoint the correct way to describe our situation.

'Of a nightmare?' Yes, I agree. This is a nightmare, and one I'd like to wake up from sharpish. I cannot believe this is happening to me, not even with all the horrific luck I've had with dating so far.

'I was going to say it's a bit weird dating a co-worker.'

'I'm not a co-worker. I'm your subordinate. Isn't this against the rules?' God, I hope so. I hope company policy says this date is forbidden and that Joshua Michaels must stand up and walk away immediately, especially as the desserts are coming out and it'll mean I'll get double helpings.

'I don't think it's against the rules per se.'

Damn it!

'I think if we were to enter into a relationship, then we'd have to inform management so measures could be put into place.'

'Well, I don't think we need to be informing anyone of this, do we?' A little plate is placed in front of me, and I seize the fairy cake that's sitting on it. The fairy cake is topped with white icing and a rainbow of sugary strands and it is perfectly fluffy and sweet when I take a giant bite. Beside me, the super-confident girl hasn't even touched her cake as she's so engrossed in conversation with her date, but I wolf mine down, rendering me unable to speak as I chomp. Joshua slowly peels back the paper case on his cake.

'Have you done this before?' His eyes scan the room, to indicate the speed dating event. I shake my head, my mouth full of fluffy sponge and icing sugar. 'Me either. I haven't dated for a while, to be honest. I thought this would be a fun way to get back out there.'

I snort. Fun? This? Not even the delicious nostalgic hit of the fairy cake can erase the cringe of this date.

'Hopefully you'll have more luck with the others.' I lick a bit of icing off my thumb. 'The girl next to me seems nice.' As if on cue, the girl throws her head back and laughs at something her date has said. 'Up for a laugh, at least.' I take in Joshua's cardigan again, and notice the way he's sitting upright, so straight and stiff there could be an ironing board stuffed up the back of it. Perhaps he won't have much luck with her after all. They're hardly a match made in heaven; she's fun and flirty and vibrant and he's rigid and serious and a humourless, miserable arse.

'Yeah.' Joshua pinches off a morsel of cake and pops it into his mouth, chewing demurely. Is he nibbling at his dessert on purpose, to make me look like a pig for scoffing my fairy cake in three bites? 'I don't think I'll have much luck with anyone, if I'm honest.'

'None of these women are your type? You haven't even given them a chance.' I scrunch up the paper case from my fairy cake, imagining it's Joshua's stupid head, and drop it onto the plate.

'It's not them. It's me.'

I roll my eyes. Is this where Joshua tells me he's too unattractive to find love, so that I'll disagree with him and tell him he's so attractive he can make a grandad outfit look alluring? Because I refuse to partake in boosting his ego.

'Is it your rubbish personality?' I dip my chin, so he won't clock the smirk on my face. If Joshua wants his ego massaging, he's come to the wrong table. My head snaps back up when Joshua barks out a laugh.

'That, coupled with the fact that my head's a bit mashed right now.' There's a teapot set out on the table with cups and saucers, sugar and milk, and Joshua pours himself a cup of tea. 'I don't think I'm actually ready to date.' He gestures at the other cup, and I nod.

'Then why are you here?'

Joshua shrugs as he pours tea into the second cup. 'My mum, mainly.' Ugh. He's a Mummy's Boy as well. 'She keeps going on at me to *get back out there* because *I'm still young* and *there's still time*.' He slides the cup and saucer towards me. 'And then I found out my wife is seeing someone else, even though we've only been separated for six months. It didn't seem long enough to me, but maybe she's got it right. Maybe my mum's right and it is time to *get back out there*.' He shudders, but there's a smile playing at his lips. 'Imagine that. My mum being right.'

I'd eat my own head before I admitted my mum was right about anything, but I don't say this out loud, not wanting to have anything in common with this man.

Joshua picks up the little silver tongs and plops two sugar cubes into his tea so daintily they barely make a splash, and I hold in a sigh. How many more minutes are there? Because if his tea-making technique is irritating me this much, it doesn't bode well for the remaining time.

Joshua nibbles at the rest of his cake and we drink our tea, and we barely say another word to each other as the minutes stretch by. Finally, thankfully, the bell rings to signal the end of the date.

'Wow, that went quick.' My tone is densely sarcastic, and Joshua huffs out an agreement as he eases himself up out of his seat.

'Let's never speak of this again?'

I didn't think I'd ever find myself agreeing with anything Joshua had to say, but this I can totally get on board with.

It's safe to say that Joshua Michaels is not the man of my dreams (and I think I'd rather remain single for the rest of my life if that was the case) but my next date isn't either. He's wearing a short-sleeved t-shirt that is a couple of sizes too small to show off his muscular frame, displaying his wrists that are bare of anything other than tattoos.

'Do you own a watch?' It probably isn't the expected first question on a date with a person you've never met before but the mini date with Joshua has put a dampener on the event and I can't be bothered messing around. There's no point putting any effort in if he doesn't own the broken watch.

My date – Bobby, according to his name tag – flinches back. 'Do I own a *watch*?' He looks down at his wrist, as if he expects to see one suddenly sitting there.

'I'm a watch enthusiast.' I shove my hands under the table, to hide the fact I'm not enthusiastic enough to wear one myself.

He shakes his head. 'I don't have one. Sorry.'

'Never mind.' I crane my head to see if I can spot the waitress with our next desserts.

My third date is wearing a watch, but it's an Apple watch and when I enquire about the possibility of another, older watch at home, he scoffs about needing anything other than the one sitting on his wrist and proceeds to list its functions, demonstrating by tapping on its screen until I feel the need to drop my head into my apple crumble and drown myself in the custard.

My fourth date doesn't own a watch; what's the point when he has a phone that tells him the time? And my fifth and final date is certainly not my dream date. I don't even get the chance to ask about his timekeeping device of choice as he looks me up and down as soon as his bum cheek has made contact with his seat and declares I'm not his type. Cracked watch or no cracked watch, this guy is a bigger knob than Joshua Michaels and there is no way I'd date him, let alone live miserably ever after with him.

–

'It was a complete waste of time.'

My friends have been waiting for me in Clementine's, ready and eager to hear the analysis of my speed dating experience. I don't leave them waiting a nanosecond more than is necessary, giving my verdict before I've even bothered to slide into the booth.

'It can't have been that bad.' Jesy shuffles over on the bench seat, and I plonk myself down next to her.

'The desserts were good. We had fairy cakes with sprinkles and American-style cheesecake and the apple crumble was *amazing*.'

'Forget about the desserts.'

My jaw drops as I look at Jesy. I haven't even told them about the raspberry cream cheese brownies or the chocolate chunk cookies yet.

'What about the dates? You know, the most important bit?'

I snort. 'Disaster. You'll never guess who showed up.'

Callum slams his hands down on the table and gasps. 'Not Ryan Reynolds?'

Jesy rolls her eyes. 'Why would Ryan Reynolds be there?'

Callum shrugs. 'He might have been hungry after the footie.'

'Woodgate is a bit far to travel from Wrexham.'

'It depends how amazing the apple crumble is.'

'But why would he be speed dating? He's happily married.'

'Again, it depends how amazing the apple crumble is.'

'It really was amazing, guys.' I shrug off my jacket. 'Hands down the best apple crumble I've ever had. We have to go back and have some when it isn't speed dating night.'

Jesy tuts. 'Will you forget about the desserts? What about *the dates*?'

'Terrible. None of them owns a cracked watch and Ryan Reynolds didn't show up. It was Joshua Michaels.'

'That guy from work?' Callum sits up straight. 'The guy who ruined your date with Oliver?' He sucks a breath in through his teeth. 'That must have been awkward, your boss turning up to date you.'

I glare at Callum. 'He isn't my boss. He's my supervisor. There's a difference.'

'And you're sure none of the others were our guy?'

I shake my head at Jesy. 'Not even close.'

Jesy winces. She places a hand on my arm. 'Never mind. We'll find him. There's still plenty of time.'

I nod, though I don't quite meet her eye. 'Have you heard back about the dress yet?'

Jesy shakes her head. 'Not yet. But we'll find that too. I promise.'

I nod again, but I'm nowhere near convinced. And my doubt only increases when the waitress stops by our table to let us know that Clementine's is now taking bookings for Christmas. Christina hands us a leaflet with the set menus and booking info, and when I turn it over there's an announcement about the New Year's Eve entertainment, which includes an Abba tribute act to bring in the new year.

Abba, not Elton John. Not like the dream at all.

Chapter Ten

I'm crushed about the dream, because it can't be real, can it? Apart from the fluke of Jesy's pregnancy, nothing is coming true: there's no guy with a cracked watch, no dress, and the New Year's Eve act at Clementine's is a foursome in glittery jumpsuits and platform boots rather than a single artist in a glittery jumpsuit and platform boots. Nearly there, but not quite. And I've checked my jewelry box over and over again and can't find a necklace with a squarish pendant and a jewel on the front.

The dream wasn't a flash forward to a life where I'm full to the brim with love. I'm not going to find the man of my dreams. I'm destined to either continue on the torturous treadmill of dating or remain single indefinitely. I'm not sure which one I dislike the idea of more.

Callum and I are in the park for our usual pre-brunch walk with Frankenstein. It's a mild day, quite warm with a gentle breeze, and I'd enjoy being out in the fresh air if I wasn't being plagued by the non-flash-forward dream.

'You throw it this time.' Callum taps the tennis ball with his foot, nudging it my way. 'My arm's aching. I hit the gym too heavy last night.' He flexes his arm, which produces very little bicep bulge.

'You haven't set foot in the gym since you set up your membership, and you only did that because Zara was a member there.'

Callum shrugs. 'We got chatting in the car park and when I asked her out, she said yes. There was no point in actually working out.' He nudges the ball again. 'Throw it before the hound wears a hole in the ground with his tail.'

Frankenstein is sitting in front of us, his tail swishing back and forth as he waits for somebody – anybody – to throw the ball. I stoop down and pick it up, throwing it across the field as hard as I can. Frankenstein bounds after it, catching it mid-air as it bounces off the grass. I grab my camera and try to capture the moment but I'm not quick enough.

'Do you think Jesy's going to make it this afternoon?'

Callum picks up the ball and throws it. I'm ready with my camera this time and take the perfect shot of Frankenstein mid-leap, his jaws open and ready to snap up the ball.

'I hope so. I need her to act as a buffer between me and my two families. It's going to be hell.'

It's Callum's birthday and his mum is hosting a barbecue to celebrate, which would be lovely if she hadn't begrudgingly invited Callum's dad and his family too. Callum's parents divorced years ago, way before I met him, but it hadn't been amicable and they couldn't seem to get past the bitterness, even when both parties had remarried. Callum and his sister, Belle, were stuck in the middle of the feuding pair, with a stepmother, stepfather and several half and step siblings on the opposing sides. The entire family was last together for Belle's twenty-first birthday party, where her mum and stepmother ended up having a full-on catfight, with hair-pulling, scratching and slapping, culminating in Callum's mum holding his stepmother in a headlock until Callum and his stepbrother managed to prise them apart. This is probably why Belle chose to celebrate her thirtieth birthday with her friends in Budapest last year instead of getting the family together, and it's definitely why Callum point-blank refused to have a party for his own twenty-first. The three of us spent the weekend in Amsterdam instead, where I had the whirliest of whirlwind romances with a Belgian backpacker. So, family gatherings were best kept separate, but for whatever reason, Debbie had decided to get everyone together in her back garden, with an open flame too close for comfort.

'Think of it as a practice run before the wedding. And you'll have me and Zara on hand, even if Jesy can't get her head out of the toilet bowl.' I aim the camera at Callum, and he gazes into the distance in a mock catalogue pose while I take the shot. 'Can you believe she's going to be a mum? I mean, it's so grown up.'

'I hate to break this to you, Daisy, but we *are* grown up. We're over a quarter of a century old. In a few years we're going to be *thirty*.'

I groan, knowing I'm going to be thirty and still single, still living with Mum and Dad and still playing make-believe that I'm going to meet the man of my dreams.

'But being a mum is *proper* grown-up.' I grab the tennis ball and throw it for Frankenstein. 'Like, moving in together is one thing and getting married is a huge commitment, but becoming a parent is on another level. You're responsible for another human being, making sure they're fed and clothed until they're a grown-up them-selves.' I'd definitely need a job that paid more than minimum wage if I had those obligations, but thanks to Joshua Michaels, that option has been snatched away. 'Do you want kids?'

Callum picks the ball up and pretends to throw it, smiling when Frankenstein scuttles off for a few steps before realising the ball hasn't sailed past. 'Yeah, one day.' He throws the ball for real this time. 'One day quite far off.'

'I want kids.' I didn't realise how much until my brother became a dad and I saw how much he adored them. He looks at Lexy and Lola as though they are the most precious things in the entire world and he would do anything to keep them from harm. I want to feel that way about somebody someday and I get a stomach-clutching ache when I think about never getting to experience it.

'How many?'

'Two?' I tilt my head to one side before shaking it. 'No, three. I'd have quite liked somebody to gang up against Oscar with when we were growing up. He could be a real pain in the arse.'

'It must run in the genes.' Callum nudges me with his shoulder. 'Three sounds like a good number to me. And I'd like them all with the same person and not scattered about like my own siblings.'

I lean my head on Callum's shoulder. 'That's the dream, but I don't think it'll ever happen for me.'

'Of course it will, you numpty.' Frankenstein has dropped the ball at our feet, but Callum makes no attempt to retrieve it and instead puts his arm around my shoulders. 'What about your dream guy? Do you not want your three babies with him?'

'That was a silly idea. You never believed it was a premonition, and you were right. Nothing is adding up. I just really, really wanted it to be true. I want to fall in love like you and Zara did – and Jesy and Ant. I see what you guys have, and I want it too.'

'Nobody's life is perfect.' Callum releases me and picks up the ball. 'People only let you see what they want you to see.' He throws the ball, and we start to move towards the park gate. 'One day you'll find someone who deserves you, whether he's this dream guy with a broken watch or not. Because you're pretty awesome, you know.'

I bat Callum lightly on the chest. 'Why can't you be single and not my best friend with dainty teenage girl knees? Then *we* could live happily ever after.'

Callum stoops down when Frankenstein sits at his feet and attaches the lead to his harness before pocketing the tennis ball. 'You don't find my dainty teenage girl knees sexy?' He looks up at me, squinting against the sun, a teasing smile playing on his lips.

'I could never find you sexy. It'd be like fancying my brother.'

'Fair enough.' We've reached the gate, and Callum leans over to peck me on the cheek. 'I'll see you at Mum's at two. Don't be late. I can't deal with that pack of animals on my own for too long.'

'You'll have Zara there with you.'

Callum shrugs. 'She doesn't know them like you do.' He holds up a hand in farewell and we go our separate ways.

Chapter Eleven

It turned out Callum's worries were unfounded and there was no violence at the barbecue, which feels like a good omen for Callum and Zara's wedding in seven weeks' time. We enjoyed the food and sang 'Happy Birthday' to a red-cheeked Callum as his mum presented him with a cake ablaze with twenty-six candles, and he opened our presents with the enthusiasm of a small child at Christmas.

The booze continued to flow late into the night, and it was probably a mistake for me to stay until the end as my head is pounding as I drag myself out of bed the following morning, wincing and pulling back like a vampire as sunlight bursts through a gap in my curtains.

Today is going to be a fun day at work, I'm sure, and I'm dreading facing Joshua when I feel as though I've been pummelled half to death, buried semi-conscious and dug up again before being deposited on the production line of Brinkley's Biscuits. I've seen him a couple of times since our inadvertent date, but we've stuck to our word and haven't mentioned it, and I think we're both trying to forget it happened. Joshua will definitely bury the incident deep in the recesses of his mind when he clocks my grey, craggy-looking skin and bags the size of a builder's heavy-duty rubble sack under my eyes.

'Joshua isn't about, is he?' I've clocked in two minutes late and I've yet to secure my hair into its net properly, and I'm really not in the mood for a stern word from our supervisor. But Melanie shakes her head.

'He isn't in.'

'He isn't?' I brighten and straighten up, as though somebody has replaced my batteries and I'm suddenly raring to go. Or maybe they've just replaced the one battery and I'm ready to limp along rather than curl up and die, because I am still horribly hungover.

'He wasn't in most of yesterday either.' Melanie leans in close and lowers her voice. 'His grandad had a stroke, so he had to rush off to the hospital. He's still not in so I'm not sure that's a good sign.'

And now I feel awful for being pleased that Joshua isn't in. Guilt makes my stomach swim. Or maybe that's the gummy bear shots Callum's stepbrother made last night after his wife had taken their kids home? Either way, I have to take a few even breaths to ward off the nausea.

'They've put Sabina in charge of the line.' Melanie scrunches up her nose. 'She's like a drill sergeant, so I'd get that sorted if I were you.' She points at my hair, which is still only half in the net. I shove it all in and hurry to get to my position on the line. We're finishing off lime sorbet shortbread today and the lurid green buttercream is not helping my stomach to settle at all. Melanie is right about Sabina, who stalks up and down the line, berating us for not working fast enough even though we're well on target, and criticising our pipe work, even though there is nothing wrong with it at all. It's almost enough to make me miss Joshua being around.

This notion evaporates as soon as Joshua returns to work a couple of days later, grumpier than usual and with the whip-cracking dialled right up. Rumour spreads quickly across the Brinkley's shopfloor, facilitated by

Melanie and Johanna from the canteen, and despite my grievances against the man, I'm saddened to learn that Joshua's grandad passed away. Still, it doesn't excuse Joshua's authoritarian behaviour as he creeps up and down the line, picking fault with absolutely anything, as though he's on high alert, desperate to find something – *anything* – to moan about.

'I can't believe I ever thought he was fit.' Melanie's up the line from me, dotting the tiniest sugar paste snowflakes onto the biscuits with tweezers. She shakes her head and puffs out a bitter laugh.

'I can't believe I miss Kath.'

I bob my head up and down and widen my eyes at Jeremy's words. 'Right? I thought Kath was the worst, but she's like Mary Poppins compared to Joshua. I keep expecting horns to appear from underneath his hairnet and I'd quite like to shove that clipboard up his arse. Sideways.'

'Nope.' The voice comes from behind me and my stomach drops when I realise it belongs to the devil-man himself. 'No horns up there.'

I peek over my shoulder and see Joshua patting down his hairnet.

'And speaking of my clipboard…' He whips the clipboard out from under his arm and scrutinises it, humming a playful tune as his eyes drop down the list. 'Ah, yes. Here we are. You seem to be way under target this morning, Daisy.'

I turn back to the line, adding a black hat and two coal eyes to the snowman in front of me as quick as a flash. I've performed the action a gazillion times this morning, but there's a backlog of snowmen waiting for headwear and eyes.

'Maybe that's because you're constantly breathing down my neck. It's quite hard to focus when you're under surveillance.'

'Or maybe it's because you've had three toilet breaks in the space of an hour.'

'That's rubbish.' It can't have been *three*. I look up the line to Melanie, who shrugs in a could-have-been way. I move on quickly, before Joshua can elaborate on his claim. 'And I'm not the only one behind. We all are. Because you're creating a hostile work environment.'

'Ah, so you *do* know this is a work environment, because you haven't been doing much actual work. Gossiping. Whining. Sneaking off for unauthorised breaks, yes, but not so much with the work thing.'

Melanie drops her gaze, concentrating hard on the snowflake placement at this bit because she's nipped off for a couple of cheeky vapes and a flirt with Dougie from packing while Joshua has been away from the line.

'You may have got away with this kind of stuff in the past, but not any more. I want you all back on target otherwise you're catching up during your break.'

There's a chorus of 'what?' and 'no way', but Joshua simply resumes his playful hum and marches to the end of the line to check the final products. I wait until his head is dipped over the biscuits to give him the finger before I dive at the snowmen with my icing bag, working extra-fast because I really, really don't want to miss my break. I feel a proper bitch-fest with Melanie is due.

–

The bitch-fest doesn't happen as soon as I'd hoped because while I'm raring to go, having warmed up to getting everything off my chest while working on the snowmen biscuits, Melanie's priority as we clock out for lunch is to make a beeline for Dougie in the canteen. The pent-up frustration of having to deal with Joshua is bubbling dangerously close to the surface so it takes every ounce of restraint I possess not to make a snarky comment when the man himself stops by my table and asks if he can have a word. Swallowing all the bad words I'd like to throw at him in response, I smile tightly at Joshua.

'I'm having lunch with Melanie. Sorry.' I am not sorry. Not even a little bit. But Joshua isn't deterred. He looks across the room at Melanie, who's attempting to wrestle a chocolate bar out of Dougie's clutches.

'I'll be quick.' He places his tray down on the table and drops into the seat opposite mine, looking me straight in the eye. I try to maintain eye contact, to show that I am not intimidated, but I'm starting to feel a prickle of discomfort almost immediately and drop my gaze to the baked potato on my plate, mentally kicking myself for losing the battle. To save face, I tilt my chin in defiance, setting my jaw as I look to the left of Joshua, eyes slightly narrowed as though I'm far more interested in something happening in the distance than whatever it is Joshua Michaels has to say.

'What's going on with your targets, Daisy?'

I'm not interested in *that*, because I know I haven't been quite meeting them over the past few days. Sabina may have been lording it over us with her temporary position of power, but she doesn't possess the same level of authority as Kath or even Joshua and we may have taken advantage of the situation.

I fold my arms across my chest, still refusing to look at Joshua. 'I'm not the only one lagging.'

'I know that, but this isn't like you.'

I narrow my eyes further and finally lock my gaze onto Joshua's. 'How would you know that? You don't know me.'

Joshua nods, his face passive. Reasonable. Which only infuriates me more. 'That's true, but I've heard about you. I know what you're capable of, but you seem to be slipping. You've become easily distractable. Distracting, even. And you seem to have a problem with me.'

I nearly huff out a laugh at that one. 'A problem' is an understatement.

'You need to act more professionally, Daisy. Telling the team you'd like to shove my clipboard where the sun doesn't shine – sideways – isn't respectful and I'd like that sort of behaviour to stop.'

Joshua's tone is level, neither friendly nor reprimanding, but I still feel as though I'm getting a telling off from the headteacher. My shoulders drop as I shrink down into my seat, all the sweary words withering away in my head. My eyes dart around the room, checking to see if anyone is listening in to this conversation, because the only thing worse than being scolded is having an audience to witness it. Nobody seems interested in us thankfully, everyone is too busy eating and chatting, but I still feel doused with shame, which fuels the fury I feel at Joshua. Throwing my shoulders back, I straighten in my seat, refusing to be cowed by this man.

'I am very sorry for saying I would like to shove your clipboard up your arse – sideways.' I smile sweetly at Joshua. 'And I am very sorry for suggesting we should shove you in a box of polar bear biscuits and ship you off to the North Pole for a laugh. Or for starting the rumour that...' I shake my head and cover my mouth

with my fingers. 'Never mind. That *was* unprofessional.'
I take a moment to enjoy Joshua's raised eyebrows as he
imagines what rumour I've spread about him. I haven't
spread any rumours but hopefully the seed I've just planted
in his mind will niggle at him for a good while. 'I haven't
been fair to you and I will try to be better.' My smile is
sickeningly sweet now and plainly fake and it slips into a
smirk when Joshua scrapes back his chair and stands up,
signalling the end of the conversation.

'I hope so, Daisy. I really do.'

I wait until Joshua has picked up his tray and turned
away from me before I stick my tongue out at him. It's
childish but it feels good.

'What were you two chatting about?' Melanie drops
into the chair next to mine, unwrapping the chocolate
bar she's successfully manhandled from Dougie.

'He was being a knob as usual.' I stab my fork into my
baked potato, a string of cheese forming as I pull it back
out again. 'Giving me grief about my targets.'

Melanie bites a chunk off the chocolate bar, speaking
as she chews. 'You know, if you two were in a film, you'd
be snogging by the end of it. I love an enemy-to-lovers
story, don't you?'

The cheese string flops back onto the top of my potato
as I dump my fork on my plate, appetite well and truly
wiped out by the very notion of me and Joshua getting
within kissing distance of one another.

Chapter Twelve

The second week of June marks Brinkley's annual Summer Family Fun Day, which takes place in the car park of the factory. All the cars are moved out and in their place are bouncy castles and other small rides, street food stalls, an ice cream van, entertainers keeping everyone amused with juggling, magic and balloon modelling, plus face-painting, a tombola and a photo booth. Employees are encouraged to attend, which most do because it's all free, including the food, and if we're going to work our arses off for minimum wage, we're going to take every perk that company founder Neville Brinkley has to offer. The best bit is that the factory is completely shut down, which only ever happens for the Family Fun Day and the Christmas period. Everyone's entitled to five tickets, which are intended for partners and children but, since I have neither of those, I've brought Callum, Zara, Jesy and Ant along.

'Do you think they'll have Canadian poutine again this year?'

I give Jesy an odd look as we pass the security booth, having shown our tickets to Richie, the one poor bugger who still has to work today. 'I thought we all agreed last year that it was utterly vile and looked like a cat had vommed on chips and gravy?'

'We did.' Jesy places a hand on her stomach. 'But baby likes the idea.'

'Remind me to never, ever get pregnant.' I snort. 'As if I'd ever get the chance.'

'You had no luck with the speed dating thing then?'

I shake my head at Zara. All her hard work on braiding my hair had been wasted. 'No luck at all.'

I find myself scanning the car park for Joshua, but the place is crammed with employees and their families. I spot Drill Sergeant Sabina bossing her kids around at the photo booth, making them pose again and again, Melanie waving to her niece as she passes by on the carousel, and Johanna from the canteen is tucking into a Greek kebab while nodding along to whatever the managing director, Jasper Brinkley, is saying.

'You'll find someone. There's no rush.'

I push my lips upwards into a smile at Zara. I keep hearing words to that effect, but it's usually from people who are already married or are about to be and it doesn't quell the rising panic that I'm going to be single forever while my friends move forward with their lives, with husbands and wives and children.

'Shall we go on the bouncy castle before we get something to eat?'

Zara rolls her eyes and tuts at Callum. 'The bouncy castle is for little kids, not big ones.'

'Says who?' Callum grins at me and I know what he's asking without the need for words. I whip my camera from around my neck and push it into Jesy's hands and Callum and I race towards the pink and yellow inflatable castle, kicking off our shoes and yelping with joy as we throw ourselves around. Callum performs a messy-looking somersault, landing on his back, and I scissor-kick my legs as I propel myself higher and higher. It's really fun until a stern-looking woman yells at us for being on there and ushers us back onto solid ground. Being kicked off the bouncy castle is bad enough, but it's made even worse when I realise one of the dads is waiting for us to get out of the way so his daughter can have a turn.

'Having fun?'

I groan, recognising that voice from the finishing line and my nightmares. I peek up from tying my shoelace and there he is: Joshua Michaels, towering over me with his arms folded and an eyebrow quirked.

'I was.' My chest is rising and falling rapidly, and my words are slightly wheezy. Forget the gym, they should start a membership for bouncy castle workouts. I'm knackered but it's much more fun than running on a treadmill. Not that I've ever run on a treadmill but it looks about as entertaining as watching *Gardeners' World* with Mum, but without the cute factor of Monty's dogs.

'You should try it.' I pull my lace into a bow and push myself up onto my feet so that Joshua isn't towering over me quite so menacingly.

Joshua narrows his eyes. 'I don't think so.'

I shrug, in a 'it's your loss' kind of way, but I can't imagine Joshua going wild on a bouncy castle. He's dressed a bit more casually than he was during our speed date; tie-less with his shirt's top couple of buttons open, and he's wearing navy jeans instead of trousers, but he doesn't look bouncy castle-ready. He looks rigid and intense, although some of that could be down to the grief of losing his grandfather, to be fair.

'I can't believe I've been relegated to cloakroom assistant.' Jesy stomps her way over and holds my camera out towards me.

'Sorry.' I take the camera and loop the strap around my neck. 'But you're pregnant, so no bouncy castles for you.' I remove the lens cap from my camera and turn towards the bouncy castle, lining up a shot and capturing the moment a little girl is at the peak of a star jump, her hair flying, eyes wide, grin wider.

'What are you doing?' Joshua glares down at my camera, trying to look at the image on the screen, but I whip it away from him.

'I said I'd take some photos of the fun day for the website.'

Joshua quirks his eyebrow again. 'And don't you think you should ask permission from parents before you start paparazzi-ing their kids?'

'It's in the terms of service for the tickets that photos or videos may be taken for promotional use.' I try to quirk *my* eyebrow at Joshua, but I can't quite manage it. 'Didn't you read them?'

'Everything okay?' Callum has sensed the hostility between us and he's at my side, his arm a comfort against mine.

I smile sweetly at Joshua. 'Everything's fine. Right?'

'Yep.' Joshua shoves his hands in his pockets, his face as stony as ever. 'Everything's fine.'

There's a hand on my other arm and Jesy nods towards the food stalls when I turn to her. 'I need food, or I'll throw up.'

'You need food, or you'll throw up?' I frown at my friend. 'Aren't you more likely to throw up if you eat?'

Jesy shrugs. 'I don't make the rules. It's a pregnancy thing. If my stomach feels empty for too long, I'll vom.'

'Let's get you some food then.' I thread my arm through Jesy's as we head for the stalls, grateful for an excuse to get away from Joshua. Callum spots Zara and they head over to join the queue for the photo booth.

'Who was that?' Jesy glances behind us, where Joshua is still standing at the bouncy castle.

'My new supervisor. And the biggest arsehole in the world.' I line up a shot of the crowds around the street food stalls. There's a good variety on offer this year: burritos, Yorkshire pudding wraps, Korean-style fried chicken, tapas and paella, Chinese pancakes, NYC-style subs and bagels, Caribbean stews. There are also sweet treats on offer, with doughnut and candyfloss vendors, cake stalls and the ice cream van, and, of course, Brinkley's biscuits.

'*That's* Joshua Michaels?' Jesy turns her whole body to have another look at him. 'You never said he was hot. Jeez, Daisy, that's the first thing you tell your mates.'

I give her arm a tug, to keep her on track to the food stalls. 'He isn't that good looking.'

Jesy splutters. 'Not that good looking? He's gorgeous, babe, especially with that broodiness going on.'

'First of all, I think your hormones are going haywire. And second of all, that isn't broodiness. It's grief. His grandad just died.'

'Aww, poor bloke. You should go and console him.' Jesy nudges me and bobs her eyebrows up and down.

'I'm not going to go and hit on a grieving man, and I'm definitely not going to go and hit on Joshua Michaels.'

'But he's *hot*. Don't you think he's hot?'

I glance back at Joshua, who's still hovering around the bouncy castle. Maybe he's contemplating having a go himself after all?

'Okay, he's quite good looking if you can get past the fact he's been a knob.'

'By accepting a job he wanted?'

'By blackmailing me into working that shift?'

Jesy looks up at the sky before giving a reluctant nod. 'Alright, that was pretty knobhead-ish. But look at him, Daisy. *Look at him.*'

I do. And I have to admit that Jesy's assessment of him is on the nose; Joshua Michaels is a fine-looking man when he isn't wearing that daft hairnet or carrying around the clipboard of doom. But I'm not interested. Not in Joshua. Not in men in general. I've officially given up on finding my dream man as it turned out it was all a load of hooey, with nothing adding up apart from Jesy's knocked-up state, and I've officially given up on dating because I simply cannot bear the thought of putting myself through it one more time. After two years of hunting for love, I'm done.

–

Jesy wolfs down a Yorkshire pudding wrap followed by a bagel with a marmalade filling and she's now got her head stuck down the toilet. Ant's with her, saying soothing things over the sound of retching, and Callum and Zara are being cute on the carousel. I watched them for a couple of rotations and captured the moment on camera but if I have to watch the loved-up couple holding hands across their horses for any longer, I'll be joining Jesy in the bogs to hurl.

Instead, I'm wandering around the car park with a massive pink fuzz of candyfloss on a stick, stopping occasionally to take photos of the family fun. The candyfloss is gone by the time I make an entire loop of the car park and end up back at the carousel, where Callum and Zara have dismounted and taken their display of devotion elsewhere. I'm about to make another circuit to search for them when I spot Joshua sitting astride a horse with sparkly purple hair, and I'm so shocked at the sight, at Joshua's enthralled face as he glides up and down on the ride, that I watch him pass by two more times before I reach for my camera and capture his delight. The aura of grief has lifted momentarily, taking away the dullness in his eyes and allowing him to smile and whoop as the horse plummets.

But the stoniness snaps back into place when he spots me taking the photo and he's scowling at me when the ride rotates him back into my line of vision again. He looks really, really angry. Hopping mad. More hopping than two days ago, when I'd yelled at him about having irregular periods after he'd pulled me up on the fact I'd been using the same excuse to nip to the loo for the past three-and-a-bit weeks. Just as I'd yelled the words, Jack from HR had strolled past and had definitely heard, even over the din of the machinery.

The ride is starting to slow down so I make a swift exit before Joshua dismounts and vents his fury at being caught having a bit of fun, scurrying towards the crowds surrounding the food vendors so I can try to blend in. I grab a doughnut, just for something to do, and head for the toilets to check on Jesy. My trainers squeak on the floor as I make an emergency stop in the corridor, and the noise alerts Joshua, who's waiting outside the ladies'.

'You took my photo without my permission.' He nods at the camera. 'You need to delete it.'

I shake my head. 'I don't need to do anything. Terms and services, remember?'

'So technically you don't *have* to, but what about being a decent person and doing it because I've asked?'

A decent person? The cheek! This is the man who blackmailed me into working a shift that potentially ruined my chances of living happily ever after. The man who begrudges bathroom breaks. Even Kath let us use the bog.

'You didn't ask though, did you?' I try the eyebrow quirk thing again. Why can't I do that? 'You demanded.'

'Fine.' Joshua huffs out a massive sigh. 'Will you please delete the photo?'

I grab my camera and tap at the buttons until I find the one of Joshua on the carousel. 'You mean this one? The one where you're smiling and looking human?'

'Yes.' Joshua grits his teeth and sighs again, but smaller this time. Less audibly. 'That one. Please.'

I shrug and smile sweetly, enjoying getting under *his* skin for a change. 'Okay.' I delete the photo. 'Done.'

Joshua nods once. 'Thank you.' He leans against the wall and glances towards the ladies' toilets. 'What's taking so long?'

I snort as I let the camera rest against my chest. Joshua Michaels really doesn't like bathroom breaks.

Joshua tuts and pushes the sleeve of his shirt up to check the time and I have to place a hand over my mouth to smother the squeak of astonishment. Because Joshua's watch has a shiny, conker-brown leather strap with gold edging to the face and, most staggering of all, there's a crack through the glass.

I am absolutely certain this is the watch from my dream.

Chapter Thirteen

Joshua covers the watch with his sleeve, and I have to curl my fingers into tight fists to prevent myself from grasping him by the arm and peeling back the sleeve to reveal the watch again, so I can take a really, really close look. Because it can't be *the* watch, can it?

We've established the dream wasn't a glimpse into the future, that it was simply a fuzzy brain blip where I invented the perfect New Year's Eve scenario after a particularly bad date. But it's there anyway, the watch my imagination presented to me, exactly as it was. There's the argument that I saw the dress on the cover of a magazine and unwittingly stored it away, but I hadn't met Joshua before the dream, so how could I have plucked his broken watch from the recesses of my memory?

'Daisy?'

I drag myself from my thoughts at the sound of my name. Jesy emerges from the ladies' with Ant and is so close she's practically standing on my toes but I hadn't noticed until now as I'm so focused on Joshua. He's pushed his hands into his pockets, and I can't help but stare at his wrist, sitting on the edge of his pocket. It's covered but I know the watch is there.

'Daisy?'

I snatch my eyes away and look up at Jesy. There are deep furrows on her face and she's peering at me closely.

'Sorry. Miles away.' I shake my head to try to dislodge the thought of the watch, sitting there, right in front of me. It doesn't work but I edge past it to focus on Jesy. 'All better?'

'Pretty much.' She threads her arm through mine and guides us towards the exit. 'There was the sweetest little girl chattering away in the next stall to her grandma. Or *gan-ma*.' She catches Ant's eye, and her worry wrinkles melt away from her face as she smiles wistfully. 'I wonder if we'll have a girl?'

'Fifty-fifty chance, I guess.' Ant lifts a shoulder and lets it drop. 'Happy and healthy, that's all I care about.'

Jesy pulls her chin back. 'Well, duh, me too. But that doesn't mean we can't imagine what he or she will be like. Or called...'

Ant shakes his head vigorously. 'Nope. No way. I am not naming my child Halo or Czarina. Happy and healthy and not with one of those names.'

'What do you think?' Jesy squeezes my arm, but although I've been listening to the conversation, the details have slipped away already because my mind can't help wandering back to the watch. *Joshua's* watch. The watch from my dream. It *can't* be right. Joshua cannot be the man of my dreams because he is the biggest dickhead I've ever met and I can't stand the thought of spending a shift with the bloke, never mind the rest of my life.

'Daisy?' Jesy's peering at me again, her head tilted to one side as we emerge out of the Brinkley's building and into the sunshine.

'Yeah?' I glance behind, desperate for one last glance at Joshua down the corridor, but the door has already swung shut.

'Never mind.' Jesy huffs out a sigh. 'Let's go and find Callum and Zara.'

We find them at the tombola, unfolding little blue tickets, and Zara whoops when she matches one of her tickets to a Brinkley's biscuit hamper.

'I never win anything.' Zara is almost physically buzzing with excitement as she lifts the cellophane-wrapped basket from the table.

Callum pulls back his chin and pushes his eyebrows together. 'Er, you won me.'

'And this biscuit hamper is the better prize by far.' Zara sticks her tongue out at him. 'I'm going to go and put this in the car. It's pretty bulky.'

I grab Callum's arm as soon as Zara has been swallowed up by the crowds. 'I need to speak to you and Jesy. Now.'

Callum's eyes widen. 'Are you okay?'

I splutter out a laugh. Am I okay? *Am I okay?* No, I am very much *not* okay. I've just discovered that my work enemy is the man I've been gushing about for weeks. The man I've been trying to find so we can live happily ever after. I'm on the brink of *freaking the fuck out*.

'Can I borrow Jesy for a teeny second?' I'm desperate to talk about Joshua and the watch but I can't do it with Ant within earshot. It's one thing letting your best friends see your bat-shit crazy side, but I can't display that in front of Jesy's fiancé.

'I'll go and grab a burrito.' Ant nods towards the street food stall and Jesy places a hand over her stomach.

'And I'll be as far away from that as possible.'

'I'll come and find you when I'm done.' Ant nods at us before heading off for the food stalls. I position myself in the middle of my friends and thread my arms through theirs as we start to wander in the opposite direction.

'Brace yourselves.' I take a deep breath. 'I've found the watch.'

'Which watch?'

I roll my eyes at Callum. *Duh.* 'The *watch*. From my dream.'

'You found the watch?' Jesy's mouth drops open. 'So does that mean you've found the guy?'

I nod. I wince. 'It's Joshua Michaels.'

'Your boss?'

I give Callum a pointed look. 'He isn't my boss. He's my supervisor. There's a difference. But yes, that Joshua Michaels.'

There's a low wall around the edge of the Brinkley's car park and Jesy unthreads her arm from mine, carefully lowering herself onto it.

'But why haven't you seen the watch before? You work with the guy.'

'We can't wear watches to work. Health and safety. I didn't see him with a watch on the date, but I saw it today.'

'Definitely?'

I nod and plonk myself next to Jesy on the wall. 'I'm absolutely sure.'

'Wow.'

I nod again. 'What am I going to do?'

'Do you have to do anything?' Callum sits on my other side. 'It isn't like you still believe the dream was real. None of the other stuff is adding up.' It's true. I don't have the dress and Jesy hasn't even had a reply about her dress enquiry, which is both rude and frustrating, and the Elton John tribute act isn't happening. 'Maybe it's just a coincidence? And you don't even *like* Joshua Michaels.'

'Right?'

Callum's eyebrows shoot up. 'What if it's a magic watch and it makes you fall head over heels in love with him?'

I nudge Callum's calf with the toe of my shoe and scrunch up my nose. 'There isn't enough magic in the world for that to happen. But he *does* own the watch and that must mean something.'

Jesy jerks upright on the wall. 'But wouldn't you have recognised him in the dream if it *was* Joshua?'

I shake my head. 'I hadn't met him when I had the dream and by the time I did, my memory was fuzzy. All I remembered was the darkish hair.' I gasp, my eyes widening. 'Joshua does have brown hair.'

Callum throws his hands up in the air. 'It must be him then. That's concrete proof right there. *Brown hair.*'

'I think the watch is concrete proof, don't you? And the fact that Jesy is going to be the size of a blimp by New Year's Eve.'

Jesy places a hand on her stomach. 'Am I really going to be that big? Do you think there's more than one in there? Because I'm only just coping with the idea of one.'

I give her hand a squeeze. 'Slight exaggeration. Just trying to make my point.'

Jesy puffs out a breath and nods. 'Good.' She gives my hand a squeeze this time. 'So, do you really believe Joshua is the man in your dream?'

I close my eyes and try to recreate the vision. I ignore the Elton John tribute act, block out the sounds of 'Crocodile Rock' and brush past the pregnant Jesy bit and focus on the man holding my hand. He is tall and he has brown hair and stubble across his jaw. He looks down at me and smiles and I see him. Properly see him. The fuzziness washes away and there is Joshua Michaels, clear as day.

'It was him.' I squeeze Jesy's hand with bone-crushing intensity as it hits me. 'It was Joshua in the dream. I *know* it was. I *know* I was in love with him.' I clutch Jesy's hand even tighter as I'm hit with a slightly mad thought. 'This could be perfect! We hate each other right now but it could be like one of those enemies-to-lovers things, like in the films. *You've Got Mail. The Bounty Hunter. 10 Things I Hate About You.*' I could easily name way more than ten things I hate about Joshua Michaels... Callum groans. 'You've been watching rom-coms with your mum again, haven't you?'

I shrug. 'I've got to fill my lonely spinster days somehow, and they're slightly better than watching *Vera* on repeat.'

Jesy sighs with relief when I finally release her hand from my grip so I can clap my hands together.

'It seems like we need a new plan then, guys. A really, really simple one.' I look at Jesy, my heart pounding in anticipation of what the new plan will involve. 'I need to seduce Joshua Michaels.'

A bubble of laughter erupts from my friends. Jesy does her best to disguise her mirth as a coughing fit, while Callum openly mocks me.

'Seduce Joshua Michaels? You? You've never seduced anyone in your life.'

Callum's right; I'm not the seducing type. I don't have it in me. I'm not flirty. I'm not a vixen. And it's hard to seduce someone when you're wearing dumpy shoes, coveralls and a hairnet, not to mention when the man in question makes your skin itch with fury.

'I need to get Joshua away from work. I need to ask him out on a date.'

My words sound so simple, but how can I do that? I've only ever asked one man out and he ended up cancelling, and I only had the opportunity to ask him out because it was part of my apology for snagging his shopping bag. I clap my hands together as I'm hit with another rom-com idea. 'I need to create a meet-cute situation with Joshua!'

'Even though you met weeks ago?'

Jesy shushes Callum and I continue. 'I could throw something over him – a load of flour? – and offer to buy him a drink to say sorry. I'll probably get bollocked for wasting flour but it'll be worth it.' I fidget on the wall because I can't seem to sit still as the excitement of it takes over the nerves and the doubt.

'Should it be this hard, though? If Joshua is your dream guy, The One...' Callum rolls his eyes, as though the notion of a 'One' is ludicrous and he isn't marrying his in a few weeks. 'If he's the person you're fated to be with, should it need all this manipulation, to be this forced? And shouldn't you at least *like* the guy?'

I'm stung by the harshness of Callum's words. It's like he deserves to be happy but I don't. Like I'm supposed to sit back and watch my friends fall in love and get married without ever experiencing it myself.

'Some of us have to work harder at finding love than others.' I push myself up from the wall. 'But that doesn't mean that we're less deserving and should accept the fact that we're going to end up alone.'

'I didn't mean that.' Callum reaches for my hand, but I snatch it away. He calls out my name as I walk away but I ignore him and head home. Later, as I'm scrolling through *Vinted*, Callum messages me to apologise for being a dick but I don't respond and continue my comfort scroll. I've been given the chance of happiness and I'm going to take it, no matter how much Callum scoffs at the idea.

Chapter Fourteen

I'm not one to blow my own trumpet but the photos from the family fun day have turned out really well. I've sent them on to the marketing team so they can add some of them to the website, and I've chosen a few of my favourites to pin up on the staffroom noticeboard. I've been the unofficial photographer for Brinkley's events ever since our work's Christmas bowling trip a couple of years ago. Like today, I pinned a few of the best shots on the noticeboard including Jeremy snorting raspberry slush out of his nose after laughing so hard when Sabina slipped, landed on her arse and sent her ball into the neighbouring lane, Johanna kissing the ball for luck moments before chucking it into the gutter, and Marvin and Richie hugging when their team won. They garnered such a positive reaction that I was asked to take photos of the Easter egg hunt a few months later. I've captured special moments from Brinkley's events ever since and though I'm not paid for the service, I do get a kick out of the reaction to my photos.

I'm pinning a picture of HR manager Jack giving a thumbs up as he takes an enormous bite of a burrito when Joshua stops behind me to study the photos. As well as the burrito shot, I've added a group photo of the canteen gang on the carousel, Melanie feeding a fluff of candyfloss to Dougie from packing, and Marvin mid-lick of an ice-cream in the security hut, his eyes wide as he clocked me and my camera.

'Just checking you deleted that photo of me on the carousel.'

I stand back to study my handiwork. 'We wouldn't want anyone to see you having fun, would we?' I squeeze my eyes shut and mentally kick myself. I'm supposed to be seducing Joshua, not sparring with him, but I can't help the sniping. It's become my go-to response when it comes to my supervisor. I take a deep, calming breath and turn to him to try again. 'It's a shame you made me delete it. It was a great photo.'

Joshua nods at the noticeboard. 'They're all great photos. I still don't want one of me prancing around on a rainbow-coloured horse on display though.'

'Got a macho image to keep up?' I don't mean to sound so sneering but come on! The guy's standing in front of me wearing a hairnet and bags over his shoes. It doesn't get much worse than that, image-wise. An image of the two of us on New Year's Eve flashes in my mind and I can't quite believe my dream guy is here, standing right beside me.

I pin another of my selected photos to the noticeboard – another group shot, this time of a few of the packing lot trying and failing to spell out the word 'Brinkley's' with their bodies – and I can feel Joshua behind me, scrutinising my choice.

'I really did delete that photo. I'm not a liar.'

Joshua holds his hands up. 'I never said you were. I'm just taking an interest in my co-worker's hobby. So much so that I'm not even going to reprimand you for clocking in late.'

I twist around and groan when I see the time on the clock. I should have clocked in three minutes ago and I haven't even got my protective gear on yet. I swallow the bitterness of the words I'm about to utter and smile as sweetly as I can at Joshua.

'Thank you.'

See, that wasn't so hard. I can say pleasant things to this man. I could even ask him out...

I inhale long and slowly through my nose and open my mouth to say the words.

Would you like to go for a drink some time?

Simple. To the point. No pressure.

But the words don't form on my lips because the door to the staffroom bursts open and Melanie is standing there in the doorway, panting and almost bent double.

'Good. You're here. It's Sabina and Jeremy.' She points in the direction of the shopfloor. 'Arguing. Headlock. Need help.'

'Which one's in a headlock?' Joshua shakes his head. 'Doesn't matter. Let's go.'

I slot the remaining photos into my locker and grab my hairnet and disposable overshoes before legging it after Melanie and Joshua. It turns out it was Jeremy in the head-lock and Sabina is now facing disciplinary action, which under normal circumstances would make me dizzy with giddiness as there isn't enough drama on the Brinkley's shopfloor for my liking, but today I feel rather flat because my chance to ask Joshua out has been scuppered. My mood is further subdued when I meet up with Jesy and Callum at Clementine's and I notice the posters for the Christmas and New Year festivities have been put up, making the Abba tribute act more official and proving yet again that the dream was nothing but a figment of my imagination. But I can't explain seeing Joshua's watch or forget the way I felt when I was with him that night. We're already halfway through June, which means I have six months to get Joshua to feel that way about me.

–

The days tick by and although I see Joshua multiple times, I can't find my voice when it comes to asking him out. I see him in the staffroom and the canteen and in my head I say something outrageously flirty, but in reality I am neither outrageous or flirty. I'm feeling dejected as I head home and the news that my brother and his family will be joining us for tea doesn't lift my spirits.

It isn't that I don't enjoy seeing my nieces, and I get on well with my brother's wife, Carmen, and even Oscar doesn't grate on me quite as much as he used to when we were growing up, but I don't need to see the happy-family star prize I'm missing out on right now. It would help if Carmen bitched about my brother's lack of washing up or his inability to pick up his dirty socks, and I'd love it if Oscar moaned about his wife pecking at him twenty-four-seven every once in a while, but my sibling is actually very good at pulling his weight at home and with the twins, and he never has a bad word to say about his wife. Quite the opposite. He is utterly in love with Carmen and is annoyingly vocal about it. When you're as unlucky in love as I am, it can be a real kick in the tits to witness it.

So I cocoon myself up in my bedroom before Oscar and his family descend and have a scroll through *Vinted* in a bid to cheer myself up. There's a cute navy blue and gold mini skirt with a diamond pattern that would look good with thick black tights and boots, but we're about to burst into full-on summer so it doesn't feel like the best time to tap buy. I scroll on and a denim jacket catches my attention. It's a decent price, but do I really need another denim jacket? Probably not. I'm scrolling again when I hear the doorbell downstairs. That'll be Oscar and the gang so I should go and show my face, even if it's only to say hello before I scuttle off back to my room. I tap away from the denim jacket and have one more absent-minded scroll as I push myself up into a sitting position and that's when I spot a long-sleeved silver sequinned wrap dress with a V neck and high waist. I sit up straight, one hand covering my mouth while the thumb on my other taps on the dress for more info.

It's my dress. The dress from the dream. And it's in my size.

I think I might pass out. My breaths are quick and shallow and it's making me feel lightheaded. This is another piece of the puzzle slotting into place. First Jesy being pregnant, then the watch, then remembering Joshua's face, and now the dress. It's happening. My dream is coming true. But to ensure it does, I'm somehow going to have to shed my utter distaste for Joshua and ask him out so we can fall in love.

Chapter Fifteen

I'm desperate to call an emergency meeting to discuss the dress and what it means with Jesy and Callum, but I can't flee while Oscar's here for tea, so I'm forced to sit down with my family and listen to their chatter while I shovel food in my mouth as fast as humanly possible. I'm hoping to slip away as soon as we've eaten but Carmen whips her tablet out of her handbag so she can show us the resort they've booked for their holiday. I make all the right noises as we're shown images of the pool area with its toddler-friendly slides and all-inclusive bar, the blocks of smart-looking apartments, and the relaxed restaurants. I'd usually be fizzing with jealousy (the family pool really does look like fun) but all I can think about is the dress and I'll burst if I don't tell the others about it very soon. I could reveal all in the group chat, but I want to see my friends' faces when I announce that I've located it, especially Callum's, whose doubts almost had me convinced that I was drifting into madness.

The holiday slideshow finally comes to an end and I'm about to make a break for it when Lexy tugs on my arm and asks me to drag the toy box out from under the stairs. I set the box out in the living room and step back as she dives in, but I don't get any further as she insists on making me a cup of tea. I crouch back down and accept the plastic cup while Lexy pours air out of the teapot.

'You sugar?' She holds up a tiny blue spoon.

'Two, please.' My thighs are burning, so I drop down onto my bum and cross my legs. Lexy taps the cup twice with the spoon before vigorously waggling it around inside the cup. If there had been tea in there, it would have sloshed over the sides and scalded my legs.

'You milk?'

'Yes, please.' I hold in a sigh. This fake tea is taking up a lot of time that could be spent strategising with my friends over real alcohol.

Lexy dives into the box in search of the little plastic jug. Books, a doll with matted hair, three cars and a fire engine come hurtling from the box before she triumphantly lifts the jug.

'I do milk.' Her sister snatches the jug from Lexy's hand and attempts to splash some into my tea, but Lexy snatches the jug back. Again, if there really had been milk in the jug, there wouldn't be a drop remaining inside.

'My milk. Lola, no.' Lexy shakes her head solemnly before pouring the milk into my cup, which is surely now overflowing with the length of time the jug is tipped upside down above the cup.

'Lola tea! Lola tea!' My niece launches herself at me and makes a grab for the cup. I relinquish it without putting up a fight. If Lola wants the fake tea, she's welcome to it because I'd rather be discussing my crazy New Year's Eve plan with my friends and a very big, very real, cocktail.

'Let's have some real tea, shall we?' Mum's been reading the reviews of the holiday resort, but she hands Carmen the tablet back. 'Put the kettle on, Daisy, love.'

Holding in a scream of frustration, I head for the kitchen. It takes a cup of tea, a detailed account of Oscar's recent work trip to Helsinki – complete with photos on the tablet – and the video of Lexy and Lola's baby ballet showcase before I'm able to escape. I tap out a message to the group chat as I scuttle along the garden path and fling open the gate, all the while expecting to hear Mum calling me back so I can sit through the story of the man who farted every time there was turbulence during Oscar's flight home again.

Clementine's. Urgent. Re NYE! I'll pick up. Y/N?

I throw myself into the car and head for Callum's first. I check the group chat and he's responded with a Y to say that he's up for the meet-up and he's making his way out of the building before I even get the chance to let him know that I'm outside. Jesy has also responded with Y (a HELL Y, in fact) so I make my way to her flat, where she's perched on the wall of the small garden in front of the block. I'm desperate to spill about the dress right here in the car but I somehow manage to keep it zipped until my bum cheek is half a millimetre from the bench seat of our chosen booth at Clementine's.

'The dress.' I flop down fully on the seat. 'I've found the dress.'

Jesy motions that I should budge up. 'The dream dress?'

I shuffle along the seat and nod. 'The dream dress. It's on *Vinted* and it's in my size.'

'No way.' Jesy drops into the seat and grasps my arm tightly. 'Did you buy it?'

I roll my eyes. 'Of course I bought it. It'll be arriving in a few days.' I place my hand on my chest as my eyes start to sting with the threat of tears as it hits me, full force. 'I can't believe I've found it. I'm going to wear that dress on New Year's Eve just like in the dream. Now all I have to do is ask Joshua out and fall in love.'

'Do you think it'll be that easy to fall in love and live happily ever after?'

I shrug in response to Callum's question. 'Why not? It was that easy for you and Zara. Do you think I'm too hideous to have someone love me?'

Callum's eyes widen and he reaches across the table to place his hand on my arm. 'I didn't mean that at all. Sorry. I'm being a grump.' He releases my arm so he can rub his forehead. 'I'm feeling a bit stressed about the wedding, to be honest. It's getting close and Zara and I are still trying to work some stuff out.'

'Is there anything we can help with?' Jesy places the palms of her hands down on the table in front of her and straightens her spine. She's in full-on business mode. 'Because I've got many folders of wedding stuff. Seriously, we'd have enough room for twins if I dumped the wedding prep in a skip. What is it? Are you over budget? Because I know some fantastic websites where you can find amazing deals. Or is it the seating plan?' Jesy pulls a face. 'Even ours is a nightmare and we don't have all your family branches complicating things.'

Callum shakes his head. 'It's not that. It's just something Zara and I have to figure out.'

Jesy reaches across the table and takes Callum's hand in hers, giving his fingers a reassuring squeeze. 'You need to relax. Things will fall into place and you'll have the best day ever.' She lets go of his hand and pats his arm. 'Remind me of those wise words in the next few months when I'm stressing about my own wedding.'

Callum flickers a smile and nods. 'I will.'

The dress arrives a few days later and it fits perfectly. I can't help but twirl around my bedroom wearing it as I imagine arriving at Clementine's with the love of my life. It's happening. It's actually happening. My dream is coming true. Sort of. There are a couple of niggles – the Abba tribute act for one and the fact that Joshua and I aren't even dating, never mind utterly in love, and I still have a simmering rage every time I set eyes on him – but that is going to change. I'm going to be brave and ask him out. The next time I see him, no matter how difficult it will be for me to choke the words out. No matter how much the thought makes me itch on the inside. Joshua is The One and I need to take control of my life for once and make it happen.

I march into Brinkley's the morning after the dress arrives with my head up, shoulders back and my steps firm and determined. There is no shuffling for Daisy Grant today. Today, I am resolute. I am unwavering in my desire to command my own destiny. Today I am going to ask Joshua out – absolutely no excuses – and we are going to begin our journey of falling in love.

Fate is on my side as I find Joshua in the staffroom, because as determined as I am, it's quite difficult to conduct a love affair on the noisy shopfloor when you're both wearing earplugs to muffle the racket.

'Joshua.' My tone matches my stride, which is far too businesslike, so I take a deep breath and push my lips into a smile and when I speak again my voice is much softer. 'Did you have a nice evening?' I cringe. I'm supposed to be seducing this man, not sounding like a distant aunt on a visit to his stately home.

'Yeah. It was good, thanks.' He should perhaps let his face know, because his mouth is downturned, and his eyes have that hooded look again. Maybe the grief at losing his grandfather has hit him all over again? 'Anyway.' He sighs and scrapes back his chair. 'I'd better get onto the floor. See you down there. Two minutes.' He nods at the clock, and I watch him leave. Seriously, this is the man of my dreams? But, like it or not, I know how I'll feel about Joshua one day very soon so I need to put my current feelings aside and get on with the task at hand.

I don't get the chance to speak to Joshua for the rest of the morning as his attention is mainly focused on the girl who has been moved over to our line to cover Sabina's temporary suspension after the headlock incident, but I spot him in the canteen during my lunch break, his shoulders hunched as he pokes at the untouched baked potato in front of him. I tell Melanie that I need to speak to our supervisor and head over to his table while Melanie makes a beeline for Dougie and a couple of the other guys from packing.

'Mind if I sit here?'

Joshua drags his eyes away from his baked potato and blinks up at me, as though he's trying to focus. 'Yeah. Sorry. Miles away.' I wish he was miles away. Preferably on another continent. But I ignore the snarky voice in my head and place my tray down on the table and pull out the chair opposite Joshua.

'Anywhere interesting?'

He shakes his head and sighs. 'I'm afraid not.'

I sit down and pick up my knife and fork, though I don't start eating yet. I'm not sure whether Joshua wants me to pry so I hold back, waiting to see if he wants to share. After a moment, he sighs again and starts to speak.

'It's my ex. Olivia. She's seeing someone.'

'And you're not happy about it.' I spear a piece of chicken and add some rice to my fork.

'It's not that I'm unhappy about it. I knew she was dating again, and I was fine with that. But it sounds like it might be getting serious between them and I guess I'm a bit weirded out about it. The thought of Olivia having a *boyfriend*.'

'I can see how that could feel strange.'

'I don't want it to. I want Olivia to be happy and she deserves to have someone in her life who'll treat her nicely and love her.'

'How long were you together?'

'Seven years.' One corner of Joshua's mouth lifts. I could almost kid myself that it's a smile. 'I guess we got the itch.'

Seven years is a long time in my world – my longest relationship was two years, when Harvey and I were together – so I can imagine how difficult it must be for Joshua to see his ex with someone else.

'Maybe it's time you started dating again? It might not feel so weird that Olivia's moved on if you have too. You already gave it a go with the speed dating thing.'

Joshua narrows his eyes. 'I thought we were never going to mention that again.' He shakes his head and, admitting defeat with the baked potato, drops his fork onto his plate. 'That made me realise I wasn't ready to start anything new. I thought Olivia and I were going to be together forever, and I can't get my head around the fact our forevers are now completely separate.'

Well.

That scuppers my plan for him to fall head over heels in love with me then, doesn't it?

Chapter Sixteen

There's a mini heatwave happening right now, so I'm scrolling through *Vinted* in search of suitable summer attire as I wait for Callum to emerge from his building. Callum moved into The Wellington, a former pub that was chopped up and converted into flats, soon after he landed his first job after uni, and Zara moved in a couple of years ago. I glance up every now and then as I scroll through cute floaty tops and strappy dresses but Callum is taking his time. I'm about to message him when the door to The Welly finally swings open and he emerges, head down, his feet shuffling as he makes his way to the car.

'Jesy will have had the baby by the time we get there.' I'm teasing but Callum doesn't so much as crack a smile as he slumps into the seat beside me. 'Aren't you excited to hear all about the scan?' I know I am. I've been buzzing with anticipation all day.

'Yeah. Course I am.' Callum says the words, but they don't translate into his features. His tone is dull and there isn't even a flicker of the excitement I'm feeling on his face. He looks as though I've just picked him up to take him to the dentist for an extraction. Our best friend has just had a scan of her first baby, and she'll expect nothing less than for me and Callum to show up with cheerleader levels of enthusiasm. I'm not going to let her down but I can't say the same about grumpy-faced Callum.

'Everything okay?' I shove my phone in my pocket and check my mirrors before moving off. 'Nervous about the stag next weekend? Because Jesy's trying to get hold of a tranquilliser gun for Robbie if you're worried about him ruining it.' Callum's stepbrother is okay in the very smallest of doses, but anything more than a couple of minutes will have the calmest of people wanting to wrap their hands around his neck.

'It's not the stag.' Callum rubs his hands over his face. 'It's nothing. I'm just a bit stressed about a work thing.'

I try to think of something helpful to say but Callum's a mechanical engineer and I have no idea what his work entails. I've brought some non-alcoholic champagne to toast Jesy's scan but perhaps I should have bought some of the real stuff too. Callum looks like he could do with a proper drink.

'I'll pull myself together by the time we get to Jesy's, I promise.'

'You'd better, because if you don't gush over that scan photo, she'll dangle you by your ankles from her fifth-floor window.'

The corners of Callum's mouth flicker and I can see the fog is already starting to shift, which is fortunate as Jesy's flat is only around the next corner. I tell him a couple of really bad dad jokes I saw on TikTok to make sure he's properly fog-free and while he groans at the first, he full-on belly-laughs at the second and we're still giggling when Jesy buzzes us into the block of flats. She greets us at her door with the black and white image of her baby.

'There's only one in there!' She places a hand on her chest. 'You have no idea how relieved I am.'

'And everything's looking healthy.' Ant joins Jesy at the door and kisses the top of her head. 'Which is the most important bit.'

'Obviously, but it's also important that *there's only one.*' She steps back and opens the door wider, leading us into the living room. 'Can you imagine us squeezing two babies in here?' Jesy and Ant live in a two-bedroom flat, but the second bedroom is little more than a walk-in cupboard.

'It's not squeezing two babies in here that you'd have to worry about. It's squeezing two babies out of... Ow.' Callum rubs his arm, where Jesy has just whacked him. She prods him, gentler this time, in the direction of the sofa and he sits, his face set in a scowl.

'So everything went okay?' I sit on the opposite end of the sofa to Callum, refusing to look at his face in case it sets off another bout of giggles.

'Everything went great.' Jesy hands me the scan photo and plops herself between us. 'I'm twelve weeks, which means I'm due on the second of January. A New Year's baby.' She gives me a pointed look. She can't say it out loud with Ant being in the same room because although we can be as bat-shit crazy as we want in front of each other, we try to mask that part of us from others, but she's trying to say *see, the dream is coming true* with her eyes. She raises her eyebrows. *Have you asked Joshua out.* I bulge my eyes at her. *I will, when the time is right.* Jesy rolls her eyes. *With you, the time will never be right.*

Who needs words to have a conversation with your bestie?

'I brought champagne to celebrate this little one.' I give the scan photo a little wave before delving into the carrier I brought with me from the car. It's the perfect distraction from our body language convo. 'Non-alcoholic, of course, so Mummy-to-be can join in.'

Jesy points out all the bits and pieces of the baby while Ant nips off to the kitchen to grab some glasses, although one very important bit won't be visible until the next scan in a few weeks.

'Will you come shopping with me?' Jesy places a hand on her stomach, where you can see the tiniest bump is forming. 'I need something to wear to the stag weekend and nothing really fits any more. If I actually manage to get it on, it isn't comfortable, and I don't want to show up in leggings and one of Ant's rugby shirts.'

'I wouldn't waste your money shopping for clothes for the stag weekend if I were you.' Callum opens the fake champagne when Ant returns with the glasses.

Jesy folds her arms. 'If I can't drink, I want to at least be able to breathe.'

'The thing is.' Callum stands up so he can start to pour the champagne. 'The stag weekend has sort of been cancelled. In fact, the whole wedding's been called off.'

A stunned silence envelops the room, with the only sound coming from the champagne glugging into the glasses as Callum continues to distribute it. Callum's tone is so matter of fact that I'm sure I've misheard him. The wedding's been called off? That can't be right, although it would explain Callum's mood when I picked him up.

'What do you mean the wedding's been called off?' It's Jesy who manages to form words first. 'What's happened? Why has Zara called it off? Is there someone else?'

Callum passes a glass to Jesy. 'Who said it was Zara who called it off?'

'Was it *you*?' Jesy points a menacing finger at Callum. 'Is there someone else? How could you do that to her?'

Callum passes a glass to me, which I take numbly. I can barely think of words, never mind voice them.

'It wasn't me who called it off. It *was* Zara.'

'Why? What happened? Is there someone else?' Jesy reaches for Callum's hand but he pulls away and continues to pour the champagne.

'Zara wouldn't do that. She just doesn't think we're in the right place to get married. She doesn't think *I'm* in the right place to get married. Zara wants a fairytale wedding, a fairytale marriage, with babies and everything, but she doesn't think I want to build that life with her.'

Jesy splutters. 'She's talking crap.'

'Is she?' Callum hands Ant a glass before pouring one for himself. 'I think she could be right.'

Jesy shakes her head, her foot tap, tap, tapping against the floor. 'But *you* proposed to *her*. Why would you do that if you didn't want to marry the girl?'

Callum shrugs before lowering himself back onto the sofa. 'I guess it just felt like the next step. You get together. A few years later you move in together and then you get married. That's what you and Ant did.'

'Because we love each other and *wanted* to do those things!'

'And I thought I wanted those things too.'

'And now?'

Callum shrugs. 'I'm not sure.'

'You're not sure? You planned a whole wedding but *you're not sure*? What kind of A-hole does that if they're not a hundred per cent into it?'

'But I thought I *was* a hundred per cent into it. It was Zara who started questioning it and the next thing I know she's called off the wedding and packed a bag so she can go and stay with her sister.'

'So you do want to marry her?'

Callum shrugs again. 'I really don't know.'

Jesy's hand is trembling so much she has to put her glass down. 'Then you don't, because if you really, truly wanted to marry Zara there wouldn't be the tiniest doubt.' She shakes her head. 'I can't believe you've done this.' Slamming her hands down on either side of her thighs, she pushes herself up onto her feet and storms from the room. A moment later, the front door slams.

'I'm sorry.' Callum drops his face into his hands. 'I've messed everything up.'

'I'll just go and see if she's alright.' Ant points at the door before he hurries off to check on Jesy. I take Callum's hand in mine and give it a squeeze.

'Is this really it for you and Zara? It's not a pre-wedding wobble? Cold feet?'

Callum shakes his head and gives a juddering sigh. 'I don't think so. I feel kind of… relieved. Confused but sort of *free*. I should feel devastated, but I don't. I'm sorry that Zara's hurt but a huge part of me feels like I've been released. Does that make me a monster?'

'Maybe it's the shock of Zara leaving? Your way of coping?'

'Maybe.' Callum nods. 'But what if…'

The front door is forcibly opened and Jesy marches into the living room, jabbing a finger at Callum.

'This is my house. You need to be the one leaving, not me.'

'Sorry.' Callum eases himself up off the sofa and leaves, leaving me stuck in the middle. Do I stay with Jesy, who's still shaking as she lifts her glass to her lips, or do I go after Callum, whose life has just been turned upside down, even if he had a part to play in it?

'I really wish this was the real thing.' Jesy pulls a face at the fake champagne, but she downs the rest of it anyway.

I go after Callum, leaving Jesy in Ant's safe hands, catching up to him as he steps into the lift. I duck inside and slip my arm through his. 'You okay?'

'I'm fine.' He smiles at me, but it cracks almost immediately, and I gather him up in my arms as he gulps back tears. I rub his back and murmur soothing sounds as he has a little cry on my shoulder and it feels like my heart is cracking down the middle. Callum and Zara were one of my inspirational couples. I looked at them and wanted what they had. It's why I went on so many rubbish dates and why I'm so desperate for my New Year's dream to come true.

'Sorry.' Callum pulls away, eyes on the ground as he wipes at them with the sleeve of his jacket. 'My head's a mess.' He starts to walk away, and I call out to him and offer to drive him back home. Callum's lips shift upwards and it's the saddest smile I've ever seen. 'I'd rather walk. Clear my head a bit. If that's possible.'

My shoulders slump as I watch him slope away. I don't get it. How can you be utterly in love one minute and then out of it the next?

Chapter Seventeen

'Oh, for biscuit's sake.' I press my lips together so tightly it hurts, but the alternative is to take my frustration out on the piping bag in my hands and ruin even more of the blueberry and peach pie biscuits in front of me. I've already produced my third reject of the day and I've barely been on the line for an hour.

'Did you just say for *biscuit's* sake?'

I turn away from the production line, happy to not look at the spoiled biscuit for a moment. Joshua's standing behind me, his head tilted to one side and his lips pressed into a thin line, though I think he's trying to suppress a bemused smile rather than trying to restrain severe annoyance like me.

'I did. It's a Kath thing. She didn't like us swearing on the shopfloor, so she set up a swear jar. It's a hard habit to break.'

'Really?' Joshua places a finger on his chin and narrows his eyes. 'I've never seen this swear jar.'

'That's because I chucked it as soon as the old bat was out of sight on her last day.' Melanie glances up to grin at Joshua before she stoops back down to carry on with her task.

'And what did she do with the money from the jar?'

'She said she donated it to charity.' Melanie glances up again. 'But we reckon she used it to buy gin and cigs on the sly.'

Joshua folds his arms across his clipboard, pinning it to his chest. 'Maybe we should reinstate the swear jar.'

'No!' The entire line, apart from Sabina's cover who hadn't had to work under the barbaric no-swear rule, barks out the same reply. I'm sure I shoved an entire day's worth of wages in that jar on particularly rough shifts. It's why we had to train ourselves to use baking-themed alternatives: for biscuit's sake, son of a batch, go cook yourself, Kath.

'We'll down tools if you try it.' Melanie aims her piping bag at Joshua in as menacing a way as she can manage when it's filled with lavender-coloured icing.

Joshua releases one of his arms from his clipboard so he can hold his hand up in surrender. 'Fine. No swear jar.' He moves on but not before I clock the smirk on his face, and I wish Melanie had fired the lavender icing after all. I take a deep, calming breath and resume my piping, carefully lining the round biscuit before adding the outline of a heart in the middle, ready to be flooded further down the line. It usually takes a matter of seconds and very little thought as the action is repeated robotically after the first few but it takes all of my concentration to get it right. My attention slips at the last second, leaving a messy dollop of icing at the bottom of the heart.

'Bain-marie!'

I resist the urge to launch the piping bag at the wall and compose myself with a few more calming breaths before I move onto the next biscuit. I need to get this one right because there are only so many rejects that are tolerable per shift and I'm single-handedly reaching the limit by myself. I do my best to push all non-piping thoughts from my brain and focus intently on the lavender outline of the design and although I am better at accomplishing the simple motif, my earlier mishaps haven't gone unnoticed, and Joshua pulls me aside during the morning tea break.

'Everything alright with you? You don't seem like your normal self this morning.' Joshua's tone is soft rather than accusatory, but it still rubs me up the wrong way.

'Sorry. My mind's been elsewhere this morning but I'll sort myself out, I promise.'

'Good, because the reject bin is looking pretty full.'

I grit my teeth, fully aware of how much I've messed up this morning but I don't want to bring out the snark again. I'm supposed to be making Joshua fall in love with me and shouting my mouth off isn't going to achieve that. I've failed to ask him out so far as the opportunity hasn't come up; you can't just go smoothly from being work enemies to dating, it seems. We need something to bring us together, like the meet-cute idea I floated a while ago. I know we've already met, weeks ago, but it could be a do-over meet, where we can start again with a clean slate.

I spend the rest of my lunch break googling movie meet-cutes and by the time I'm back on the line with a piping bag in hand, I have a plan.

–

'You're going to chuck orange juice over him?'

It's the night of what was supposed to be the start of Callum's stag weekend and it's the first time I've seen him since he announced the wedding was off. It took a lot of coaxing but I've managed to drag him out of his flat so we can get very, very drunk. I tried to get Jesy to join us, but no amount of coaxing would convince her to come as she can't get drunk, very or otherwise, so she doesn't see the point.

She has, however, mellowed and apologised for her outburst and for chucking Callum out of her flat. ('It's the hormones. They're all over the place. I love you, even if you are a massive wazzock.') Callum has apologised for being a massive wazzock so we're all good again, I hope. We have, of course, decamped to Clementine's for our non-stag night out for cocktails and chips, and I've just revealed my meet-cute plan to Callum, who is less than impressed.

I chuck a chip at his head. 'I've seen it. It works.'

'You've seen someone fall in love after having orange juice thrown at them?'

I chuck another chip at his head. 'I'm not going to throw it over him. I'm going to *accidentally* spill it on him, so I can offer to buy him a drink after work to apologise.'

'You've actually seen this work?'

'Yep.'

Callum narrows his eyes. 'Where?'

I select a massive chip from the plate and take my time chewing it. 'One of my mum's films.'

Callum hoots with laughter, his eyes wide and bright so that he looks like the old, pre-wedding-cancellation Callum again. 'You saw it *in a film*? Well, that's me convinced. You drench Joshua in orange juice, he swoons, falls madly in love with you and your New Year's Eve dream comes true.

'*Ow.*' Callum scowls as he reaches under the table to rub his shin.

'You still don't believe the dream was real, do you?'

'I believe you had some sort of vision when you spaced out, but do I think it was a flash forward? A deja-*new*? Absolutely not, because unlike you and that other crackpot friend of ours, I'm sane and rational.'

'Even with the dress and the watch?'

'But what about Elton John?' Callum quirks an eyebrow and we both turn towards the door, where there's a poster for the bar's festive entertainment. Christina's blocking the poster, so we turn back to our chips again.

'Have you spoken to Zara yet?'

Callum shakes his head. 'She's blocked my number, I think, and she's definitely blocked me on social media. I withheld my number and called her sister, but she hung up as soon as I told her it was me.' He shrugs. 'Understandable, I guess. I'd do more than hang up on a bloke who messed one of my sisters around like I've messed Zara around.'

I place a hand on Callum's. 'You didn't mess her around. You thought you wanted to do the whole marriage thing.'

'Well, she could see I wasn't really up for it, so why couldn't I?'

I shake my head but I have no words to answer that. But then my attention is snatched away from Zara and the wedding. Christina has moved away from the poster and there's red tape across the Abba tribute act in the bottom right-hand corner.

'What's going on there?' I shuffle out of the booth and dash towards the poster. Scrawled on the red tape in black marker are the words 'CANCELLED. NEW ACT TBC'.

'The Abba tribute act has been cancelled.' My heart is hammering and it's making me feel a bit woozy. 'Now do you believe me that the dream is coming true?'

Callum shrugs and pulls an apologetic face. 'We don't know it's going to be Elton yet.'

'So if it turns out that an Elton John tribute act is going to play here on New Year's Eve will you believe me then?'

Callum nods. 'Yes, if that happens then I will one million per cent believe you and I will get down on my knees and beg for your forgiveness for ever doubting you.'

'You'd better practise your grovelling then, because it's going to happen.'

I just know I'm going to arrive at Clementine's on New Year's Eve with 'Crocodile Rock' in full swing and I'll be utterly in love. My heart hammers a little bit more in anticipation. 'Ready or not, I'm going to ask Joshua out the next time I see him.'

Chapter Eighteen

Adrenaline is pumping around my system as I step into the factory, and it's making my skin tingle as I hunt down Joshua. Because today is the day of the meet-cute and although I'm physically prepared with my bottle of Tropicana, mentally I'm all over the place. I want to do this because of the dream, but it's still quite difficult imagining feeling those things for *Joshua*. But the heart wants what the heart wants and I'm going to do everything in my power to deliver.

I find Joshua in the staffroom, but he isn't alone and is chatting to Jeremy. I store my things in my locker while I wait for Jeremy to bugger off for his pre-work cig, but he stays put until it's time to clock in. I've been on high alert all morning and I feel myself crash as I join the production line with the unspilled bottle of orange juice sitting in the staffroom fridge.

Sabina's back after her suspension, but she's been put as far away as possible from Jeremy while still remaining on our line and Joshua keeps a close eye on her over the course of the shift so I'm barely within sniffing distance and I don't even see him in the canteen during our lunch break. I've resigned myself to the fact that I won't be asking him out today after all when I spot him loitering around the car park after my shift. Instead of heading for his own car, he's standing beside Jeremy's. The bottle of orange juice is in my bag and I unscrew it as I rush over, flinging it towards Joshua before I have the chance to talk myself out of it.

It happens in slow motion, the juice arcing out of the bottle and flying majestically towards its prey, when Jeremy pops up from where he'd been leaning into the back seat of his car and steps in front of the liquid missile, spluttering with shock and confusion as the side of his t-shirt is splatted.

'What the fondant?'

Jeremy is standing with his arms held out, twisting to look down at the orange splodge on his torso. I'm impressed he's managed to muster an anti-swear jar expletive under the circumstances. I'd be stuffing ten-pound notes in Kath's jar if someone had chucked a drink at me.

'Oh my god.' Adrenaline has resumed pumping and is flooding my body, making me feel jittery and a little bit sick. Fight or flight mode is kicking in and I'm contemplating turning around and legging it when Joshua speaks.

'What the hell, Daisy? Why did you do that?'

'It was an accident! I tripped!' I search the ground for a crack in the tarmac or a rock or... *anything* that I could have feasibly stumbled over.

'It didn't look like you tripped.' Joshua quirks his stupid eyebrow and folds his arms across his chest, which is supposed to be damp with juice right about now. 'It looked like you threw it on purpose. In fact, it looked as though you were aiming for me.'

I shake my head aggressively, as though I'm trying to dislodge it to get out of explaining myself. 'I didn't, I swear. It was an accident, and I'm so sorry, Jeremy.' I reach into my bag and pull out the wad of pre-prepared tissue, handing it to my colleague so he can dab the juice from his t-shirt. 'Let me get you a drink, to say sorry. Not orange juice, obviously.' I titter but nobody else joins in the amusement. They don't even flicker a smile. 'Let's go to the pub.' I nod towards the pub on the edge of the industrial park and Jeremy shrugs.

'It's the least you can do, I suppose.' He pulls his t-shirt away from his body, where it's clinging stickily to his ribs. 'Sabina didn't put you up to this, did she?'

'No!' My eyes widen in panic that I could have inadvertently landed my co-worker in even more trouble than she's already in. 'Like I said, it was an accident.' I hear Joshua snort with derision and turn to scowl at him. '*It was an accident.*'

Joshua holds his hands up. 'Fine. It was an accident. Even though it didn't look like one to me.'

I continue to scowl at Joshua. How can my heart want *this*?

Jeremy closes his car door and hands the bag he's been holding over to Joshua after checking it hasn't been caught in the orange juice crossfire.

'Thanks, mate.' Joshua takes the bag and nods at Jeremy before starting to move away. 'I'll see you tomorrow.'

'Wait!' Panic makes my voice squeaky. It also makes me wave my hands in front of me like an over-enthusiastic children's TV presenter. Because I'm supposed to be going on a date with Joshua, not Jeremy. 'You have to come with us.'

'Er, why is that?' Joshua looks down at his shirt. 'I didn't get soaked.'

'Because...' I press my lips together as I try to come up with an excuse for Joshua to join us when clearly he would rather bounce up and down on a trampoline made of rusty pins than socialise with me. (And the feeling is very much mutual.) '...team bonding! I feel like we've got off to a bad start, so let's wipe the slate clean, go for a drink and get to know each other properly.'

Joshua doesn't look convinced. He's clearly itching to keep moving, to avoid spending any more time than necessary with me. But he *has* to, because at some point we're going to get past this animosity and fall in love.

'It'll be good for team morale if we're not sniping at each other all the time. If we could be...' I hold back a shudder. '...friends.'

Joshua sucks in a breath, holding it for a second before releasing it in a loud huff.

'Fine. One drink. But only if you promise to stop taking the piss with the bathroom breaks.'

I tut, but playfully. 'That's a quid for the swear jar. I'd have gone for *take the proof.*'

Joshua rolls his eyes but I swear there's a hint of a smile on his lips as we start to make our way across the car park. Not only have I mildly amused Joshua Michaels and got him to go for a drink with me (albeit with Jeremy), I didn't actually promise anything about those bathroom breaks.

–

I'm not sure it counts as a date when there's three of you and there's still the whiff of dislike in the air, but I make the claim in the 'Friends Without Benefits' group chat anyway while I'm at the bar waiting for our drinks. Jesy and Callum don't need to know right now that the meet-cute was a big, fat fail and that Jeremy is here too. As far as they're concerned, Project Deja-New is on course for a happily ever after.

'Need a hand?' Joshua's tone is gruff as he makes the offer, but I accept it anyway and he grabs the two pint glasses from the bar while I pick up the gin and tonic that's hopefully going to help me get through this.

'Isn't this nice?' I sit on the stool opposite Jeremy and take a massive glug of my drink. 'So, Joshua. How have you found working at Brinkley's so far?'

Joshua drops onto the free stool between me and Jeremy. 'Good. Mostly.' He takes a sip of his pint. 'Trying to find my feet and all that. Make my mark.'

I nod and take a daintier sip of my drink as there isn't much left. My brain is whirring away as I try to think of something else to say. I already know about his relationship status, so I'll steer clear of anything family-related in case I pick at any grief-shaped wounds.

'How would you normally relax after a long shift?'

Joshua opens his mouth to answer but Jeremy gets in there first, telling us *all about* his love of hiking; the equipment, the snacks, his top ten hikes in the North West. Joshua is finishing his pint, and my G&T is nothing but a fond, distant memory by the time he wraps it up.

'Shall I get us another?' I cross my fingers under the table, because Joshua only agreed – begrudgingly – to one drink – but he's hardly going to fall head over heels in love with me while listening to Jeremy bang on about fells and knolls and ordnance surveys. I need more time. And more alcohol.

'I'll get these.' Jeremy scrapes back his stool as he jumps out of his seat, and I'm immensely grateful for his presence as, from the look on his face as Jeremy rushes off to the bar, Joshua was about to decline. But it's too late as Jeremy is already at the bar. I've honestly never seen the man move so fast.

'So, um, Joshua.' I drum my fingers on the table while I try to conjure something witty or insightful to say to spark up a conversation now we're finally alone. 'Do you have any hobbies?' I'd been hoping for something more astute than that but it's all I've got, I'm afraid.

'I play five-a-side.'

'Really?' I sit up straighter, intrigued by this new information. Joshua doesn't look particularly sporty, but I can get on board with this update. 'My best friend's partner plays rugby.'

Joshua's eyebrows lower. 'Five-a-side *football*.'

'I know.'

Joshua huffs out a short, sharp breath and pulls his chin back. 'It's a completely different sport.'

'*I know.*'

'Then why…?' He shakes his head slowly and I find myself asking the same question. Why am I putting myself through this ordeal?

'Forget it.' I slump back in my seat and thump my arms across my chest, my eyes wandering over to the bar to see where Jeremy's up to with those drinks. The barman hasn't even got to him yet and I have to dig deep to remind myself why I'm here so I don't simply give up and go home.

The dream. The euphoria as Joshua kisses my cheek and it hits me that I'm utterly, weak-in-the-knees in love with him. The dense feeling in my chest that makes it hard to breathe but in the most wonderful way. The tingly fingertips. The calmness despite all of that going on at once.

'Do *you* have any hobbies?'

I start, not expecting Joshua to pick up the conversation baton. His tone suggests his question should be

133

accompanied by a huge sigh and an eye-roll to signal that he's not really interested in the answer but he should make an effort to be polite, but I grasp hold of it with both hands anyway.

'Photography is my main thing, I guess.'

Joshua nods. 'Ah, yes. The snapping away at the family fun day.'

'It wasn't supposed to be a hobby. I went to college to study photography and I was supposed to carry on with it but… let's just say it didn't turn out how I planned and I ended up at Brinkley's.'

Joshua lifts a shoulder in a shrug. 'You could always take it up again. You're young and good at it.'

'You think I'm good?' There's a flicker in my stomach that spreads into a warm glow that makes my cheeks pink.

Joshua shrugs again. 'I've seen the photos in the staff-room. I'm no expert but they look pretty good to me.'

'My best friend is always telling me I should go back to college.'

'What's stopping you?'

'Time. Money.' I have a small savings pot – it's one of the advantages of living with Mum and Dad, having a bit of spare cash that isn't eaten up by bills – but it's supposed to be for a deposit when I finally move out. 'Confidence, I guess. I messed up before, why wouldn't I mess up again?'

'People make mistakes. You learn from them, hope-fully. You messed up before, why wouldn't you succeed this time?'

The warm glow builds up to a tingly heat and I find myself smiling. This is the kind of Joshua I'd like to get to know better. A nicer Joshua. Softer. A Joshua who doesn't look down his nose at me and make notes about me on that stupid clipboard.

'This is nice.'

Joshua's eyes flick around the room and he gives me an odd look. 'This place?' The pub is rather drab, so I get the confusion.

'No. Us. Talking without snapping and stuff.'

'Ah.' Joshua nods. 'That. Yeah, I prefer it this way.'

'Me too.' I unfold my arms and rest them on the table. 'I'm sorry I've been pushing your buttons. I was a bit upset when you took over from Kath and I blamed you for it.'

'Really? I get the impression none of you were too fond of my predecessor.'

'Oh, we weren't.' I give a bitter laugh. 'She was a nightmare. But the thing is, I applied for the position. Which I obviously didn't get.'

Joshua tips his head back. 'Ah, that makes sense.'

'I didn't take the rejection very well. Sorry.'

'While we're apologising...' Joshua cringes. 'I've been wanting to say sorry about how I pressurised you into swapping shifts that time.'

'Pressurised?' I tilt my head to one side. 'Do you mean blackmailed?' I'm teasing because not only am I over the Oliver thing (that date would have been a waste of time), I also want to stay on this good side of Joshua. 'Forget about it. Let's start again. Clean slate?'

Joshua nods once, decisively. 'Clean slate.'

A tray of drinks is plonked down on the table, shattering the serenity that had settled between us.

'I got shots.' Jeremy throws himself into his seat and grabs a dinky glass from the tray. 'The missus has already been on my case for not coming straight home so I might as well make the cold shoulder I'm going to receive worth it.' He tips the liquid down his throat before slamming the glass back down on the tray and snatching up his pint.

I look at Joshua. He looks at me. We both shrug and pick up a shot. It looks like this evening is going to get lively.

—

'Firstly, you're not supposed to launch the drink at the guy. And secondly, you need to stop watching those old cheesy rom-coms with your mum.'

I lean into Callum and groan, threading my arm through his as we step into the park behind my house on Sunday morning. 'Firstly, that's why I need a boyfriend, so I'm not stuck at home watching old cheesy rom-coms with Mum. And secondly, it worked, didn't it? I got Joshua on a date.'

Callum snorts. '*Was* it a date with that other guy there?'

'Jeremy didn't stay the whole night.' His wife had bombarded him with calls and texts when he failed to come home after he'd promised he was ordering an Uber and in the end he'd gulped down the remainder of his pint, slammed the glass down on the table and stormed out of the pub while muttering, 'Never ever get married. It ruins your bloody life.' I'd expected Joshua to follow, but we stayed in the pub for another drink before parting ways.

'Whatever it was, we had a great time and it's the start of something very special.' I sigh, long and dreamily. 'It's a pity you're not still getting married. Joshua could have been my plus-one.'

'I am so sorry to have messed up your plans.' Callum's voice is dripping with sarcasm as he unlocks our arms and bends down to release the lead from Frankenstein's harness.

'Sorry, but it is a bit annoying. A wedding would be the perfect excuse for another date.' I ignore the thunderous look Callum is projecting my way.

'Did you manage to speak to Zara yet?' Apparently, she dropped by the flat a couple of days ago while Callum was out at work and removed all traces of herself. She posted her key through the letterbox afterwards, signalling the very end of their relationship.

Callum rummages in his pocket for the tennis ball while Frankenstein tap dances at his feet. 'Nope. I'm still blocked, and her sister has asked me to leave her alone. I hope she's okay, but I have to respect her wishes and back off.'

'I'm sorry.'

Callum launches the ball across the field. 'You keep saying that but it's my fault we're in this mess. I'm such an idiot.'

'You are, but you're allowed to be a sad idiot.'

Callum nudges me with his arm. 'Do you think Jesy will come with us to Clementine's today?'

'Probably not. This is peak puke time.'

But Jesy does come with us. In fact, she almost knocks Callum over in her eagerness to vacate the flat when we drop by on the way to brunch.

'I'm starving. My morning sickness has gone and it's left me ravenous. Look.' She prods at her stomach, where there's a small mound. 'That isn't baby. That's pasta and biscuits and doughnuts. I haven't stopped eating since Thursday and I'm not about to quit now. Come *on*.' And she'd grabbed mine and Callum's hands and dragged us to the lift.

While the first thing Jesy does when we reach Clementine's is order pancakes and croissants with jam, I hold off my brunch ordering to ask Christina whether they've replaced the Abba act for New Year's Eve.

Christina shakes her head. 'Nope, and it's probably too late to book anything decent now. We'll probably end up doing a quiz and karaoke. Which is fine.' Christina smiles but her heart isn't in it. 'Karaoke is fun.'

'I think you'll find someone.' Someone with star-shaped glasses and platform boots. Because I've almost got everything else I need for the dream to come true: the dress, the cracked watch, the man. Sort of. We haven't kissed or anything, and I'm not entirely sure we've been on a date, but we'll get there, I'm sure of it. I just need to put my brave girl pants on and make it happen.

Chapter Nineteen

It's the last week of July and I still haven't asked Joshua out on an actual, no-doubts-to-be-had date. There are now only five months until New Year's Eve so I need to get it done, and fast. Joshua did say he wasn't ready to start a new relationship yet during our accidental speed date but I know we'll be together by New Year's Eve, so I just need to go for it. I manage to catch Joshua as he's about to climb into his car after our shift and even though the thought alone is making me feel sick (or that could be a consequence of the unexpected sprint across the car park) I vow to do it right here, right now. No thinking about it. No losing my nerve. *Just do it, Daisy.*

'Do you want to go out for a drink or something?'

I mentally kick myself. 'A drink or something' is too vague and flimsy. Too throwaway. 'A drink or something' could be a date, but it could also be a couple of mates – no, work colleagues – going for a drink, or 'something'.

'A date.' I spit the words out before I can process and reject them. 'We had fun the other night. At least I did. I hope you did too. So. Would you like to go on a date? With me?' I look down at my shoes and will a sink hole to open up under my soles.

'I'm sorry but I can't.' Oh. Right. Of course. Hello, Rejection City. You look awfully familiar. 'I'm busy tonight. But I'm free on Monday?'

He isn't rejecting me. *He's saying yes.* I look up, to make sure he's not taking the piss, but he looks earnest enough.

'I'm free on Monday too.'

'Great.' He smiles and nods once. 'How about the cinema and then drinks?'

I nod. Cinema and drinks on Monday sounds perfect; there are four whole days to feel sick with nerves but also there are four whole days to mentally prepare for the first date with the love of my life. Plus, a cinema and drinks date shows we already have stuff in common as we both enjoy films and drinking.

'And I did have fun the other night, by the way.' Joshua climbs into his car and closes the door. He's about to set off when I leap forward and call out his name. He winds down the window.

'I thought you said you weren't ready to date?'

He shrugs. 'Maybe I was wrong. It happens, only very occasionally.' He lifts a hand and then he's gone. I stand watching the space he's left behind for a moment while I wrap my head around the fact that I'm going on an actual date with Joshua Michaels. *I'm going on an actual date with Joshua Michaels.* With a squeal, I scurry to my own car, where I jump into the group chat.

—

Jesy comes round after work on Monday to help me get ready for my date with Joshua. I leave her in the bedroom with a magazine while I hop into the shower to scrub myself until I tingle from head to toe.

'Did you know that the baby is now around eighty-five millimetres long?'

While normally Jesy would be flicking through *Grazia* or *Cosmo*, she's currently poring over a pregnancy mag, and she tells me this fact as soon as my big toe is over the threshold of my bedroom. Pre-shower, she'd told me all about weird non-food cravings, passed on the horrifying fact that babies can be born *with teeth*, and told me that she is not, under any circumstances, having an episiotomy. I'd crossed my legs and concurred with that.

'So, what are we wearing tonight?' Jesy flicks the magazine shut and shuffles off the bed. She joins me at the wardrobe and starts to rummage through my outfits.

'I want something comfortable, but I don't want to show up in days-old jeans and a t-shirt.'

'How about…' Jesy plucks a hanger from the rail and drags it out of the wardrobe. 'Shirt dress and trainers?' The shirt dress she's selected is calf-length with long sleeves and is navy with a white spotty pattern. It has casual chic vibes, which is exactly the look I was going for.

Jesy dries and straightens my hair for me, stopping every thirty seconds or so to scoff the snacks she's brought along, which means it takes ages. But with the morning sickness now gone, she's making up for lost time and eating as much as she wants without puking, so I can't blame her.

'It should have been Callum's wedding this weekend.' She glides the straighteners through a section of my hair before she stops, grabs a pickled onion Monster Munch from the packet and nibbles one of its claws off. 'We should do something to take his mind off it. Not a big night out or anything. Do you realise how boring it is watching other people get drunk?' She nibbles another claw off the crisp. 'Maybe we should have a sleepover, like when we were kids?'

'That sounds fun.'

'Great. We'll have it at Callum's, if he's up for it, obviously.' She shoves the rest of the Monster Munch in her mouth and wipes her fingers down her front before resuming the hair-straightening. She fires off more pregnancy facts as I apply my make-up and then it's time for Jesy to go. Joshua is on his way and the rest is up to me. I still can't quite believe this is happening, even as Jesy kisses me on the cheek and wishes me luck.

I'm pacing the hallway, waiting for him to turn up, but I still jump a mile when the doorbell rings. I take a deep breath and count to five (well, four-and-a-smidge because I really can't wait any longer) and swing the door open.

'Joshua! Hi!' On the inside, I'm a wobbly-jelly mess, but I refuse to allow it to seep out and display itself to my date. Outwardly, I am breezy and assured as I step outside, until I lose my footing on the bottom step. It's been there my entire life, you'd think I'd be used to it by now, but I stumble like a complete imbecile with no way of styling it out. Great going, Daisy.

'I really shouldn't drink at lunchtime.' The only way to get past this is to make a joke of it.

Joshua holds my elbow to steady me. 'You really shouldn't let your supervisor know you enjoy a worktime tipple. I hear he's a miserable git who'll send you up to HR.'

'You heard he was a miserable git too?'

'Everyone knows it.'

I pat Joshua's arm. 'You're not so bad, you know.'

'Not so bad? We've started on the compliments already?'

'Enjoy that compliment, because that might be as good as it gets.'

Joshua places a hand on his chest. 'Then I'll treasure the fact that Daisy Grant thinks I'm *not so bad*.'

A giggle bubbles out of me, taking me by surprise. It's almost as unexpected as the fact that Joshua Michaels is being funny – and at his own expense – and being a little bit... flirty?

Joshua has a taxi waiting and we head to the cinema. He lets me pick the film and I feel a huge amount of pressure to get it right. There's a rom-com that I really want to see, but it's more something I'd go and watch with Jesy so we can swoon at the rom bits and fall about laughing at the coms. There's a horror I'm desperate to watch too, but I want Joshua to start falling in love with me and people having their throats slashed by small children probably isn't the ideal setting for that. Jesy hates gore so I'll watch that one with Callum, who's as keen to see it as I am. I opt for a spy comedy because the trailers make it look goofy and fun but also with a smidge of romance between the two friends who find themselves thrown into a scouting mission.

The film is good and I get the chance to assess our suitability while we're forced into such close proximity. Joshua sits very neatly, with his knees pressed together so his legs don't encroach on my space, which is a positive point as nobody likes a man-spreader, but it means we don't get to accidentally touch, especially as Joshua has opted for his own small bucket of popcorn instead of sharing a larger one. Our fingers don't meet as we both reach for the snack at the same time like in a cheesy rom-com, and we don't get the chance to chat much until afterwards, when we head over to the pub near the cinema.

But we chat easily once we get the chance to, especially once a couple of drinks have loosened us up, and I'm itching to get in the group chat to tell the others how well it's going. This is definitely the start of my New Year's Eve dream and the thought of midnight striking on the thirty-first of December makes me want to jump up on the table and perform the 'Macarena'. But I'm not a dancing-on-the-table sort so I simply grin from ear to ear until my face aches.

'You look happy.' Joshua's been to the bar and he returns with more drinks, setting them down on the table before sitting on the stool next to mine. He's so close, his thigh is against mine and a rush of adrenaline makes me jittery.

'I am happy.' I pick up my glass, hoping my hand doesn't tremble and give away how eager I am for this night to go well.

'Good, because I'm happy too.' Joshua meets my eye and smiles. 'I'm glad I came out tonight. With you. For this date.'

'Does it feel weird being on a date with someone other than Olivia?'

Joshua tilts his head to one side and narrows his eyes. 'I thought it would, you know. I was nervous, to be honest, but it doesn't feel weird at all. It feels… nice.'

'*Nice?*' I open my mouth in mock outrage. 'The socks my gran gets me for Christmas are *nice*.'

'Hey, you think I'm *not so bad*. I bet your gran's socks are not so bad too.'

'We are very bad at compliments.'

Joshua nods. 'We are, but at least we have something in common.'

I groan. 'Surely we have more in common than that. What kind of music do you like?'

Joshua likes Arctic Monkeys and The Libertines. I like Taylor Swift and Ellie Goulding.

Joshua reads crime thrillers. I read *Grazia* and *Cosmo*.

Joshua is separated from his wife. I've never been in a relationship that spanned more than three Christmases.

'But the film was good. We both enjoyed that.'

I lift my glass to toast Joshua's point, and he clinks his own against it. 'We have silly spy comedies in common.'

'And Brinkley's, until you get how talented you are and go and do something you're amazing at.'

I plonk my glass down and try to glare at Joshua, which is hard when I'm dying to grin like a loon. 'You don't think I'm amazing at hand-finishing biscuits?'

Joshua places a hand on his chest. 'You are the best piper we have on the team by miles, but are you living your dream?'

I'm living my dream right now. It's coming true before my eyes and I have to pinch myself to prove that it's real.

—

We find that we have a few more things in common: we both lick the flavour off crisps before we eat them (it drives Callum mad, to the point he refuses to witness my crisp-eating), we can't stand the milk left behind in the bowl after eating cereal – unless it's Coco Pops, obviously – and neither of us can whistle, which causes us to clutch our stomachs as we laugh at our failed attempts in the pub.

'That was like a Daffy Duck concert.'

We've managed to calm ourselves down but Joshua's evaluation of our whistle attempt sends me over the edge once more which in turn sets Joshua off until we're nearly on the floor laughing again. My stomach aches but in the most glorious way.

'I was right about you.' I finish off the last drop of my wine. 'You're not so bad.'

'This has been fun, hasn't it? But...' Joshua turns his wrist so he can check the time. 'We've both got to get up early in the morning.'

'Your watch is broken.' I take Joshua's hand in mine so I can get a good look at the watch.

'It was my grandad's.'

'The one who died?'

Joshua nods. 'My grandma bought him this watch for their tenth anniversary, and he always wore it, even when it got cracked.' He runs a finger along the fracture in the watch's face. 'It's a bit silly to wear a broken watch but it makes me feel closer to him.'

'I don't think it's silly.' Aside from the sentimental nature of Joshua wearing the watch, it's what led me to him. Without the cracked watch, I'd never have known he was the man in my dream. 'I think it's sweet.'

'Sweet? You think I'm *sweet*?' Joshua's eyes widen. 'Wow, what a way to dent my ego. You don't think I'm dashingly handsome and Bruce-Willis-in-*Die-Hard* tough?'

'You can be both of those things, can't you?'

Joshua tilts his chin. 'So you *do* think I'm handsome and Bruce-Willis-in-*Die-Hard* tough?'

I'm suddenly very aware that I'm still holding Joshua's hand. 'Well, I haven't seen you fight a bunch of terrorists so I can't comment on the Bruce Willis bit, but you're definitely handsome.' My heart is racing. We are in flirty territory here.

'I am? Good to know.'

Joshua leans in and kisses me and although it's a good kiss, I don't feel the fireworks in my belly that I expected to. But this is a first date and we're in a pretty busy pub. I'm sure the fireworks will turn up soon.

Chapter Twenty

At twenty-five years of age, I'm attending a sleepover and I'm stupidly excited about it and have even bought new pyjamas for the occasion. Never before have I been so eager to get ready for bed, not even when I was a kid on Christmas Eve, and I insist we change into our PJs as soon as I arrive at Callum's flat. It isn't even seven p.m., but so what?

I sort of expected Callum's place to have transformed without Zara there, as though Callum might have chucked the squishy smoky-grey recliner sofa out and replaced it with a black leather suite and ripped up the carpet so dark glossy laminate could be laid in its place. But the living room looks very much as it did the last time I was here; the walls are still a soft grey with a cornflower blue feature wall, the rug Callum and Zara brought home from Morocco is sitting in front of the fireplace, and the coffee table is still cluttered with post and books and remotes and controllers for a gazillion gadgets. It still looks homely and not at all like the bachelor pad I was anticipating.

'Not a word.' Callum points first at Jesy then me as he steps into the living room in his reindeer-print pyjamas. 'These are the only PJs I own. Zara bought us matching ones last Christmas.' He jabs his finger in Jesy's direction again as she starts to snigger. 'Do not laugh. It's these.' He indicates the festive bedwear. 'Or a pair of boxers, because that's what I normally sleep in. I think I know which you'd prefer.'

'I think they're adorable.' I flop down on the sofa and pop up the recliner.

'Just what every man wants to hear. Not manly. Not sexy. *Adorable.*'

'I can hardly describe them as manly or sexy – there's a cartoon reindeer on the front with 3D antlers, and it's you wearing them. I could never think of you as manly or sexy.'

This isn't strictly true. I did have a bit of a thing for Callum once, briefly, a long, long time ago. I missed him terribly when he went away to uni and we'd email back and forth most days and I'd leap at my phone whenever I heard the ping of a text coming through. I marked the day he'd return for Christmas on my calendar, my stomach fluttering as the days neared because I missed my best friend so much it ached, but then so did Jesy. But when he arrived at Clementine's on that cold December evening, something strange happened to me. My knees turned to jelly, and my breath caught in my throat. Callum was here but it wasn't the Callum who'd left at the end of the summer. This Callum had tamed his out-of-control curls, so while his hair was still longish on top, the sides were short, and he'd lost the puppy fat from his cheeks, giving him a more defined jawline. Without his hair flopping incessantly into his face, I noticed how striking his slate-blue eyes were and I was jolted by the fact that Callum Cox, my best friend, was beautiful.

I never told Callum as I was afraid it would alter our friendship, and my silly little crush soon fizzled out anyway. So, it remained a secret, and I've never told a soul to this day, not even Jesy. *Especially* not Jesy.

'Anyway, zip it about the PJs.' I rub my hands together. 'What's first for the sleepover fun?'

We decide to pick a film to watch first. We've all brought a favourite to watch during the evening and we set out our snacks on the coffee table before we reveal our choices. Callum goes first, sliding a DVD out from the shelf before presenting it to us.

'*Up?*' Jesy shakes her head. 'I can't handle that right now. My hormones already have me bursting into tears at adverts for supermarkets. Can we at least fast-forward through the opening scene?'

'Nope.' He grabs a packet of tissues from the shelf under the coffee table and tosses it at Jesy. 'We're watching the whole thing.'

Within seconds, Jesy has tears streaming down her face as she rams popcorn into her mouth to muffle her sobs. I take her mind off the heartbreaking montage by dissecting my date with Joshua with her for the millionth time. Callum shushes us several times, but we ignore him.

'What do you think it means?' I've confessed my lack of fireworks-in-the-belly during our first kiss before but I'm still anxious about what it signifies.

'I think you're putting too much pressure on yourself, babe. You've built up this relationship in your head because of the dream, so you're expecting it to be full-on and loved-up like you saw it, but this is just the very beginning. I didn't feel fireworks in my belly the first time I snogged Ant.'

'You can't remember the first time you snogged Ant.' Callum drags his attention away from the film to remind Jesy of this fact. 'You were falling-over drunk. You couldn't even remember who he was when he texted you the next day and if it wasn't for his banter on WhatsApp, you'd never have met up with him again.'

Jesy smiles. 'That was top-quality banter. There definitely wouldn't have been a first date or a second kiss without it.'

'Did you feel fireworks when you kissed him the second time?'

Callum snorts. 'She must have felt something, because they went back to his place that night.'

Jesy chucks a piece of popcorn at Callum's head. 'Watch your sad film, Reindeer Boy.' She turns to me and gives my knee a squeeze. 'Relax, Daisy. You like Joshua. He likes you. Enjoy the ride.' She looks past me, at Callum. 'And don't you dare say a word about me enjoying the ride with Ant that night. Even though I did. Very much so.' She smirks as she shoves a handful of popcorn in her mouth.

–

We play Uno once *Up* has finished and Jesy has stopped crying, and then order a pizza.

'Get dough balls.' Jesy shakes the last few Pringles out of the tube into her hand. 'And cheesy garlic bread. And wings! Don't forget wings.'

Once the order has gone through, Jesy reveals her film of choice.

'Now, I don't have a DVD for my choice, because we're not all stuck in the past.' She grabs one of the many remotes from the table and loads up Netflix.

'No.' Callum shakes his head as Jesy searches for her film of choice. 'Not *Kissing Booth*. It's dogshit and you'll mess up my algorithm. Jesy. *No.*' He lunges for the remote but it's too late, the film is starting and the algorithm has been corrupted. 'I can't believe you've done this.' Callum slouches on the sofa, his arms folded across his chest, a pissy look on his face.

'And I can't believe we've run out of Pringles.' Jesy gives the empty tubs a sad little shake. 'Have you got any more?'

'Seriously?' Callum gestures at the coffee table, which is laden with empty snack bowls. 'That baby's going to come out like the Michelin man's chubbier brother.'

Jesy gasps and places a hand on her stomach. 'Are you fat-shaming my unborn child?'

'No, I'm giving you a warning. Because that baby's gotta come out, no matter how big it gets.'

Jesy quirks an eyebrow. It's her *I'm livid but I'm trying not to show it* look. 'Thank you, Doctor Cox. I shan't eat another thing all night. I will be hungry and miserable if it makes you happy.'

There's an awkward moment where nobody is really paying attention to the film any more but we don't say a word to each other either. Jesy slides the tube back onto the table, her eyebrow still quirked.

'Are you in a mood with me?' Callum finally breaks the silence when the awkward moment verges on the unbearable.

'Why would I be in a mood with you?' Jesy's face relaxes, but she's still livid under the surface. 'Just because you've insinuated that my fanny's going to be ripped to shreds because I'm a greedy pig with no self-control?'

Callum raises his hands. 'In my defence, it came from a good place.'

Jesy smiles sweetly, which is scarier than the eyebrow quirk. 'Say anything like that again and you'll find that Pringles tube lodged in a very *bad place*. Okay?'

Callum nods. 'Won't happen again. There are some more Pringles in the kitchen. Shall I...?'

'I would if I were you.' Jesy settles back down into the sofa while Callum dashes off to grab the Pringles from the cupboard.

We finish watching the film, then we play Unstable Unicorns before we put on our final film of the evening. Jesy falls asleep five minutes into *500 Days of Summer*, with her hand in the Pringles tube.

'Have you had a good night?'

The film has finished, and we've prodded Jesy awake. She's in the bathroom, leaving Callum and I alone in the living room.

'Yeah, it's been great.' Callum starts to stack the empty bowls. 'I haven't thought about the fact that I was supposed to be getting married today once.'

'It was the right decision.' I pile up the takeaway boxes and follow Callum into the kitchen. 'For both of you, even if it doesn't feel like it right now. It'll all work out in the end.'

'Yeah, you're right.' But Callum doesn't look so sure about that. 'Have you enjoyed our sleepover?'

'I've loved it.'

Callum dumps the bowls in the sink. 'Pity you have to end the night by sharing a bed with Jesy. You know she snores, right?'

I shrug. 'It could be worse. I could be sharing the sofa with you.'

'You'll wish you were sharing the sofa with me when Jesy finds her stride. I've already warned the neighbours about the noise pollution.'

'You know Jesy's behind you, don't you?'

Callum whips round, face horror-stricken, while I double over laughing because Jesy is still safely in the bathroom.

'You're a menace, Daisy Grant.' Callum places one hand over his heart as he recovers from the shock, while he pulls me in close with the other. 'I no longer pity you having to share a bed with Dora the Extreme Snorer.'

At which point Jesy obviously appears, stony-faced having heard her new nickname.

—

Joshua and I go on our second date. It's been ages since I played mini golf – I think the last time was during a family holiday to Costa Brava when I was twelve and I ended up 'accidentally' thwacking Oscar on the shin with my club when his smugness at winning became too much. But it was Joshua's suggestion and we have fun as we make our way around the underwater-themed course, and when I somehow make a hole in one, the ball gliding straight through the fish's mouth and sailing into the hole beyond, Joshua congratulates me by picking me up, twirling me around and kissing me. There aren't any fireworks but maybe that's because I'm too busy giggling at the absurdity of me getting that shot and at Joshua's reaction.

'That was awesome.' Joshua places me down gently on the ground and shakes his head in wonder.

'I wish we'd filmed that.' I wriggle my phone free from my pocket and tap on the camera icon. 'Do you think I could do that again? Press record, just in case.'

'Ugh, you're not one of those people who record every minute of their life and put it on TikTok, are you?'

I snatch my phone away and close the app before shoving it back in my pocket. 'Of course not. I'm not even on TikTok.' I am. Jesy, Callum and I went through a phase of following all the trends last summer. 'I just thought I'd get some proof, because no-one will believe I made that shot in a million years.'

'I saw it. I'll back you up.' Joshua takes my hand in his and guides me to the next hole and I forget all about being bothered by the TikTok thing (did he have to sound so sneering?) because Joshua Michaels, my Dream Man, is holding my hand. I'm gutted it only lasts a few seconds as he releases it to take his shot. There are no holes in one this time and I tell Joshua about the sleepover at the weekend while we make our way to the next one.

'A sleepover?' Joshua is stooping to place the ball down in readiness for his shot but he stands up to look at me, ball still in hand. 'Aren't you a bit old for a sleepover? Isn't that what kids do?'

I shrug. 'Why should kids get to have all the fun?'

Joshua shrugs and places the ball down on the ground and lines up his shot, wriggling his shoulders and shuffling his feet as though he's Tiger Woods and not a bloke playing a round of mini golf.

'What did you do this weekend?'

Joshua taps the ball towards the giant octopus, whose tentacles are swirling around in front of the gap that leads to the hole on the other side. He waits until the ball sails through the gap before he answers.

'I played footie in the morning and then went to a party.'

'A party?' I'm slightly miffed he didn't invite me, but then I was having fun with my own mates. 'Did you get drunk and dance to "Gangnam Style"?'

Joshua pulls his chin back. 'It was a kids' party.'

'Oh.' Now I'm not so miffed. A kids' party sounds horrific. Poor Joshua. 'Whose was it? A niece or nephew's?'

Joshua doesn't answer as he's stalked off behind the giant octopus. I follow, finding him looking down into the hole on the green, where his ball is sitting.

'A hole in one!' I lift my hand and Joshua high-fives me, his face all lit up. I can't pick him up and twirl him around like he did to me, but I do push myself up on tiptoe to kiss him. This is a much better game of mini golf than the one we played in Costa Brava.

We go for a drink after the mini golf, which turns into a bit of a session and we're in need of food to soak up the alcohol, so when Joshua suggests we grab a pizza to take back to his, I'm in. We have a bit of a debate over toppings – I'm a tuna and sweetcorn girl, Joshua is all about the meat feast – so we opt for a third option of ham and mushroom as there's no way Joshua will compromise on the tuna, claiming – wrongly – that it doesn't belong on pizza, and there's no way I'm giving in and letting him get his way.

Joshua lives in a smart terraced house that opens straight into the living room. I'm not surprised in the slightest to be met with pale grey walls with spotlights in the ceiling, or the dark grey sofa opposite a boxy fireplace with a massive TV bolted above it, and the neatness of the place doesn't jolt me. Everything is perfectly ordered, and there isn't a stray mug or magazine in sight. It's a complete contrast to my own personal space, i.e. my bedroom, the only area in the house that is allowed to be totally chaotic. But even our living room looks lived in, with knick-knacks dotted about and TV guides and books left lying around. Joshua's living room looks sterile, but it suits him and I'm not fazed by its general appearance. What does surprise me are the prints either side of the chimney breast. Two grids of nine canvases are arranged in the alcoves, depicting family shots of Joshua with who I'm presuming are his parents, his siblings and his nieces and nephews. The photos give a warm, homely feel to what is otherwise quite a cold, stark room.

'The pizza's getting cold.' Joshua threads his fingers through mine and guides me away from the photos, surprising me with a kiss when I turn around. His kisses trail down to my neck and although there's no wild explosion of fireworks like in the dream, there's definitely something happening and soon neither of us cares about the pizza getting cold. In fact, we leave it sitting there in its box, completely forgotten about until the morning.

Chapter Twenty-One

I'm wearing my new long, boho-style dress with a ruched bust, short puffed sleeves and a split thigh that is perhaps a little too much for a Wednesday night at Clementine's, but it's my birthday and I deserve to feel fabulous in my latest *Vinted* buy while I get drunk on raspberry beret cocktails. I've survived a celebratory tea with Mum and Dad and Oscar and his family, but I've left the twins scoffing my Victoria sponge (Mum says I'm too old for a caterpillar cake, but I say *WTF*) and now it's time for the real festivities to begin. I'm not even in work tomorrow so I can properly let my hair down.

Stepping into Clementine's is like a premonition of my flash-forward dream (premonition squared?) as I'm holding Joshua's hand, and my friends are waiting for me inside. Holding hands with Joshua, I've found, isn't like holding hands with Skeletor, as I'd once presumed it would be. It's rather lovely, and I'd forgotten the glow you get from this simple act. It's been a long time since my last relationship, and Harvey wasn't much of a hand-holder anyway. But Joshua isn't affection-averse. He's the first to hold out his hand for me to take and we've had several public kisses, though none at work.

Joshua has let it be known to management that there's something going on between us but we haven't shared it with the team yet as it's such early days and I know without a doubt that Melanie will be relentless in her ribbing and Sabina will be watching our every move for signs of biased behaviour so she can make a complaint. But, unfortunately for Sabina, there will be no signs of biased behaviour as Joshua and I have been utterly professional while at Brinkley's and that isn't going to change.

Callum is the first to spot us when we step into the bar, but it's Jesy who raises her hand in greeting before rushing towards us.

'Happy birthday, babe.' She throws her arms around me and squeezes me tight, which is starting to get a bit more difficult as her bump seems to have expanded every time I see her. She releases me and looks Joshua up and down. 'Hello. You must be Joshua.'

Joshua and I have been dating for three weeks now and this is the first time he's officially met my friends. My birthday seemed like the perfect excuse to get us all together without making it into an awkward meet-the-boyfriend scenario. Not that Joshua is my boyfriend yet. We haven't put any labels on it, but Jesy, Callum and I know it's a given. By New Year's Eve we will be as loved up as Romeo and Juliet, but without all the death and family drama.

'You must be Jesy.' Joshua holds his hand out towards Jesy, who ignores it and pulls him into a hug instead. Joshua looks stricken and gives Jesy an awkward pat on the back.

'I'm Callum, but I'm not much of a hugger.' Callum joins us and when Joshua holds out his hand, he shakes it. 'Happy birthday, Daisy. You look…' Callum takes a step back so he can take in my fabulous new dress. 'Amazing.'

'Thank you.' I pinch the edges of my skirt and curtsey. 'I thought I'd make the effort for my birthday. Speaking of which, get me a cocktail and gimme my pressies.'

We slide into the booth Callum and Jesy have already bagged and Callum heads for the bar to get a round of drinks. Jesy waits until I've had my first sip of raspberry beret before she hands me a gift bag. Inside is a squishy wrapped present and when I open it, I find a cushion with Jesy's grinning face printed on it.

'You're an absolute knob.' I half-stand as best as I can in the booth so I can hug Jesy across the table. 'I love you.'

'Do you make a habit of calling your friends knobs?' Joshua looks bemused. Or perhaps appalled. Probably a mixture of the two.

'It's just how we are.' Jesy reaches for my hand and gives it a squeeze. 'It's meant with the utmost affection.'

Joshua doesn't look convinced, his brow furrowed as he tries to marry up an insult and affection, but Callum moves us along by passing me a gift that is sort of wrapped. It looks like my nieces have wrapped it while fighting over the sellotape. Like Jesy's gift, this one is also squishy, so it isn't the biggest shock when I find a cushion with Callum's face on it beneath the paper.

'You are also a knob.' I do the half-stand to hug him. 'And I also love you.'

'I didn't want the Jesy cushion to be lonely.' Callum claims he isn't a hugger, but he totally is and he gives the best cuddles. His arms seem to grow several inches as they wrap around you, so you feel completely bound by warmth and love and I always let out an unintentional contented sigh as I lay my head on his shoulder. They should prescribe Callum-hugs on the NHS because no matter how down you're feeling, you'll feel a million times better with his arms around you.

I'm not expecting an actual gift from Joshua – we've only been on a handful of dates and we're not officially a couple – but he reaches into the inside pocket of his jacket and hands me a small rectangular gift. I tear open the paper to reveal a cream box and when I ease it open I find a silver necklace inside.

'Thank you so much.' A lump in my throat causes my voice to crack as I gaze down at it. 'It's perfect.' I touch the little silver camera charm and the lump in my throat grows. We haven't known each other for long but this is such a thoughtful, personal gift and I'm honestly blown away.

Joshua helps me to put the necklace on and when I move the charm into place with my fingers, I'm jolted by a feeling of familiarity. The squarish shape of the charm. The jewel on the front, which isn't a jewel at all but the camera's lens. This is the necklace from my dream. I catch Jesy's eye to try to telepathically impart this new information to her, but she simply smiles at me and places her hand on her chest.

'That is the sweetest gift.'

'Sweeter than this face?' Callum holds up the cushion printed with his face and rolls his eyes.

I don't answer. I twist so I can see the New Year's Eve entertainment poster beside Clementine's door. The act for New Year's Eve is still TBC, but it doesn't matter because I'm a million per cent certain that I'm on track to living happily ever after with the man of my dreams.

'So.' Callum rubs his hands together. 'Are we ordering? I'm starving.'

We dive into the menus, musing over the options even though we'll be getting the same as we always do. I've come to terms with this fact when I notice Joshua hasn't bothered to grab a menu.

'What are you having?' I slide my menu towards him and tap my usual option. 'I'm having the pancakes. They're the best.'

'I'm not hungry. I've already had breakfast.' He shrugs. 'I don't really do brunch.'

Jesy's eyes widen. 'What? Brunch is the best meal of the day.'

'Is it?' Joshua pulls his chin back. 'It isn't even a meal, really. It's a mash-up of two meals that serve their purpose individually.'

'But... pancakes.' I don't understand how you wouldn't jump at the chance to work your way through a tower of pancakes laden with syrup. It's like sneaking a dessert in where you shouldn't.

Joshua holds his hands out, palms up. 'I'm more of a breakfast and lunch type of guy, I guess.'

Callum smirks. 'I bet you shampoo and condition separately too.'

I kick him under the table and he presses his lips together so he doesn't yelp.

'I do shampoo and condition separately. It's the proper way to do it.'

'A two-in-one saves time though.' I'd two-in-one way more things if I could but Joshua doesn't seem to be on the same page. He shrugs.

'I guess I'm not a rushing-around kind of guy.'

Callum snorts. 'Daisy is definitely a rushing-around kind of girl.' He scoots his legs out of the way as I take aim under the table again.

'Then it's a good job opposites attract. And I'll make sure I skip breakfast next time.' Joshua kisses my cheek and I beam, my fingers finding the charm of my new necklace again. I have to wait until Joshua pops to the loo before I can tell Jesy and Callum about the significance of the necklace and the wait almost kills me.

'So he's definitely The One then?'

I give Callum my best *duh* stare, but I can't hold it for more than a second or two because we're on borrowed time. He holds his hands up and pulls back as much as he can in the booth.

'Just checking, because you don't seem to have that much in common, to be honest.'

I frown across the table at Callum. 'Yes we do.'

'Like what?'

'Like…' I lift my hands, palms up. 'Lots of things.' Callum stares at me until I elaborate. 'The licking-the-crisps thing.'

Callum fake-gags.

'We both can't whistle.'

Callum rolls his eyes.

'And we both work at Brinkley's.'

'That's it?' Callum shakes his head and snorts.

Jesy scrunches up her nose. 'It isn't much, babe. But he is seriously *hot*. If I wasn't pregnant and about to get married to my soulmate and he wasn't dating my bestie, *he would get it*. Repeatedly.' Jesy shrugs. 'Sorry. Hormones. I'm horny, like, all the time. It's getting a bit embarrassing, actually. Ssh!' She bats her hand around. 'He's coming back. Talk about something else.'

'Like what?'

Jesy shrugs at Callum. 'Anything. Oh, I know! My hen weekend plans. They've changed. We're not going on a bender in Benidorm any more because that will be zero fun for me.' She pats her bulging stomach. 'So, we're doing a relaxing spa weekend instead. Facials. Pedicures. Body scrubs. I'm having *everything* waxed because I won't be able to reach by then.' She flashes Joshua an apologetic look as he slides into the booth next to me and he responds with a tight smile, clearly uncomfortable at the over-share. 'There's this place in Cheshire I'm interested in. It's an actual castle. I'm going to try and book the same weekend as we'd planned for Benidorm since everyone's already requested the time off. Are you in?' She looks first at me and I nod.

'Sounds fun.'

She looks at Callum, who also nods before holding up a finger. 'But I'm not having anything waxed under any circumstances.'

'Wait a minute.' Joshua tilts his head to one side, his eyes slightly narrowed. '*You're* going on the hen weekend?'

'Yep.' Callum meets Joshua's gaze, eyebrows raised as though in challenge. *Got a problem with that?* 'As one of Jesy's best friends, I'm an honorary hen.' He flicks his gaze towards Jesy. 'But I mean it about the waxing.'

'That's fine by me.' Jesy edges her way along the booth and eases herself up off the bench. 'Time for another wee. My bladder's the size of a pea right now. I'll get another round in on my way back. Same again?'

Jesy may need to wee every two minutes but she's glowing right now and I wonder if I'll look half as wonderful as she does if I ever have babies. I know it's too soon to be even thinking about stuff like that, but these aren't normal circumstances I'm dealing with. I may be in the midst of a three-week relationship with Joshua but I already know how powerful my feelings are going to be in four months' time. What I don't know is whether Joshua wants children, but obviously I can't discuss any of this with him yet. I may be clued up with what the future holds but he has no idea, and my dream stands zero chance of coming true if I scare him off with baby talk.

Chapter Twenty-Two

'If it's a twenty-week scan, why are you having it at twenty-three weeks?'

Jesy and I are browsing through rails of maternity wedding dresses, which aren't the sacks that Jesy feared they would be. They're beautiful and Jesy is going to look radiant in whatever she wears. She's lost the greyish pallor now the morning sickness has packed up and left for good and she's really starting to blossom. She has her next scan tomorrow and I'm trying to get my head around the timing.

'Honestly, I think I'm lucky to get booked in before the baby's first birthday.' Jesy pulls out a cream dress with a frilly neckline but puts it straight back on the rail. 'When Anna needed her wisdom tooth removing in hospital, she had to wait for over a year. She was in agony. She'd have gouged the tooth out with a spoon if she could have.'

I suck in a breath and wince, but my features brighten when I pull out an ivory dress with a lace bodice and floaty sleeves. I hold it out to Jesy, who appraises it for a moment before giving a sad shake of her head.

'The train's too long. I'm going to be waddling like a penguin at that stage – I don't want to trip over my dress as well.'

'You're not going to waddle.' I replace the dress on the rack. 'You're going to glide majestically like a goddess.'

'You're a good friend.' Jesy runs her fingers over a lace and pearl bodice before moving on to the next dress. 'A terrible liar, but a good friend.'

'I'm not lying. I've seen you, remember? You looked incredible. Womanly and stunning and—'

'As fat as a pig?'

I tut and give Jesy a stern look. 'And *divine*. Honestly, Jesy. You're going to make the most beautiful bride. Ant is a very lucky man to be marrying you.'

Jesy nods at this. 'I know, and if he wasn't repulsed by me chucking my guts up every day for weeks, then he isn't going to be put off by this bulging out of a wedding dress.' She places a hand on her stomach. 'Pushing a whole human being out of my fanny might just do it though.'

I decide to side-step that one, because I have no idea how to add a glamourous tint to childbirth. 'Are you going to find out the sex of the baby tomorrow?'

'We're not sure.' Jesy pulls a bright ivory dress from the rack. It has a crossover neckline and an empire waistline with a simple but elegant diamante-encrusted band sitting above the bump. The sleeves are long, which is perfect for a winter wedding, and while the dress is floor-length, there's no train to trip over. 'Ant wants it to be a surprise, but how can we wait that long to know if it's a boy or a girl? I want to go shopping for clothes that aren't white or cream or beige.' Jesy wrinkles her nose. She has always been about a colour pop when it comes to fashion. 'I want to halve my list of baby names because it's getting out of control. I swear, my list is bigger than Santa's naughty or nice list.' She holds the dress against her frame and fans the skirt out. 'What do you think of Silas for a boy?'

'Wasn't there a serial killer called Silas on *Hollyoaks*?'

Jesy's shoulders slump. 'Oh, yeah. I don't want a soap serial killer name.'

'That rules out Richard and Pat then.'

'Which were top of my list. Damn.' Jesy smirks as she places the dress back on the rail. 'Baby needs cake. Shall we go and get a brew?'

We leave the wedding dresses behind and head to the nearest coffee shop. I join Jesy in having a sugary treat and select a Black Forest Danish.

'So how are things going with you and Joshua?' Jesy digs into her chocolate fudge cake with a fork. 'Are you head-over-heels in love?'

'I like him. A lot. We're having fun.' I bite into my pastry and swipe the cream off the tip of my nose with a napkin.

'But?'

I shrug as I chew before finally answering. 'There is no but.'

'It sounded like there was a but.'

I shrug again. 'I haven't had that overwhelming rush of love that I felt in the dream, but it's still early days. We've only been going out for a few weeks.'

'Seven.'

'So less than two months. That's still really early.'

'For marriage and babies, yes, but for feeling passion?'

I sit up straight and flash Jesy a satisfied smile. 'There is passion.'

Jesy flicks her eyes up to the ceiling. 'You've had sex. That isn't the same. Like, when I think about Ant all muddy after rugby I get all tingly.' She shivers with delight. 'And he only has to look at me across a crowded room and I melt.'

'But you've been together years. I'm sure I'll feel that way about Joshua one day.'

Jesy leans across the table towards me. 'But you're supposed to feel that way about him *now*, in the beginning. I *still* feel that way about Ant. It didn't grow after weeks or months. It's always been there.'

'But Jesy.' I place my hands on the table and hold eye contact with my friend. 'I *know* I'll feel that way about Joshua, because I've felt it already in my dream.' Jesy puts a forkful of cake into her mouth and chews while I digest her point. Finally, she shrugs.

'If you're sure?'

I nod once, decisive. 'I'm sure.'

—

The excitement of Jesy's scan leaves me feeling jittery all through my shift the following day, though I manage to make it through without ruining the figgy pudding design on the biscuits we're currently making. Callum and I have arranged to meet Jesy at Clementine's and we're the first to arrive, which means we can have a guilt-free alcoholic drink before the mum-to-be gets here and have a last-minute wager.

'I say... boy.' Callum is the first to place his bet, and there's a tenner up for grabs.

'I guess I'm saying girl then.' I spot Christina across the room and raise a hand to get her attention. She makes her way over to the bar and takes our order. 'Have you had any luck finding a replacement for the New Year's Eve act?' I twist to glance at the poster, which still says TBC but I'm clinging onto the hope that Elton's booked in.

Christina shakes her head as she places a pint on the bar. 'Not yet, I'm afraid. We did find a Beyonce tribute act who was available, but one look at the website told us why. She looks good but sounds awful. Like someone's trampling over a bag of cats.' She reaches for a glass from the shelf above the bar. 'We had a drag Bananarama act last year and they were amazing, so we need something just as entertaining.'

'I remember them.' I nudge Callum as Christina turns to add gin to the glass. 'One of them took a shine to Callum.'

'Can you blame her?' Callum runs a hand from chest to thigh. 'Who wouldn't want a piece of this? If all else fails, I can stick on a skirt and a pointy bra and belt out some Madonna. My stepmum is a massive fan and she played her songs constantly when I was growing up, so I know all the hits. I can't be as bad as the cat-stomping Beyonce act.'

'That's a brilliant idea.' I pat Callum on the shoulder. 'You could open with "Like a Knobhead".'

Callum pulls back his chin. 'Ouch.'

'"Papa Don't Screech"?'

'Hey!'

Christina places my gin and tonic on the bar. '"*Do* Cry For Me Argentina"?'

Callum folds his arms and huffs. 'So you're going to gang up on me now? Fine. I'll hang up my ice cream cone bra and revoke my kind offer.'

Christina blanks Callum and grins at me. '"True Spew"?'

'Harsh!' Callum looks from Christina to me, his jaw hanging open, but Jesy arrives and Madonna is forgotten about as she waves the scan photo at us. I melt over the photo while Callum demands to know whether it's a boy or a girl. Whether he's a tenner up or a tenner down. Jesy reaches into her bag and pulls out a pair of pink bootees.

'It's a girl!'

I squeal. Callum throws his arms around Jesy and congratulates her, even though he's now out of pocket, and I join in the huddle.

'What do you think of the name Otter?'

We've bought Jesy an orange juice and taken the drinks over to a booth. Callum and I side-eye each other at Jesy's suggestion, but it's Callum who's brave enough to respond.

'I think it's *otterly* ridiculous.' He holds his hands up as Jesy glares at him. 'Sorry, I'm on the attack after Daisy and Christina pounced on me.'

Jesy makes a pfft sound. 'Daisy and Christina pounced on you? You wish.' Callum looks down at the table but not before Jesy and I have clocked his pink cheeks. 'Oh my god. Do you fancy Christina? Because I think she's single now.'

Callum rubs the back of his neck. 'I do not fancy Christina.'

'Why not?' Jesy cranes her neck so she can see the barmaid serving at the other side of the room. 'She's cute, and if you're both single...'

'But Callum's not ready to start dating again.' Callum flashes me a look of gratitude as I come to his rescue. 'It's too soon after Zara.'

'Rubbish.' Jesy rolls her eyes, but she doesn't push it and, under the table, Callum takes my hand in his and gives it a squeeze.

Chapter Twenty-Three

Over the past few weeks, I've bounded into Brinkley's, eager to see Joshua even if it means putting in a shift. The alarm clock hasn't been met with swear words and I haven't wished for an asteroid to take me out as I wait at the traffic lights during the drive over. The sight of him in his coveralls might not make me tingle but it's exciting getting to know him more, knowing that we're moving closer and closer to the day when – bam! – I'm hit with all the feels.

I'm sliding my bag into my locker when the door to the staffroom opens and my lips stretch into a mega-watt beam when I spot Joshua. He checks behind him before placing his hands on my hips and kissing my neck.

'Hey, you. I was hoping to find you on your own, because I'm dying to do this.' He kisses me, pushing me back until I'm pressing into the lockers behind me. It doesn't matter about fireworks and butterflies because this feels pretty damn good, even if we're in danger of being caught. Probably *because* we're in danger of being caught.

Placing my hands on Joshua's chest, I push him very gently away, part of me hoping he won't notice and will carry on kissing me. But he pulls back, so slightly I can feel his breath on my lips.

'Someone might come in.' I whisper, in case someone's already at the door, ready to catch us. We still haven't told anyone except those higher up than Joshua about our relationship yet.

'I know.' Joshua presses his lips against the side of my neck.

'And you like the idea of being caught?'

Joshua places his forehead against mine and grins. 'A little bit.'

'Even by Melanie, who'll tell everybody, from Brinkley's and beyond?'

Joshua scrunches up his face and groans. 'Good point.' But he doesn't move away.

'And I thought we were going to be professional at work?'

Joshua peels himself away from me. 'How about dinner tonight then?'

'What's the occasion?'

Joshua lifts one shoulder and drops it. 'Does there have to be a reason to take my girlfriend out for dinner?'

Girlfriend. I've referred to myself as Joshua's girlfriend lots of times over the past few weeks, but never out loud and Joshua hasn't identified us as boyfriend and girlfriend either. Until now. Excitement fizzes in my stomach like a can of Coke that's been shaken up. The dream is coming true. First step: girlfriend. Next step: love.

'What's going on here, then?'

Joshua leaps away as Sabina's voice catches us off guard. Neither of us heard the door opening but there she is, standing in front of us with a smirk. From the stricken look on Joshua's face, the reality of getting caught kissing his co-worker doesn't quite live up to the fantasy.

'I was just showing Joshua some more of the photos I took of the family fun day.' I snatch the leftover photos still sitting in my locker and present them to Sabina as exhibit A.

'You were just showing Joshua photos of the family fun day?' Sabina arches an eyebrow as she takes the proffered stack. 'So, the rumours about the two of you aren't true?'

'Rumours?' Joshua swallows hard. 'What rumours?'

Sabina sniggers. 'Everyone's talking about the two of you getting it on. There's a sweepstake on when you'll come clean. I'm down for two more weeks, so if we could keep this between us…?' Sabina grins, Cheshire Cat-like, and she hums to herself as she flicks idly through the photos, enjoying the fact we're both mortified and that her presence is increasing our discomfort. 'Aww, this is a nice one of your little girl.' She turns the latest photo over to flash at Joshua and it takes a moment for the words to sink in.

Joshua snatches the photo from Sabina and holds the image against his chest.

This is a nice one of your little girl.

I peel the photo away from Joshua's chest and take it in. It's a photo of a little girl in mid-air on the bouncy castle, her blonde hair wild around her face, her mouth wide open with delight.

Your little girl.

I look at Joshua, my eyebrows pulling down low.

Joshua doesn't have a little girl.

Except Joshua can't meet my gaze and his breathing is shallow.

'How do you know about…?' I flip the photo to face Sabina. *And why don't I know about… whatever this little girl is called?*

'Annika was playing with her at the fun day. They had such a good time.' Sabina turns to Joshua. 'We should set up a play date. Maybe that pirate-themed play centre?' She hands the photo back to me and heads to her locker, sliding her handbag inside. I watch Joshua but he still won't look at me. I have so many questions right now, but I can't ask them while Sabina's shuffling around in her handbag, ready to scoop up the gossip and pass it around the canteen.

Joshua has a daughter?

Why hasn't Joshua told me he has a child?

Sabina has met this daughter and wants to set up a play date with her little girl but I, Joshua's *girlfriend*, am only learning about her now? By accident?

Joshua has a daughter?

What does this mean for us?

Sabina's revelation plays on my mind for the entire shift, so while I may be busy covering biscuits with gingerbread-flavoured icing and adding tiny, intricate details, I'm constantly thinking about Joshua and the child he has kept secret. He picks me up that evening and we head out of Woodgate and over to Salford Quays, where Joshua has booked a table at a restaurant with gorgeous waterside views. There are tables outside but although the view is super romantic with the lights shimmering on the water, I'm glad when we're seated inside because my dress really isn't suited for al fresco dining in autumn. We're seated at a table in the middle of the restaurant, where I can still see the water if I almost tip myself out of my chair and *really* crane my neck. The waiter leaves us with a couple of menus while he heads off to get our drinks order.

'I think we should talk.' I feel discomfort in my stomach and not because I'm hungry. 'About your daughter.' We've chatted in the car, about nonsensical things, and I've been waiting for Joshua to bring up the fact that he's a father, but it seems he's quite happy to brush the fact back under the rug and ignore it. But I can't do this. I can't pretend I don't know. Can't pretend that I'm not confused and hurt by the omission. Can't pretend that I'm not freaking out that my boyfriend has a child. Because I'm not ready to be in a child's life. Not ready for the responsibility. I'm hardly the prime example of someone prepared for this; I still live at home with my parents, I get fed up after more than two minutes of fake tea parties with Lexy and Lola, and baby ballet bores me to tears (it isn't even real ballet, and it's proper yawnsville looking at a gazillion photos of my nieces pointing their chubby toes).

'Hallie. Her name is Hallie.' Joshua puts his menu down and takes my hand in his. His fingers are warm and comforting as they squeeze mine. I can't believe I ever thought his hands resembled an evil skeleton's. 'She's three and she means the absolute world to me.'

'Then why didn't you tell me about her?'

'I'm sorry about that. I *should* have told you. I wanted to tell you, but I guess I was scared.'

'Scared? Of what?'

Joshua rubs his forehead with his free hand. 'Rejection, I guess. I thought it might put you off, me being a dad.'

I dip my gaze and study the menu so I don't have to meet Joshua's eye. Because his fears aren't totally unfounded. Joshua having a child wasn't part of the plan. Part of the dream. It's a massive complication that I'm simply not ready to deal with.

'Daisy.' Joshua squeezes my hand and waits until I look up from the menu before continuing. 'I know this is a shock. I know I've been an idiot. But it doesn't change the way I feel about you. About us.' He lifts my hand and presses his lips to my fingers. I hold my breath as I wait for it to happen.

I love you.

Is a couple of months too soon to make a declaration of love? I think it was about six months before Harvey and I said it; me saying it first because I was fed up waiting to hear it from him. I'd thought I was in love with Harvey, but I didn't feel that overwhelming rush, as though I was being knocked over by a wave from the inside, like I did in my dream. I'd thought I was in love with Rhys too, but I was young and incredibly naïve and caught up in my first romance and I know now that it wasn't love. Not even close.

But I don't feel that connection with Joshua yet either. I like him. He's kind and funny and we've been having a great time, but I've yet to feel a single flutter when I think about him, and now this hurdle has been chucked in the way.

'I'd love for you to meet Hallie.' Joshua traces a pattern on the table with his finger. 'But only if you want to. I understand if it's too soon. Or just… too much. But Daisy, this is me. I'm a dad. I come with a daughter. There's no getting away from that.'

My stomach feels tight, as though it's being squeezed. Joshua is right; there's no getting away from the fact that he's a father and he'll never have a clean break from his ex-wife. As the mother of his child, Olivia will always be in his life. The question is, am I willing to put my reservations aside and go with it to fulfil my dream?

Chapter Twenty-Four

It's been a couple of weeks since I've been free on a Sunday, thanks to work and my new relationship with Joshua, so I'm excited to meet up with Callum for our pre-brunch walk. We have much to discuss after Joshua's revelation as I didn't think it was a discussion to have over group chat. Something as big as this needs a face-to-face with a drink or two.

I'm the first to arrive at the park and it's much cooler than the last time we took Frankenstein for a stroll so I'm rubbing my hands together for warmth when I spot Callum. He's clearly feeling the cold too as he's wearing a woolly hat pulled down over his ears.

'Hey, it's *Where's Wally?*' The hat is red and white striped with a big red pom-pom on top. He wore the same hat last year and when I pointed out the resemblance, he'd claimed it was exactly the look he was going for and he'd made me close my eyes before darting off to hide behind a bush. Today, however, there's no game of hide and seek and he takes the hat off and tries to stuff it into his pocket. He throws the ball for Frankenstein and tucks his hands under his armpits for warmth.

'Ooh, that one looks like a good cruncher.' I point at a yellowing leaf that's curling at the edges just ahead of us on the path. Normally, Callum and I would battle to get to it first, with elbows out and hands to faces as we attempt to victoriously crunch the hell out of the leaf with our feet. But when I leap towards the leaf, Callum doesn't join in and the sound of the leaf noisily crinkling underfoot isn't nearly as satisfying as it should be.

'Hey, you.' I fall into step with Callum again and nudge him with my arm. 'What's wrong?'

Callum shakes his head. 'Nothing.' Frankenstein stops by his feet but instead of dropping the ball, he snatches his head away when Callum reaches for it. When Callum tries again, Frankenstein lowers his chest so his bum is sticking up in the air, which is the signal that he wants Callum to wrestle the ball from him. But instead of crouching to the ground and putting Frankenstein in a playful headlock so he can ease the ball from his jaws, Callum simply walks on without the ball.

'Seriously, what's wrong?' Because there's something going on. I know Callum and this isn't like him at all. He's playful and silly and loves nothing more than a bit of light rough play with his dog. It's as though the lights have been switched off inside him.

Callum shrugs and I think he's going to say *nothing* again, but then he sighs and answers honestly. 'I'm just realising life can be really shit sometimes.'

I hook my arm through Callum's and rest my head on his shoulder. 'Are you missing Zara?'

'We were together for ages.'

'You were.' She was his first serious girlfriend after uni. We all assumed they'd be together forever. 'It must be strange, being on your own after so long.'

'It is, but she made the right decision. We'd be married by now if she hadn't ended things. Zara would be my wife, and I'd have been fine with that. Happy, even, but

I've never felt what you describe feeling in your dream for Zara and she deserves that.'

I give Callum's arm a squeeze. 'You do too.'

Frankenstein finally gives up on the idea of rough play and drops the ball on the path. Callum stoops to pick it up, pretending to throw it so the dog bounds away for a few steps before barking and leaping back towards the path. He does this twice more before Frankenstein cottons on to the trick and refuses to budge until he sees the ball arc through the air.

'Are you worried Zara's seeing someone else? Because Joshua says it's weird for him to think about his ex having a new partner.' My stomach churns at the mention of Joshua. I'm dreading having the conversation with my friends and updating them on our relationship because I can guess it won't be good. Callum's always been sceptical about the dream thing so throwing a surprise kid in the mix isn't going to convince him that I'm about to live happily ever after.

'I'd have no idea if she was seeing someone. She asked me to leave her alone, so I have. It feels like the least I could do under the circumstances.'

'You need to stop beating yourself up. You couldn't marry someone you weren't totally in love with.'

'But I was going to.' Callum stoops to half-heartedly wrestle the ball from Frankenstein's mouth. He gives up and stands up again. 'I wasn't man enough to face up to it.'

I resist the urge to punch him on the arm for being an idiot and thread my arm through his instead as we continue to amble along the path.

'And you're only being nice about it because I'm your friend. Imagine if Ant had done this to Jesy, causing her to call off their wedding a few weeks before the big day.'

He's right. I want to argue against it, but I can't. 'I'd cut off his bollocks with a rusty butter knife.'

'You'd have to wait your turn, because I'd be the first in line to maim him. Which I know makes me a massive hypocrite.' He takes Frankenstein by surprise and manages to snatch the ball from his mouth. Frankenstein *oofs* and tap-dances on the spot as Callum pulls his arm back.

'When do you think is the right time to say I love you?'

Callum releases the ball and whirls round to face me. 'Has Joshua said he loves you?'

I shake my head. 'Not yet. But that's okay, right? It's too soon?'

Callum shrugs. 'Is there such a thing as too soon, if that's how you feel? Because sometimes you can leave it too late, and you miss your chance.'

'But it's only been a couple of months.'

'That's all it takes sometimes. Even sooner. I don't think there's a *right time*. A couple of months. Six months. Longer. However long it takes.' Callum shrugs. 'But what do I know? You're asking the wrong person for advice on love.' There's such sadness in his eyes but also something else. Something vaguely familiar. And then it hits me. I'm remembering the first time he came home from uni and I noticed how strikingly beautiful his eyes were, and I'm remembering the way they made me come over all flustered and jelly-kneed. What an idiot I was.

'What's so funny?'

I press my lips together to stop them from reaching upwards. I shake my head. 'Nothing. But don't move.' I hold my hand up and take a step back as I grab my camera which, as it always is during our walks, is around my neck. 'Stay still. No silly poses. Stay just as you are.'

'I'm not really in the mood for silly poses anyway.'

I shush Callum before lining up the shot. With the autumn sun in the background, I capture a truly beautiful shot of my friend.

'Now take one with the hat.' Callum pulls the *Where's Wally?* hat from his pocket and shoves it haphazardly onto his head. He tilts his face and stretches his mouth, Jim Carey-like.

'I thought you weren't in the mood for silly poses.' I take the photo anyway, laughing at the result.

'What silly pose? That was a sexy pose and you know it.'

I laugh again as I push the cap over the lens. 'You are a very sexy man, Callum Cox. It's such a shame about those teenage-girl knees though.' I yelp as Callum lunges at me with his fingers poised for tickling and I take off, veering off the path and onto the damp grass with Frankenstein yapping at us as he joins in the chase.

—

Callum is still wearing the stripy hat when we arrive at Clementine's, despite Jesy insisting he looks like a dork (this encourages him, if anything) but he does take it off as we slide into our preferred booth. I wrestle my coat off and try to calm my breathing, which is coming out in manic little puffs. Because I can't put it off any longer. It's time to have the conversation, but how do I dive into that? *Hey, guys. Guess what? Joshua's got a child! And he wants me to meet her! How amazing and non-scary is that?*

Maybe not.

So, guys. I sort of found something out about Joshua the other day. He's sort of got a child. And he wants me to meet her.

Not perfect, but better.

I take a deep breath to calm myself and place my hands down on the table. 'So, guys.' I take another deep breath. This is hard. I don't know how *I* feel about Joshua having a child and I'm not sure I'm ready to know how my friends feel about it, but I need advice, and quickly, because I'll be seeing Joshua in the morning.

'What can I get you today?' Christina's arrived at our table with her pad and pencil before I can spit out the rest of my speech. 'The usual?'

Callum and I nod, while Jesy requests her usual, plus toast with jam. And a hash brown. She eyes Callum as Christina walks away with our order, but he's learned to keep it zipped when it comes to Jesy's appetite. I take the silence as my cue to restart the conversation, but Jesy gets in there first.

'What do you think of the name Cricket?' She looks across the table at me, but it's Callum who answers.

'As in Jiminy?'

'As in you're a knobhead.' Jesy fixes Callum with a glare until her features soften and she looks across the table again. 'Daisy, what do you think?'

I feel like a deer caught in headlights with my wide eyes and slack jaw. I look down at my hands, which are still planted down on the table. 'It's, er, different. Pretty unique. Which is good if unique is your goal.'

'Hard to get a personalised mug at the gift shop if you're named after a bug though.' Callum's mouth opens wide and he slams his hand down on the table. 'Oh! I get it! Ant. Cricket. Both bugs. But why not Mosquito? Or Slug?'

Jesy's mouth twists. 'Why not Callum's-a-prick?'

Callum nods and shrugs at the same time. 'Also hard to get on a personalised mug at the gift shop. Better than Cricket though.'

'You really don't like Cricket?' Jesy looks wounded. Her shoulders have slumped, and her mouth is down-turned. 'I think it's cute.' She turns back to me and I'm hoping she doesn't probe any further on the name, because it's a bit *out there*, isn't it? 'How did Oscar decide on two names when the twins were born? Because finding one is hard enough.'

'I'll ask his advice.'

Jesy places a hand on her chest and tilts her head to one side. 'Would you? You're the best.'

'I'm, er, also needing advice.' It isn't my pre-prepared opener to the conversation, but it'll have to do. 'It's about Joshua.'

Jesy sits up straight. 'Ask away.'

I take a deep breath and jump right in. 'So, it turns out that Joshua has a child. A daughter. Hallie. She's three, and he shares custody of her with his ex. And he wants me to meet her.'

I slump in my seat, utterly spent, as though I've run a marathon. I hadn't realised how exhausting it was, keeping that bottled up for the past few days.

'Wait, what?' Jesy pulls her chin back and observes me across the table, a smile playing on her lips, as though I'm going to crack a smile any second now and declare I'm winding her up.

'Joshua's a dad?' Callum huffs out a humourless laugh. 'Since when?'

'Since his daughter was born?' I shake my head at Callum. He can be a right numpty sometimes.

'But how long have you known about this?'

'Only a few days.'

'So he's kept this secret from you? Why?'

I shrug at Callum. 'He was scared it'd put me off.'

'And has it?'

I wince. 'Would it make me a bad person if I said maybe a little bit? It's just this isn't what I signed up for. I thought I was getting the man of my dreams, the man I'd fall in love with, marry, and have babies with. He wasn't already supposed to have done those things with someone else.'

'That doesn't make you a bad person at all.' Callum places his hand on top of mine. 'You're allowed to feel how you feel, and it must have been a shock to find out this very important information after a couple of months.'

My head bobs up and down enthusiastically. Yes! Callum gets it! 'It *was* a shock.' Especially as I had to learn the information from Sabina. 'I had no idea.' Though I'm now guessing not all of those photos of children on his living room wall were of his nieces and nephews.

'The question is.' Jesy covers my other hand. 'Can you get over the shock and move on with the relationship? Or is it a line you're not willing to cross?'

That is the question, but unfortunately, I don't have the answer.

Chapter Twenty-Five

Monday rolls around too fast. The question has been bubbling around in my brain and I still have no answer. I'd told Joshua that I needed a bit of time to get my head around the new dynamics of our relationship, but I can't keep him hanging on forever. But maybe just a little bit longer? I sneak across the car park like a bad actor in a spy film and scuttle along the corridor to the staffroom, where I throw my stuff in my locker so I can make a dash to the toilets to hide out until it's time for my shift to start. But the door swings open as I'm jamming my bag into the small space and my stomach plummets.

'Morning, Daisy.'

I sag with relief at Melanie's voice.

'So, you and Joshua seem awfully chummy lately.' She stops by my locker and plays with the padlock on the neighbouring door. 'There's no more bickering over bathroom breaks and he seems much more pleasant. Much less grumpy. Almost like he's in love?'

I snort. 'In love? With who?'

Melanie rolls her eyes. 'Come *on*, Daisy. We all know you're getting it on. Isn't it about time you admitted it?'

I narrow my eyes at my workmate. 'Do you have today on the sweepstake?'

Melanie gasps. 'You know about that?'

I tut and shake my head. 'You *do* have today on the sweepstake. You know this is cheating, don't you? Trying to get me to admit it so you can win the cash.'

'So there *is* something to admit then?'

I give my bag one final shove and push the door against it, securing it into place with the lock. 'No, there's nothing to tell. Joshua is just a guy I work with.'

Melanie rolls her eyes again. 'Yeah, right. We've all noticed how you are around each other. You're definitely having sex.' She backs up and heads for the door. 'I'm so jealous, by the way. And if you could announce it by the end of the day, that'd be great.' She holds her thumbs up at me, grinning as she backs out into the corridor.

—

'I have something for you.' I think it's a magazine he's holding up in the air until I get closer and realise it's a college prospectus. 'There's a photography course starting in January. I know it's a while off but you'd need to apply quite soon.' He flips open the prospectus, which has a little pink note stuck to the page he wants to show me. 'There's a part-time option, which I'm sure you'd be able to fit around your shifts if your supervisor has a word with management about your schedule. I hear he's decent like that.' He winks at me as he hands over the booklet. 'What do you think?'

I think Joshua is very sweet for remembering our conversation about my passion for photography and for taking the time to not only pick up the prospectus but to mark out the appropriate page for me. This encouragement is exactly what I'd want in a long-term partner. Someone to hear me, to know what I need to do to bring out the best in me, someone to give me the massive kick up the arse to get me to do it. This must mean something, like maybe it's a sign that Joshua is The One for me? That no matter how many obstacles are put in our way (even child-sized ones) we're meant to be. The dream has shown me what could be, and I'd be a fool to run away from it, surely?

'I think I should take you out for a drink to say thank you.'

Joshua claps his hands before rubbing his palms together. 'I won't say no to that.'

'Are you free after work today?' I'd have taken it for granted that he would be a few days ago, before I knew he had extra responsibilities, but there are three of us to consider in this relationship now and it leaves me feeling uneasy.

'I have no plans.' Joshua takes a quick look around, to make sure we're still alone, and stoops to kiss me on the lips, nudging the uneasiness aside for the moment. 'I have to rush off, but I'll see you on the floor in two minutes.' He nods at the clock before he dashes away. I slot the prospectus in my locker and head out too.

—

'You do *not* iron your sheets!' I gape at Joshua with a mixture of disgust and admiration at his admission. 'You know that isn't normal, don't you?'

Joshua shrugs as he takes a sip of his pint. 'I don't like wrinkled sheets. And you haven't complained when you've stayed over.'

I snort. 'I haven't exactly been focusing on the sheets, only what's happening between them.' I shake my head, still perplexed by what I've just learned. 'Please don't tell me you iron your undies as well. I couldn't cope with someone *that* neat-freaky.'

Joshua frowns. 'I'm not neat-freaky. I'm just not a slob.'

I nearly choke on my wine, because if not ironing your bed sheets and your underwear makes you a slob, what will he make of me when he sees my clothes-and-mug-strewn bedroom? My room is hardly a pigsty, but it isn't clinically tidy like Joshua's place.

'Anyway.' Joshua taps the college prospectus between us on the table. 'Have you thought about signing up for this?'

'I'm still thinking about it.' I drain my glass, mainly so I don't have to elaborate. I *have* thought about the course a little bit, but there's so much going on in my life right now, so many decisions to make, that it hasn't been at the forefront of my mind.

'Another?' Joshua is already scraping back his chair and reaching for my empty glass before I have the chance to respond. Another plus point: understanding my needs before I've had the chance to voice them. Being with Joshua isn't as simple as I'd originally thought but it'll be worth the sacrifices and the compromises to feel so completely head-over-heels in love.

I take a quick snap of the prospectus photography page while he's at the bar and add it to the group chat.

Daisy:
Joshua's found a photography course he
thinks I should apply for

Jesy:
Are you going to?

Daisy:
Maybe. Do you think I should?

Jesy:
YES

Callum:
I've been telling you to do this for years.
Clearly my opinion means nothing

Jesy:
It isn't like you make good decisions

Callum:
Maybe not for myself…

Jesy:
Or Zara

Callum:
Uncalled for!

Daisy:
Before this turns into an argument, I feel I should tell you that I'm going to tell Joshua that I'd like to meet his daughter

Jesy:
OMG!

Callum:
Are you sure?

Daisy:
Yes

Daisy:
I think

Daisy:
Do you think I shouldn't?

Jesy:
It's a big step, but if you're ready, go for it, babe

It's been years since I've been to the zoo. Joshua already has Hallie when he picks me up and I twist in my seat as I'm putting on my seatbelt so I can say hello to her in the back.

'This is my friend, Daisy.' I feel a little jolt at Joshua's term 'friend', but he squeezes my knee in solidarity and it's fair enough, really. Hallie is only three – she probably doesn't even know what a girlfriend is, and we've only been seeing each other for a couple of months, so it's best to ease her into the relationship slowly.

'We're going to see lots of animals today.' I click my seatbelt into place and Joshua moves away from the kerb. 'Do you have a favourite?'

'I like ellie-phants.' Hallie says the word carefully, her brow furrowed as she concentrates on getting it right. 'I sleep with my ellie-phant, Bubbles. He's squishy and I love him. Will gave him to me.'

I glance at Joshua, who clears his throat and rolls his shoulders. 'Olivia's new fella.' He shifts so he can see Hallie in the rear-view mirror. 'But we're going to see real elephants today.'

'Real ellie-phants are very big.' Hallie stretches her hands as far apart as she can. 'But they are not scary.'

'Real elephants are the cutest. I also like giraffes. Did you know there's a new baby giraffe at the zoo?'

Hallie's eyes widen. 'Will we be able to see him?'

'I hope so, but sometimes baby giraffes are sleepy or just a bit shy, but there'll be lots of other animals to see, like monkeys and lions and penguins.'

Hallie gasps. 'I like penguins!'

I feel a hand on my knee and when I turn to Joshua, he gives it a squeeze and smiles while keeping his eyes on the road. I was anxious about meeting Hallie properly and spending the day with her as Joshua's girlfriend, and maybe Joshua was apprehensive too, but I seem to be doing okay. Granted, we're only a couple of minutes into the trip but I've managed to engage the child in conversation. Being an aunt to two-year-old twins has its advantages.

We arrive at the zoo and the first thing we see are the elephants, who are very big but not at all scary as they squirt themselves with water. Joshua hoists Hallie up on his shoulders so she can get a better look, and she giggles as they amble along with their trunks swinging.

We move on, stopping at the face painting station, where Hallie has a pair of elephants painted on her cheeks before we cross the bridge and head down to the butterfly garden. Hallie is delighted as a massive indigo butterfly flutters by before landing on the rail next to her. I have my camera at the ready and I manage to capture her wide-eyed wonder as she leans in close. The butterfly flutters away but I'll be able to give Joshua the image to keep forever.

'Can we see the bats now?' Hallie takes my hand as we emerge from the butterfly garden and even though the fruit bats are on the opposite end of the zoo and we don't get to see them for ages, she keeps her hand tucked in mine as we make our way from one animal enclosure to the next.

I'm exhausted by the time we make it back to the car, but I can't stop smiling. It's been such a fun day, and I enjoyed the zoo even more while seeing it through the eyes of a small child.

'Today was great.' Joshua nods at Hallie sleeping in her car seat in the back as we zoom along the motorway. 'I think you've made a new friend.'

'I think Hallie has too.' She's clutching the penguin toy Joshua bought her from the gift shop, resting her head on him as it lolls to one side. I catch a yawn with my hand. 'It's been a brilliant day, but I'm knackered. How do you do this full-time?'

Joshua lifts one corner of his mouth in a rueful smile. 'I don't. Not any more.'

'Sorry.' I could kick myself for being so clumsy with my words, but Joshua smiles, properly, at me.

'It's fine. I know what you mean. The truth is, I didn't do much of this when I was with Olivia. We had the occasional day out, but I wasn't all that enthusiastic about it, to be honest. I only did it to stop Olivia from nagging at me to spend more time with them.' He shrugs. 'I was an idiot. I didn't realise what I was pushing away.' He glances at his daughter in the rear-view mirror. 'It's why I make more of an effort now, because I know how precious my time with Hallie is.'

'You're a good dad.'

Joshua shrugs. 'I'm trying to be.'

I yawn again. I can't help it. A day out at the zoo is draining, but in the most fun way. I've loved every single minute of our day together and I've taken a gazillion photos. I can't wait to go through them and pick out the best ones to print.

I suddenly straighten in my seat and my eyes fly open. We're back in Woodgate. I look at Joshua, who grins back at me.

'Hello, sleepyhead.'

'Did I…?' I shake my head as a yawn takes over. Of course I fell asleep. 'Sorry. Couldn't help it. Good job I'm not driving, eh?' I rub my hands over my face and yawn again. I clearly have zero stamina when it comes to childcare.

'I'll drop Hallie off at Olivia's and then we can pick up a takeaway if you fancy it?'

I place a hand over my stomach as it rumbles at the mention of food. Napping makes me ravenous, apparently. 'Sounds lovely.'

Hallie, as though sensing she's home, stirs in the back as Joshua pulls up. The door to the house next to us flings open and a woman stomps across the drive. I try not to notice that she's thinner than me or that she's very pretty, even when her lips are screwed up and her brow is furrowed.

'We're late, I know.' Joshua slips out of the car and meets her at the end of the drive, his hands held up. 'Time sort of got away from me.'

'And you couldn't text to let me know?' Olivia stoops and catches my eye. I look away but I can still hear her voice through the open window, and I don't want to draw even more attention to myself by closing it. 'Oh, sorry. You were too busy playing happy families with your new *friend* and *my child*.'

'I'm sorry?' Joshua shoves his hands under his armpits and tilts his head to one side. 'Do you have a problem with me seeing someone new? Because wouldn't that make you a massive hypocrite since you're shacked up with Will?'

'I am *not* "shacked up" with Will.' Olivia performs the quotation marks by flicking her fingers up and down angrily. 'He stayed over *one time*.' She jabs her index finger practically up Joshua's nostril, and he takes a step back. 'And it was an accident. He fell asleep on the sofa.' Joshua snorts but doesn't say anything. He doesn't need to; he clearly thinks his ex is lying. 'Hallie woke up early and found him asleep on the sofa.' Olivia pauses when Joshua snorts again, but he doesn't say anything and she continues. 'That isn't the way I wanted to introduce them, believe me, and I wanted to talk to you about it first, which is what you should have done. I'm not bothered that you're seeing someone, Joshua. I'm happy for you. But it's about having respect.'

She stalks away from Joshua and heads towards the car. I sink down in my seat, wishing with all my might that I could disappear, but it's the back passenger door she stops at. She yanks open the door and pokes her head into the car.

'Come on, Hallie. Let's get you inside.' Her voice is much softer now, playful rather than laced with scorn. She unfastens the car seat and Hallie wriggles free. 'Go and say goodbye to Daddy.' She moves out of the way and helps Hallie out of the car before shutting the door. She steps over to my window while Hallie flings herself at Joshua.

'I'm sorry we had to meet like this. Maybe next time it'll be on friendlier terms.' She nods at me before she retrieves Hallie from Joshua's arms. 'Next time, if you're going to be late, please let me know.' Settling Hallie on her hip, she returns to the house while Hallie waves frantically over her shoulder.

Joshua sighs heavily as he sits beside me in the car. He closes his eyes for a moment before he turns to me. 'So. Takeaway. What do you fancy?'

I fancy melting into the car seat and vanishing from Earth, but that isn't an option, unfortunately. I really didn't expect to end our zoo trip with a domestic.

'I'm really tired. Do you think you could drop me off home instead?' I fake a yawn and I'm fooling no-one.

Chapter Twenty-Six

Despite the altercation with the mother of his child, my relationship with Joshua is going extremely well. Everyone knows about us at work now, thanks to Melanie who spread the word like Buddy the elf spreading Christmas cheer for all to hear when we finally let slip that we are a couple, and he fits into my friendship group to the point that he even gave his honest opinion on Jesy's latest name suggestion (seriously, I love Jesy to death, but she cannot name her child Echo, as though she's an AI device) and he didn't freak out when I accidentally left my toothbrush in the pot in his bathroom. And no, there shouldn't be quotation marks around the word *accidentally* as Callum suggested. It was a mistake. A reflex. I am not trying to stealthily move myself into Joshua's place. Our relationship may be going well but nobody moves in together after ten weeks, even if they are destined to be together.

We may not be hitting the moving-in milestone any time soon, but Joshua is about to meet my family for Sunday lunch.

It'll mean missing my walk with Callum and brunch afterwards, but the others don't seem to mind. Callum says it'll be nice to spend some quality time with Frankenstein without me hogging the ball and Jesy can't wait to find out how Joshua's first meeting with the parents goes.

My stomach is a jumble of nerves when the doorbell chimes. What if Mum embarrasses me so much I'll be forced to jump out of the window to escape? What if the twins are a whirlwind of mischief? What if Oscar is himself? The only ones I'm not worried about showing me up are Dad and Carmen; Dad's so laidback he's horizontal and Carmen is simply delightful. I often wonder what she sees in my brother, because whatever it is, it's invisible to me.

'You don't have to do this if you don't want to.' I look behind me as I stand on the threshold with Joshua, checking that Mum hasn't descended yet, because once she does, that's it. There's no going back. 'I can tell her you're ill and can't make it.'

'It's fine.' Joshua presses a kiss to my forehead. 'Honestly.'

I hesitate for a moment before I lead him inside and along the hallway to the living room. Mum leaps up as we step inside and beams at Joshua as she takes his hands in hers.

'Joshua. It's so lovely to finally meet you. Daisy has talked non-stop about you for weeks!'

My eyes bulge as I look at my mother. First of all, that is a whopping lie. I've barely said a thing to Mum about Joshua. And second of all, *shut up, woman*.

'All good, obviously.' Mum tinkles out a laugh while I continue to glower at her. 'Come and sit down, Joshua.' She starts to tow him towards the sofa. 'Would you like a cup of tea?'

'That would be lovely, Mrs Grant.'

Mum tuts. 'You must call me Veronica. We're practically family now.'

I want the ground to open and gobble me up. In fact, I want the ground to open and gobble Mum up.

My brother and his family haven't arrived yet, so Joshua is able to get settled with a cup of tea (from a pot I didn't even know we owned) in the living room before chaos (aka Lexy and Lola) descends.

'So, Joshua. You work with Daisy?' Mum smooths down her trousers before she perches on the sofa. Mum never wears trousers at the weekend. She's very much a jeans or leggings woman when she isn't at work, and I notice she's also wearing her stiletto-heeled court shoes with the pointy toes, which she only wears for special occasions (weddings, funerals, christenings – mainly things that involve church and sitting a lot) because they pinch her toes to the point that she can barely walk, but they were expensive so she can't throw them out.

'I do. I joined Brinkley's a few months ago.' Joshua takes a sip of his tea from his cup before returning it to its saucer (another piece of kitchenware I didn't know we possessed). The cup is so small, the tea must be almost gone after that one sip. Dad, I note, is cradling his usual 'No.1 Dad' mug that Oscar and I gave him for Father's Day over a decade ago. There's a chip on the rim but, like Mum's shoes, he refuses to chuck it in the bin and instead drinks from the other side.

'Are you red or blue?' Dad points his mug at Mum. 'That's the question you should be asking.'

Mum tuts. 'He might not even like football, Peter, and what does it matter if he likes City or United? It isn't as though you're a huge fan yourself. It's just an excuse to go down the pub.'

Dad shrugs. 'That's as good a reason as any other.'

Mum shifts her attention back to Joshua, morphing the scowl she's been aiming at Dad into something much more pleasant. 'Daisy has seemed happy these past few weeks. I guess we have you to thank for that, young man.'

Young man? Joshua is thirty-two. He's a father. He isn't some seventeen-year-old I've brought home from college.

'We've never seen her this happy with a boy before, have we, Peter? I think it might be love.'

Oh, sweet baby Jesus, no. I want to leap up and clamp a hand over Mum's mouth, as though I can somehow bundle her words up and shove them back in, erasing them from everyone's ears, but I'm frozen to the spot, my eyes wide, mouth wider. I thought the teapot and the toe-abusing shoes were bad enough, but this is something else.

'So, whatever you're doing, keep doing it. You have my blessing.' Mum beams at Joshua. He smiles back, more tentatively, before taking another sip of his tea. I bet he's planning how to make a swift getaway. I'm praying for an asteroid to sweep down and take us all out but something even more destructive happens: the front door bangs open, followed by thunderous footsteps in the hall before the living room door crashes open and my nieces charge into the room. Never before have I been so happy to see them.

'Nanny!' Lexy throws herself at Mum, distracting her from saying any more mortifying things. Although, can it get any more mortifying? I suppose she could probe Joshua about his performance in bed. I slap my hand over my mouth, as though I've said the words out loud and have given her ideas.

'Who you?' Lola has stopped in front of Joshua and is scrutinising him with narrowed eyes.

'I'm Joshua, your aunty Daisy's boyfriend.'

My heart flutters at the mention of the 'B' word, but my joy is short-lived as Oscar strides over to Joshua and holds out his hand.

'Alright, mate?' He jostles Joshua's hand up and down so vigorously, the teacup rattles on the saucer in Joshua's other hand. Luckily, there's barely any tea left after two sips, so none is spilled. 'So you're the new boyfriend. Got any criminal convictions I should know about?' Oscar laughs as though he's remotely funny before Carmen pulls him away with a roll of her eyes. I pray again for the asteroid.

—

We have twice-baked spinach and goat's cheese souffles for a starter. I have to ask what it is, because it looks like a cow has coughed up phlegmy chewed-up grass into a bowl of yellowish sick before someone added a little white hat to try to mask its revoltingness. We never have starters, not even at Christmas, and although Dad is mainly in charge of the cooking in this house, this addition to the meal has Mum's stamp on it. I'm not saying she's cooked it herself – Mum could burn a salad – but I'd bet my *Vinted* log-in details on the fact that there's a recipe page torn out of a *Good Housekeeping* magazine in the kitchen somewhere.

I poke at the mound of grass-phlegm with my fork. I need to try it so I don't hurt Dad's feelings but I really, really don't want to. I hold back, waiting to see Oscar's reaction as he shoves a forkful into his mouth. He chomps and swallows before going back for more, but I realise gauging my brother's reaction isn't the way to go; that boy would eat roadkill without a hint of hesitancy. He'd even give Mum's efforts a go if he was hungry enough.

I turn to his offspring instead. Kids don't muck about with pleasantries. If it's minging, they'll let me know. Lexy is the first to get the grassy mixture from bowl to mouth and I watch her face closely as she chews. Her nose scrunches as she eats, but that's just a Lexy thing. It's cute but unhelpful in this situation. I turn to her sister, whose face is all squished up, as though she's trying to push all her features into the middle of her face. But it isn't down to the food as she hasn't even picked up her spoon yet.

'Don't want.' She shoves her elbow on the table so she can drop her chin onto her upturned hand. 'Want nuggies.'

Mum tinkles out a laugh, her gaze flicking to Joshua before returning to her granddaughter. 'We're not having nuggets today, sweetheart.'

Nope, we're having pre-chewed grass. I watch as Carmen plunges her fork into her starter. It's already been hacked into a couple of times so either she's really enjoying it or she's trying to get it over with as quickly as possible. Carmen is far too nice to show if she didn't like it.

Mum's picking at her food, taking tiny mouthfuls, but I'm pretty sure she's trying to be dainty rather than reluctant. Dad's bowl is already half empty but Oscar inherited his cast iron stomach so this is no indication of whether the dish is palatable or not. Joshua isn't giving much away either; he's eating the food at a normal rate without showing outward signs of disgust, but perhaps he's being polite?

'Don't you like it, love?' Dad nods at my untouched food so I'm forced to dig my fork into the green mass. I fork up the tiniest bit and shove it between my lips while praying I don't throw up on the table in front of Joshua. I narrow my eyes at Mum as I swallow, because this is all her doing. If she'd acted normally about Joshua being here, if she'd let Dad serve his usual non-starter Sunday roast like he would have if it had been Callum or Jesy sitting next to me, I wouldn't be on the verge of humiliating myself and hurting Dad's feelings all at once.

Oh. It's actually not bad. Quite nice. I take another tiny bite. It's not bad at all if you ignore the fact it looks as though it's been partly digested. I eat a few more small forkfuls before placing my cutlery down and declaring I'm saving myself for Dad's roast potatoes.

Mum's pompous behaviour continues after we've eaten as she insists we play 'parlour games'. I'm not even sure what a parlour game is, but it turns out it's charades and the Eighties music quiz we forgot to play last Christmas. The twins do colouring at the dining table while the rest of us troop through to the living room.

'What are you doing?' I hiss the words at Mum even though we're the only ones in the kitchen. The others are still in the living room, carrying on with the game of charades while we make a brew.

'Tea.' Mum's eyes widen as she places a hand in front of her mouth. 'Does Joshua not like tea? I'm sure I asked him when he arrived. Does he prefer coffee?'

'He prefers acting like a normal person and not a Victorian gentleman.' I snatch the teapot away and replace it with a couple of mugs. 'Parlour games? We don't even have a parlour because we're a working-class family, Mum, and so is Joshua, so why are you trying so hard to be Violet Crawley?'

Mum gasps, her mouth hanging open for ages. 'Violet Crawley is ancient. I'm more like Lady Mary, surely.'

I snort as I add more mugs to the worktop. 'Whoever you are, we're not the posh people from *Downton Abbey*.

We'd be downstairs, scrubbing chamber pots. So, can you act like a normal person? You didn't act like this when Oscar brought Carmen home. You bonded by salivating over Daniel Craig. And there was no starter whenever Harvey came over for tea.'

Mum opens the tea caddy and starts to plop teabags in the mugs. 'It's different with Joshua. I was married with two children by the time I was your age. You can't afford to mess around any more.'

'I'm not messing around.' The kettle clicks off so I lift it up off its base and begin to pour into the mugs. 'But I'm not going to pretend to be something I'm not. I want Joshua to fall in love with *me*, not some pimped up version you've created in your head.'

Mum nods and places a hand on my arm. 'You're right. Sorry, sweetheart. I'll try to be myself.' She drops a few inches as she kicks off her shoes. 'These nasty buggers can go back in the wardrobe for a start.' She winks at me as she stoops to pick them up. 'I'll save them for your wedding.'

With Mum back to normal, I start to relax and have fun with the second half of the game of charades. Afterwards, we split into pairs to compete in the Eighties music quiz, which Oscar and Carmen win hands down. I don't think Oscar answers a single question, but Carmen's knowledge of Eighties pop is unparalleled. I'm having a really good evening until Joshua receives a phone call from Olivia. His ex does not sound happy and when Joshua takes the call outside, I scurry to the back door to listen in as best as I can. From what I can gather, Olivia is upset that Joshua forgot to pack Hallie's favourite soft toy when he dropped her off at home earlier, while Joshua insists the elephant was in the bag. A heated debate ensues as Joshua paces up and down the garden. I wish he'd stop stalking around because after a few steps I can't hear him, even with my ear pressed right up against the door. When he sets off across the lawn, they're still arguing about the soft toy but by the time he strides back, the conversation has moved on.

'When did you break up?'

I press my ear harder against the door but it only muffles the sound, so I pull away again.

'I had no idea. I'm sorry, Liv. And I'm sorry if I didn't pack the elephant. I'll go home and check. Right now. As soon as I've hung up, I'll leave.'

I leap away from the door and dash back to the living room as Joshua hangs up and heads for the door, so he'll never know I was earwigging.

Chapter Twenty-Seven

'Do my hands look massive?' Jesy shoves a hand right in my face, as though she's high fiving my eyeballs. There's no hello as I join her in the booth at Clementine's. No *how are you?* or *how did it go with Joshua meeting the family?*

'This one looks huge.' I bat her hand out of my face and move further along the bench so that I'm out of her reach and am now sitting opposite Callum. 'But only because you've just slapped my retinas with it.'

Jesy holds her hands out in front of her, palms up. 'They've grown, I swear. My fingers are like sausages. Big fat ones that are about to pop. Look.' She wafts her hands in my face again. 'My hands are like shovels on the ends of my arms.'

I ignore the hands and turn to Callum. 'Have you told her she's being ridiculous?'

'Many times. In many different ways.' He shrugs and takes a sip of his drink. 'How did it go with Joshua and the parents?'

Finally! I could leap across the table and hug the man for remembering.

'It was a bit traumatic at first. Mum was doing this weird trying-to-be-posh thing. It turns out she bought a teapot to "make a good impression".' I pull a face as my fingers perform the quotation marks. 'But it turned out okay once she stopped trying to make out we're landed gentry. Until…' I scrunch up my nose and drop my gaze down at the table. I'm not sure I want to go into the phone call I overheard between Joshua and his ex. And by 'overheard' I obviously mean 'purposely earwigged on'.

'Until?' Jesy nudges my calf with her foot when I don't respond. 'What happened?'

'Did Oscar attempt to burp the alphabet again? Because I hate to admit it, but getting to M is impressive.' Callum grimaces. 'The vomiting into his hands afterwards, not so much.'

I shake my head. 'He was less of a knob than usual, actually. I think having kids is making him grow up.'

'Did Lola draw on your bedroom wall with your Tom Ford eyeliner again?' Jesy is still examining her hands, looking first at the left, then the right, and then pressing them together, palm to palm.

'Nope, the twins were fine too. They played quite nicely for a change.'

'Nobody got bit?' Callum's eyebrows shoot up. 'Then what's the problem?'

I pull the sleeves of my jumper down over my hands and refuse to look at my friends as I answer. 'I sort of overheard a phone call.'

'You listened in on purpose?' There's no accusatory tone to Jesy's question, and when I nod and sneak a peek at her, she motions for me to continue.

'Joshua was talking to his ex, Olivia. It was quite heated.'

Jesy gasps. 'He was having phone sex with his ex at your house?'

'Not heated like that. Heated as in angry.'

'Sorry.' Jesy shrugs. 'Hormones again. It's all sex, sex, sex in my head. I've started to fancy the guy who runs the corner shop. I keep going in for chewing gum and scratch cards. I'm either going to win the jackpot or cheat on my hubby-to-be. I even bought a Peperami the other day. I don't even like Peperamis and it gave me indigestion.'

'I love a Peperami. Give it to me next time.'

Jesy tuts and whacks Callum on the arm with her shovel-hand. 'Don't say things like that.'

Callum rubs his arm. 'Things like what?'

'*Give it to me.*' Jesy adopts a gruff voice to quote him. 'I'm already hot and bothered without any sexy talk.'

Callum splutters. 'Sexy talk? Wow, the bar is low for you these days.'

Jesy widens her eyes at him. 'Well, duh. Did you not hear the corner shop story? The guy is, like, seventy plus. He has a grey moustache and a *combover.*' She drops her face into her giant hands. 'What is wrong with me?' Her head snaps up as Callum starts to laugh at her predicament, which earns him another whack on the arm and a few not-nice names.

'Why was Joshua angry on the phone?' Callum brings the conversation back to me as he rubs his arm again.

'It wasn't really him who was angry. Not at first. His ex said he forgot to pack Hallie's toy and he said he didn't.' I wave my hand to show the topic's irrelevance. 'But things were a bit awkward afterwards. I was feeling guilty for listening in and Joshua had to rush off so he didn't piss her off even more and now I'm feeling...' I heave in a breath and let it out in a heavy sigh. 'A bit glum. I thought everything would be perfect when I met my dream guy.' I shake my head. 'No, it is. It's great and we're moving forward. I'm pretty sure Joshua enjoyed meeting my family – even Oscar – and they liked him. So that's good, isn't it?'

Jesy and Callum have sat back while I've waffled on, but now Jesy leans forward and places her hand on mine. Her hand isn't giant at all. It's exactly the same as it's always been. Same size. Same comfort.

'What is it that's bothering you?'

'Nothing. Like I said, everything's great.' I try to wrestle my hand free, but Jesy presses down firmer to keep it in place.

'Daisy?'

'Nothing's bothering me. We're moving forward, just as we should be.'

'But?'

I wasn't going to add a 'but', but I can feel it there as much as Jesy can. I try to push it away but it won't budge.

'But?' Jesy repeats the prompt and when I sigh, it's like I'm not only releasing air but the feelings locked inside me.

'But I guess being in love doesn't feel like I was expecting it to. I like Joshua. A lot. And I fancy him like mad.'

Jesy shrugs. 'I fancy the corner shop dude like mad. It doesn't mean I want to spend the rest of my life with him.'

'But you're not in love with the corner shop dude. You're in love with Ant, who you *do* want to spend the rest of your life with.'

Jesy grins. 'I also fancy him like mad. He's really hot, isn't he? Don't you love a rugby bod? And when he comes home all filthy...' She shivers with delight while Callum gives the biggest eye-roll I have ever witnessed.

'Do you need a moment alone?'

'I need a moment alone with my fiancé.' Jesy closes her eyes and takes in a deep breath, a smile playing on her lips. 'Anyway.' Her eyes snap open and focus on me. 'Back to you and Joshua. If you fancy him like mad and you're in love with him and the relationship is moving forward, what's the problem?'

I think back to my dream months earlier and the overwhelming rush of love I felt for him. 'I guess I'm not feeling it. Not like I did in the dream.'

'Maybe you're not actually in love with him?' Callum asks the question slowly, cautiously, and he inches away from Jesy in case she whacks him again.

'But I am.' I frown. 'Aren't I?' I'm not sure. I know I'm supposed to be, but I've yet to experience what I did during the dream. 'Maybe I'm not in love with Joshua.' Panic starts to boil in my belly, and I look at Jesy with wide, startled eyes. 'What if I'm not in love with Joshua?'

Jesy's hand is a comfort on mine again. 'It's still early days, babe. You can't force these things. It'll happen when it happens. You've only been dating for a couple of months.'

'Ten weeks. Two and a half months.' The panic starts to boil over, hot and frothy, and my breathing is coming in fast, shallow puffs. 'Shouldn't I be feeling... something? Butterflies? Racing heart?' My heart is galloping right now but it's with alarm rather than adoration.

'Maybe he's not The One?'

My lips twist as I glare at Callum. 'But he is.'

'Even though you have nothing in common with him?' Callum holds up his hand as I open my mouth to dispute this. 'Like what? The whistling and crisps thing? What about the things you *don't* have in common?'

I shrug. 'There isn't that much.'

Callum holds his hand up so he can tick items off his mental list. 'He's a TikTok snob and you can scroll for hours. He doesn't think tuna belongs on a pizza and it's your favourite.'

I snort, really loudly. 'That doesn't mean anything. Not everybody likes the same food.' I give Callum a sly look. 'Not everybody will eat absolutely anything that's put in front of them.'

'You will eat anything. Even Peperamis.' Jesy fake-gags. 'You're like a walking wheelie bin.' She smirks. 'You like food almost as much as Daisy does.'

My jaw drops in outrage. 'Excuse me? Who ate *two* brunches the other day?'

Jesy places a hand on her stomach. 'The baby. I don't usually demolish food like a Henry Hoover on speed.'

'And I do?' My eyes bulge as I look across at my friend, who's gone back to examining her hands, just, I suspect, so that she doesn't have to look at me.

'No, of course not. But back to Joshua.' She sneaks a peek at me, to see if I'm still miffed. I am. Very much so. 'He's super neat and tidy and you're… not.'

I shove my arms across my chest and slump in my seat. This is turning into a Daisy-bashing session. 'I'm not that bad. And neither is Joshua. He isn't militant about mess or anything.'

Callum gives me a pointed look. 'He irons his *sheets*, Daisy.'

Damn. I wish I hadn't told my friends about that.

'And he's a bit boring.' Callum flicks his hands up in the air as I glare at him. 'What? He is.'

'He isn't boring. He's mature. He's a father, remember?'

'Which he didn't bother to tell you about for ages.'

'He had his reasons.' I jut my chin in the air. 'And none of that matters. He's the guy from my dream. I saw him. I was in love with him. *That's* what matters.'

'But you can't force yourself to fall in love because you think you dreamed about him.'

My mouth drops open, and I turn my glare at Callum up to the max. 'I don't *think* I dreamed about him. I *did* dream about him. How can all the other stuff come true if it wasn't real?'

Callum looks down at the table and shrugs. 'But it hasn't all come true.' His head rises and he twists in his seat so he can look at something behind him. I follow his gaze and find the poster for New Year's Eve, where the Abba tribute act has been replaced by a karaoke and quiz night. They haven't managed to find a replacement act. They haven't managed to book an Elton John-alike to make my dream come true.

I reach for the camera pendant on my necklace and squeeze it. The dream was real. It *was*.

I look away from the poster. Wasn't it?

Chapter Twenty-Eight

Halloween has taken over the baby section of the clothes shop but in the cutest way possible. Tiny sleepsuits are patterned with smiley-faced pumpkins, miniature t-shirts are emblazoned with cheeky ghosts and sparkly skulls, and I can't help reaching for a pack of minuscule socks, each with a different Halloween design: teeny-weeny witch, purrfect black cat, scare-free skeleton. I need these in adult sizes but they only go up to six to twelve months.

'Next year.' Jesy sighs and hooks the black vest with attached purple and green tulle skirt back on the rack. 'I'm going to have so much fun dressing little Moon up next Halloween.'

I side-eye Jesy. 'You're still keen on Moon? Even though Ant said he'd divorce you if you name his child that?'

Jesy sticks her chin up in defiance before slumping almost immediately. 'No. I guess not. It's just so hard trying to find a name that we both agree on.'

'You could consider something…' I try to find a diplomatic word that's the opposite of my friend's suggestions so far. 'Normal?'

Jesy snorts. 'What, like *Jessica*? Normal is boring. There's a reason I insist on being called Jesy with one S and a Y. Do you know how many Jessicas there were in my year at school? Four. So we all had to go by our full names.

Jessica Wilson-Jones. Jessica Myres. Jessica Abbott. Jessica Bottomley. That was the worst one. Imagine having to be reminded that your name contained a bum every time someone referred to you. It was her idea to switch up our names to Jesy, Jess, Jessica and Jay. No need for surnames then.'

'That does sound complicated.' We start to move away from the Halloween-themed display. 'But you cannot name your child Moon. Getting married, giving birth and then getting divorced within weeks sounds way messier than someone ending up with the same name as you at school.'

Jesy ignores my advice and reaches for a pair of pumpkin-patterned leggings and matching jumper, draping them on her bump. 'What are you coming as for the Halloween party? The obvious choice for me is a big, fat pumpkin.'

The youth centre where Jesy holds some of her art sessions is hosting a Halloween party, and Jesy and the kids have been making decorations for the past couple of weeks.

'You'll be the most beautiful pumpkin there has ever been.' I rest my head on Jesy's shoulder and give her arm a squeeze. 'I'm not sure what I'm going to go as. I thought we could look for a costume today.'

'And what about Joshua?'

I focus on the display of bat-themed sleepsuits so Jesy doesn't see me scrunch up my face. Because Joshua isn't all that keen on dressing up and I doubt I'll get him to wear anything more adventurous than a pair of socks with a Halloween design.

'I'm not sure yet. Oh.' I stop and grab hold of Jesy's arm as we move around the Halloween display, as I spot

Zara up ahead. Callum's ex is sifting through dinosaur-emblazoned t-shirts, checking the sizes on the hangers until she finds the one she's been searching for. It's very small. Newborn, perhaps.

'Oh my god.' Jesy leans in to hiss the words in my ear. 'Do you think she's up the spout? We could be baby buddies. What?' Jesy pulls back her chin as she takes in my aghast expression. 'I don't have any pregnant friends. It'd be nice to share some of the more unpleasant stuff with someone else.'

'More unpleasant stuff?' My aghast expression morphs into one of surprise. 'What on earth have you been holding back? Because you've shared some pretty horrific stuff with us. You nearly made Callum throw up when you were describing... Zara! Hi!' I lift my hand in greeting when Zara looks up and sees me and Jesy loitering. 'I didn't expect to see you here.' I look around at the baby stuff. At the little T-rex t-shirt in her hand. Does Callum know his ex is shopping in the baby department? Because their relationship only ended three months ago. Either she's moved on super-fast or... My insides turn to liquid at the thought. Callum's worst nightmare would be having kids from a broken home.

'Are you...?' Jesy's eyes land on Zara's stomach, which doesn't look as though she's shoved a small cushion up her jumper like Jesy's does. She's asking the question I'm too afraid to voice.

'Am I having a baby?' Zara's eyes widen as she takes in the t-shirt she's holding, as though she's only just realised it's in her hand. 'No! Not me. My friend is. She's popped to the loo. Again.' Zara rolls her eyes and shoves the t-shirt back with the others.

Jesy seems to deflate beside me as the hope of having a mum-to-be friend fizzles away. 'I know what that's like. When's she due?'

'Three days ago. She heard a rumour that someone went into labour in here and was gifted a basket of baby stuff, so we've been hovering, just in case.'

'Really?' I can see Jesy's mentally storing that fact for later.

'I think it's an urban myth, but she's going crazy at home so we needed to get out for a bit.' Zara's fingers trail across the t-rex t-shirt that's back on the rail. 'How's Callum doing?'

'He's… okay.' Jesy's tone suggests 'okay' is a generous assessment, because although Callum is coping with the break-up, he's hardly doing cartwheels around the flat.

'Is he seeing anyone?' Zara asks us the question, but she isn't looking in our direction. A pair of blue polka-dotted mittens are on the receiving end of her gaze.

'No.' I almost laugh at the question, because I can't imagine Callum dating anyone else. Not yet. Not for a while.

'Oh.' Zara's gaze flicks towards us but doesn't quite land before it's back on the mittens. 'I thought that maybe…' She shakes her head. 'Doesn't matter.'

'You don't think Callum was seeing someone behind your back, do you? Because Callum would never do that.'

Zara meets Jesy's gaze as she answers her question. 'No, I don't think he was seeing someone else while we were still together. But I've had my suspicions for a while that he likes someone more than he's willing to admit.'

'Who is it?' Jesy steps forward, eager for a bit of gossip. 'Is it that girl he works with? What's she called?' Jesy looks to me for help. 'Mia? Leah?'

'Ria. But she flirts with everyone.' I look at Zara to drive home the point. 'Callum doesn't like her. Not like that. And I've never got the impression he likes anyone else.'

Jesy shakes her head. 'Me either.'

Zara shrugs. 'Maybe I got it wrong. Or maybe he doesn't even realise it himself. I don't think she does either.' She looks over her shoulder and smiles. 'There's my friend. It was nice to see you.' She raises her hand in farewell before moving away. Jesy and I watch her head towards a heavily pregnant woman before turning to each other.

'Who do you think she is?'

I shrug. 'Someone she works with? A friend she's known since school? I don't recognise her. She isn't the maid of honour, or who would have been the maid of honour, because we've met her.'

Jesy nudges me and tuts. 'Not the pregnant girl. The girl Zara was talking about. The one Callum likes.'

I shake my head. 'I don't think there is a girl. We'd know about her if there was.' I look over at Zara, who's nearing the exit with her friend. 'Maybe it's Zara's way of rationalising what happened, because it makes more sense to break up if there's someone else involved rather than feelings just sort of fizzling out.'

'I guess.' Jesy picks a long-sleeved t-shirt up from the rack and places it across her stomach. 'But maybe it's time Callum got back out there.'

I wrinkle up my nose. 'It's a bit soon, don't you think?'

Jesy gapes at me. 'It's been three months.'

'Which isn't that long when you've been knocked so hard by a break-up.'

'Has he been knocked that hard?' Jesy returns the t-shirt to the rack and picks up another. 'It was more of an escape for Callum than a devastating loss.'

'Of course he was devastated. He was going to marry Zara. They were supposed to be spending the rest of their lives together. Then suddenly, Zara's moved out of the flat and he's on his own. He might not have wanted to marry her deep down, but it was still a shock. I don't think he's ready to move on from that yet. Can you imagine Callum setting up a *Love Today* profile? He's never used a dating app before.'

Callum's always been lucky enough to meet women the old-fashioned way; he met his uni girlfriend at the library, and he got chatting to Zara in the car park of the gym. He's never had to agonise over dating profiles, editing every single word over and over again so that they project fun and flirty rather than a full-on cheese-fest. He's never had to spend ages doing his make-up only to have to tweak with filters for the profile pic afterwards. Not that Callum wears make-up (apart from that time he lost a bet with Jesy and the penalty was having to wear false lashes for a week).

'Then maybe we should set him up?' Jesy practically throws the t-shirt back on the rack so her hands are free to clamp down on my shoulders. 'We have to set him up! Who do you know who's single? What about that girl you work with? The cute one with the nose ring?'

'Melanie?' I shake my head rapidly. 'No way. I can't set Callum up with Melanie. She's fun but she's flaky. I can't see her and Callum together.'

'Did you imagine me — creative, dainty but with a big gob — with someone like Ant?'

I can't say that I did. I always imagined Jesy would end up with someone similar in personality and not with someone with shoulders the width of a bendy bus who could pick my friend up with his little finger. But they fit. Jesy's big gob doesn't clash with Ant's quieter nature off the pitch, and his more rational mind reins in Jesy's flare for mixing colours and prints so their flat is the right side of kitsch, flirting with gaudy without overstepping the mark. And nobody has ever looked more secure than Jesy when her tiny frame is wrapped up in Ant's tree-trunk arms.

'Melanie has a thing for Dougie in packing.' I shrug an apology but Jesy isn't deterred. Eyes narrowed, she taps a finger against her bottom lip.

'I think I might know someone. She's recently divorced and has been dating again but I don't think she's met anyone she likes enough to take seriously yet.' She claps her hands together. 'This is so exciting. We get to play Cupid.'

I try to muster some level of enthusiasm for the notion but there's nothing there but a sense of foreboding. I'm certain that it's too soon for Callum to be dating someone new but I'm also certain that nothing I can say or do will steer Jesy off this track.

'I'm going to invite her to brunch. See if sparks fly.' Jesy claps again and emits a little squeal of joy. I sigh, resigned to the fact that this is going to happen.

'Can we go and find my Halloween costume now?'

–

I haven't been trick or treating since Oscar and I were kids, and I haven't dressed up for Halloween since then, other than a sparkly pumpkin clip in my hair or a pair of dangly skeleton earrings, so I've gone all out with my witch costume. My pointy hat sits upon a purple wig and I'm wearing purple and black stripy tights with a handkerchief-hemmed black dress that's cinched in at the waist with a bat-topped belt. I'm wearing laced-up heeled boots to complete the look and have gone heavy on the eyeliner and very red on the lips. I think I look pretty hot for a hag but unfortunately the cheap material and the wig is itching me like mad, so the effect is marred by my constant clawing at my skin. I have a thorough scratch before I set off for Joshua's but the urge to scrabble at my crawling skin is dangerously distracting as I drive.

I have a good scratch once I've pulled up outside Joshua's place, trying my best to get it out of my system so I don't turn up looking like I've been infested with fleas. Once I'm as itch-free as I'm going to get, I climb out of the car and knock on the door. I'm expecting some sort of reaction from the get-up but a grimace from Joshua wasn't quite what I hoped for. But it's what I get.

'You didn't get my text.'

I glance back at the car, where my phone is stowed in the glove compartment. There are no pockets on this itch-fest dress, and I don't have a suitably witch-like bag.

'Is everything okay?'

Joshua scratches the back of his neck. I'm desperate to copy him. 'Hallie decided that she wanted me to go trick or treating with her and Olivia.'

'Oh.' This isn't awkward at all. My friends are expecting both of us at the party and I know Callum is going to chalk this down as another reason why Joshua isn't The One. But he's a father, of course he has to put his child first.

I try to smile, to show that I understand, which I do, but it won't come. 'Don't worry about it.' I take a couple of steps back. Joshua only has a narrow strip of walled-in yard at the front of his house so I'm back on the pavement. 'Have fun.'

'Sorry.' Joshua scratches the back of his neck again and I could weep with the need to gouge at my skin too. 'You look amazing, by the way.'

I manage to smile this time. 'Thank you. You should have bought a costume after all.'

Joshua shrugs. 'Dressing up really isn't my thing. I'll save you some sweets.'

My smile widens into a grin. 'You'd better.' I lift my hand in farewell. 'Wish Hallie a happy Halloween from me.'

I scurry to the car because I really, really need to scratch. Once I'm somewhat relieved, I head for the youth centre, which is decked out for a monsters' ball. I find Callum — or rather he finds me when he pokes me in the side with a foam sword. He's dressed as a pirate, with red-and-black striped leggings, thigh-high leather boots and a belted tunic over a long-sleeved white shirt. He's wearing a patch over one eye while the other is heavily lined with smoky eyeliner, and he's adopted a moody, glowering expression as he demands that I walk the plank. My breath catches in my throat, as though there's a real pirate standing before me, but the spell is broken when Callum breaks out in a goofy grin.

'Happy Halloween! Are you ready to party?' He holds his arm out to me, and I take it, relieved that he hasn't asked about Joshua's absence. I push the thought of Joshua spending the evening with his ex away as 'Monster Mash' starts up on the sound system and Callum and I push our way onto the dancefloor.

Chapter Twenty-Nine

I grab Joshua's hand as we step through the doors to Clementine's, to try to recreate the moment from the dream, but it's almost midday on a regular November Sunday so the New Year's Eve party atmosphere is lacking. I missed my walk with Callum and Frankenstein this morning as I stayed over at Joshua's. It's been two weeks since the Halloween party and my skin has finally recovered from the assault from the nasty fabric of the witch outfit.

I spot Callum, Jesy and Ant at our preferred booth, already tucking into pancakes and waffles and all-day breakfasts, so Joshua and I head to the bar and place our brunch orders with Christina before joining them.

'You can't sit in the corner.' Jesy reaches out across the table to grab Callum's arm as he starts to shuffle along the bench to make room for us.

'Why not?' Callum pauses, now halfway along the booth's seating.

'It's this feng shui thing I read about in a baby magazine. You need to sit in the middle.'

'But why?' Callum still hasn't budged but his facial expression says he would very much like to.

'I don't know the science of it.'

Callum snorts. 'There is no science to it. It's mumbo jumbo.'

Jesy quirks an eyebrow. 'So, you want my baby to come out sideways?'

Callum's eyes bulge and he shakes his head at Jesy. 'Your baby isn't going to come out sideways because I've moved over to the corner.'

'Are you sure about that?'

Callum nods. 'A million per cent.'

'So, you're willing to risk my vagina being ripped to smithereens? You won't humour me and sit in the middle?' Jesy folds her arms and looks at me. 'Can you believe this? My *best friend* won't sit in the middle *just in case* it stops me being mutilated during childbirth.'

I don't know what to say, because Jesy is clearly on another planet with this one and the thought of the baby ruining her fanny is making me feel queasy and putting me off the French toast that haven't even arrived yet.

'*Fine.*' Callum huffs as he shuffles out from the booth seating. Joshua sits down and nudges his way to the corner, followed by Callum who dutifully sits in the middle and I'm about to plonk myself on the end when Jesy shakes her head.

'You need to sit here, with me.' She pokes Ant in the side, and he edges to the corner of their side of the booth and she moves to the middle, freeing up the end for me. 'Baby will be born with a full set of teeth if you don't, and I'm not breastfeeding a baby with gnashers.'

I sit next to Jesy. There's no point arguing. The woman has clearly gone mad. Hormones, hopefully, with the insanity being only a temporary thing.

Christina arrives with our brunch order and the smell of the apple and cinnamon French toast I ordered fills me with early festive spirit. It's a reminder that Christmas will be here in just over a month, with New Year's Eve not far behind. Christmas cards, tubs of chocolates and mince pies have been filling the shelves of the supermarket since September and I feel all tingly at the thought of my special night with Joshua, right here at Clementine's in a matter of weeks.

'My final dress fitting is on Thursday at six. Will you be able to make it?' Jesy runs a piece of pancake through the syrup pooled on her plate and pops it in her mouth. Also on the horizon is Jesy and Ant's wedding, which is now just five weeks away.

'I'm on earlies all week so I can be there.' I glance across at Joshua. It'll be our last week working together on the same line as there's been a management shuffle and Joshua is being moved from the hand-finishing line to packing and distribution. Joshua assures me that it's nothing to do with our relationship, that several supervisors are switching lines, but I can't help but think that we're being pulled apart, even if it's only at Brinkley's.

'Good, because Mum's going to be there, so I'll need you to mop up her tears before she snots all over my dress. I'm the first of her offspring to get married and she's a mess. She's getting worse the closer we get to the wedding. You should have seen her when the invitations arrived – she burst into tears and the ink ran so I had to give her a new one to frame. It's in the hallway, so everyone can see it as soon as they step through the front door.'

'That's sweet.'

Jesy shakes her head at me. 'It's more of a reminder for the others, to be honest, especially Tina and Anna. *Look, your little sister's settled down. How about you try it too?*'

'But Tina's been with her boyfriend for, like, three years?'

'Four.' Jesy shrugs. 'But it isn't marriage and babies, which is what Mum really wants.' She stabs another piece of pancake with her fork and loads it up with syrup but it doesn't make it to her mouth. The fork clatters onto her plate as she shoots up from her seat suddenly (or as suddenly as she can, being in the third trimester of pregnancy and in the middle of a booth).

'Gia! How lovely to see you.' She barges me out of the way to free herself from the booth and throws her arms around a woman who's approaching our table. 'Come and meet the others.' Releasing the woman, Jesy takes her hand and tows her the rest of the way to the table. 'Guys, this is my work colleague and friend, Gia. Gia, this is my best friend, Daisy and her boyfriend, Joshua, and you've met Ant already.' Ant nods in acknowledgement while Joshua smiles in greeting and I raise my hand. 'And this is Callum.' Jesy holds her hands out towards Callum like a magician presenting a conjured-up assistant in a tiny, sparkly dress.

She returns to her place next to me, leaving Gia to sit next to Callum. Jesy catches my eye and winks and the feng shui nonsense suddenly makes sense. It isn't hormone-induced madness. It's meddling. *We get to play Cupid*, she'd gushed while we were shopping a couple of weeks ago, just after we'd bumped into Zara. This is a set up. Poor Callum.

'Gia's an administrator.' Jesy does the magician-hands again, but this time aimed at her colleague. 'And Callum is a mechanical engineer, which sounds really boring, but he assures me it isn't.'

'That doesn't sound boring at all.' Gia twists so she's looking directly at Callum. 'What sector do you work in?'

Callum is taken aback by the question, probably because we never ask him about what his job entails. Like Jesy said, it sounds pretty dull.

'I'm working as a fire engineer at the moment.' Callum has recovered enough from the shock of someone being interested in his work to answer and Jesy pokes me on the thigh under the table as Callum starts to tell Gia about his current project. She grins when I look at her, but I turn back to Callum, who's chattering away to a rapt-looking Gia. She's smiling and nodding along, eyes wide with intrigue, and when she asks more questions so he can elaborate on his role I feel a squirm of guilt that I've never asked those sorts of questions before. I mean, I sort of get the gist of what Callum does for a living, but I've never got down to the nitty gritty of it. But then I never go into the day-to-day of hand-finishing biscuits either.

Jesy pokes me on the thigh again and leans in close, lowering her voice to a barely audible mumble. 'Am I the best matchmaker or what?'

I open my mouth to answer but I have no words. I'm not sure how I feel about Jesy foisting an unexpected would-be-match on Callum. It isn't really fair to put him in this position and I don't think he's ready to be dating again, as I stated during our shopping trip conversation, but I also know Jesy only wants Callum to be happy and this is her way of trying to make that happen. I want Callum to be happy too, but I don't think this is the way to go. Callum, however, disproves this when he suddenly erupts with laughter at something Gia has said. He certainly sounds happy right now and he looks it too as Gia, head thrown back as she laughs too, pats him on the chest. His cheeks are pink and his eyes are sparkling and he kind of reminds me of Frankenstein when Callum tells him he's a good boy moments before a gravy bone is produced from behind his back. All that's missing is the sound of paws tip-tapping on the floor in anticipation of the treat.

'I need a wee.' Jesy prods at me until I emerge from the booth, and she takes my hand and drags me to the loo with her. 'What do you think? Isn't Gia amazing? And *gorgeous*.' Jesy doesn't even wait until the door is closed behind us before she jabbers out her questioning. 'Do you think Callum likes her?' Jesy waves away her own question with her hand. 'Of course he does. Like I said, she's gorgeous. And she's so funny. Honestly, Daisy, you're going to love her. Though not quite as much as Callum.' Jesy winks at me before she dips into one of the cubicles because she really does need a wee.

Gia is gorgeous, with big bouncy curls and freckles across her cheeks, and she's already made Callum laugh. Why wouldn't he like her, apart from the fact he was supposed to be getting married this year and is still getting over the break-up?

'But... don't you think Gia might be a bit much for Callum?'

'Too much how?'

'She's lovely, obviously, but she's pretty vibrant and quite loud.' I can hear her booming laughter right now, from across the bar and through a closed door. 'And Callum's more... reserved.'

'Are you saying he's boring?'

'No.' I see my eyes widen in the mirror above the sinks. 'Of course not. He's witty and interesting but he's also sweet and Gia might be a bit much for him.'

'Opposites attract? And Zara was hardly meek.'

'That's true, but he's still vulnerable after his break-up with Zara.'

The toilet flushes and the lock slides open before the cubicle door opens. 'Gia's divorced, so she knows what it's like when a significant relationship ends. Plus, she can lick his wounds for him.' Jesy joins me at the sinks and nudges me. I'm still not sure, which I can see is written all over my face in the mirror. 'Look, Callum's a big boy. He can decide whether he's ready or not.'

I can't really argue with that, and Callum and Gia are still giggling about something when we return to the table. He doesn't appear to be overwhelmed by Gia's personality or uncomfortable with how tactile she is. I watch as she pats him and holds onto his arm, roaring with laughter at something that wasn't even that funny.

'Joshua says you met at work.'

I sit upright, astonished that Gia has dragged her attention away from Callum to speak to me. I'm surprised that she evidently spoke to the others while Jesy and I were in the loo.

'I love a work romance.' She bites her lip and fans herself with her hand. 'Very swoony.'

She'd definitely swoon if she heard the full story of me and Joshua, about how I dreamed we were in love before I even met him. That – or she'd have me sectioned for my own safety.

'Do you have a crush on anyone at work?' I ignore Jesy's foot jabbing at mine under the table.

'Ha! As if!' Gia looks at Jesy and they both snigger, which I think is a bit mean unless they work with a bunch of actual trolls. Joshua catches my eye and raises his eyebrows, and I think he's conveying his distaste too until he glances down at his watch.

'Sorry guys.' He nudges his plate away from him. 'I need to get going. I've got a date with Santa.'

'Santa?' Gia edges out of the booth, with Callum following to let Joshua out.

'I'm taking my daughter to see him.' Joshua meets my gaze as he passes by shuffling along the bench, but he looks away quickly. Olivia didn't want to miss out on Hallie's visit to Santa and as neither she nor Joshua were willing to go second (it just isn't as magical second time round, according to Joshua, and he'd missed the grotto visits the previous years and had some catching up to do) they'd decided the fairest option was to take her together. So, the trio are off to see the big man in red this afternoon. Joshua did invite me along, but I imagine it'd be pretty awkward intruding on a family moment.

'Isn't it a bit early for Santa?' Gia pulls her chin back and I'm pleased to see it gives her three chins, because I'm petty like that when it comes to super-gorgeous women. 'It's only the middle of November. It's ages until Christmas.'

Joshua shrugs. 'It isn't that long, and there's loads of stuff we need to do before Christmas.'

'Like my wedding.' Jesy clasps her hands in front of her and does a little wiggle. 'And my hen weekend, which is in *four weeks*. A whole weekend in a real-life castle, being pampered. And watching my friends and family get drunk.' Jesy unclasps her hands and her shoulders slump. 'I might make it an alcohol-free weekend, actually.'

'Alcohol-free?' Callum scrunches up his nose. 'I might be busy that weekend after all.'

Gia's eyebrows pop up her forehead. 'You're going on the hen weekend?'

'Why shouldn't he?' I don't mean to snap, but the words fly out of my mouth, sharp and hostile, before I can stop them. 'It's his best friend's hen weekend.'

'It's just unusual, that's all.' She turns to Ant. 'Are you inviting any women to your stag?'

Ant grins. 'Only the stripper.'

Jesy whacks him on the arm. 'There will be no strippers. The only boobs and fanny you're going to see for the rest of your life are mine.'

Gia shrugs. 'I don't see anything wrong with a man window-shopping. My man can look as long as he doesn't touch. As long as he's coming home to me, I don't care.'

I feel a really big eye-roll coming on and have to fight really, really hard to stop the motion. She doesn't mind her boyfriend ogling naked women? Pur-lease. I try to catch Jesy's eye to share a bit of sisterly solidarity, but Jesy is giggling along.

Joshua's phone pings. He drags his phone out of his pocket and reads the message. 'I really need to go – Olivia says they're waiting.' He stoops to kiss me goodbye. Great. So I have to sit here with the soon-to-be-weds and Callum salivating over Gia like a fifth wheel. It'd be less awkward shoving myself between Hallie and her Mum and Dad for the Santa pic. I cross my arms and sigh, body deflating like a petulant child as I watch Joshua leave to spend a magical day with his daughter and his ex, but I sit ramrod straight when I spot the New Year's Eve poster on the door when it swings shut behind him. The 'TBC' notice has been replaced.

Grabbing Callum's hand, I drag him across the bar, ignoring his squeak of pain as his arm is almost yanked from its socket and his shrieked request to tell him what the hell is happening. I stop at the door and jab my finger at the Elton John tribute act announcement, letting my smug face do all the talking.

My dream is coming true! All the pieces have fallen into place and in just over six weeks, I'll be right here in Clementine's, totally in love.

Chapter Thirty

Christmas has been nudging its way in over the past few months, ramping up with festive TV adverts and town lights switch-ons in November, but there's been no holding back since December rolled around. Advent calendars were opened on the first (and some weirdos only ate the one choc), boxes of decorations were dragged out of lofts, festive jumpers and socks were donned, and nativity plays have been performed in primary schools across the country. Joshua had been buzzing with pride after he'd been to see Hallie's performance as a sheep and he was so happy, I couldn't bring myself to mind that he'd taken her and Olivia out for hot chocolate afterwards, even if it did sound super cosy and affectionate.

It's a good thing that Joshua is on friendly terms with his ex, as that's what's best for their child. And that's why I wasn't overly miffed when, after we'd planned to go to the town's lights switch-on event, Joshua had gone with Hallie and Olivia instead. I'd tagged along with Callum, Jesy and Ant and had a blast, so it's no big deal. And it isn't as though we haven't got plans to do festive things together. Right now, for example, we're being crushed in the crowds of the Manchester Christmas markets as we attempt to drag ourselves to the hot chocolate kiosk, but being pressed against your boyfriend is never a bad thing. I just wish I wasn't also being pressed into the roll of Christmas wrapping paper that's sticking out of the shopping bag of the woman in front of me.

'Isn't this romantic?' I could pinch myself, because this is everything I've always dreamed of. It's a cold, crisp evening and I'm decked out in a fluff-topped bobble hat and matching scarf, my mittened hand clutching the leather-gloved hand of my beloved while Christmas music plays and lights twinkle. I've seen this in the Hallmark Christmas movies that Mum insists on devouring every December, but I've never experienced it for myself. Until now.

'What?' Joshua leans down to shout right in my ear over the sound of The Jackson 5 singing about Santa Claus coming to town. The sound system is uncomfortably loud but it's all part of the experience.

I reach up on tiptoe and yell in Joshua's face. 'I said, isn't this romantic?'

Joshua shoots out a puff of air. 'Hardly. It's freezing. People are pushing in the queue, and I can hardly hear myself think.'

'But it's Christmas! It's so magical!' I breathe in the scents; sugary sweetness mingling with roasting meats and fried food, with an undercurrent of festive spice. I squeeze Joshua's hand, to make sure he's really here, with me, as pure joy pulses around my body at the prospect that I, Daisy Grant, have a boyfriend at Christmastime. And not only a boyfriend; the man who will turn out to be the love of my life. It doesn't get any more magical than that.

'Mmm, delicious.' We've finally got our mitts on a hot chocolate, topped with whipped cream and marshmallows, and I swipe my mitten across my mouth in case my sip has left a moustache.

'It should be, for the price.'

We've moved away from the crowd to enjoy our drinks so Joshua no longer has to yell, and I can easily pick up the morose tone of his voice, though I choose to ignore it. Nothing can ruin this precious moment for me – not the overbearing rabble, not the overinflated price of a hot chocolate, and not the grumpiness of my boyfriend.

'Shall we have a wander?' I nod towards the stalls set up along Market Street, and Joshua offers me his arm. The crowds aren't as intense here and I manage to peruse the stall's offerings, picking up a bracelet for Mum, a bar of fudge for Dad and hand-crafted wooden jigsaws for Lola and Lexy.

'What do you think of this for Hallie?' I indicate a ragdoll with a pretty floral dress and sunshine-yellow shoes. She's beautiful, but I don't know Hallie well enough to make the judgement. I've only met her a handful of times, usually in quick snatches before Joshua has to take her back to her mum's.

Joshua pulls me gently away from the stall. 'You don't need to get Hallie anything.'

'But it's Christmas. And I want to. It doesn't have to be the doll.'

Joshua shrugs. 'There's plenty of time to find something.'

But there isn't. Not really. We're over a week into December. Christmas Day will soon be upon us.

'Do you not like the Christmas market?' Taking Joshua's arm, I move us along to the next stall. 'Because we don't have to stay. We can go home.'

There's much more to see – there are stalls beyond Market Street, the giant Santa perched above St Peter's Square, and all the festive lights – but I can't ignore the fact that Joshua's heart doesn't seem to be in it any longer.

'You wouldn't mind?'

I shake my head, squashing down the disappointment. 'Not at all. Let's go.'

It's no big deal. I can always come back with Jesy and Callum another day.

—

We're now midway through the most festive of months and Christmas has exploded, and no more so than in the Wilson-Jones's house. Carolina and Terence Wilson-Jones take the season extremely seriously and they have the biggest wreath they could possibly fit on the front door, its garland filled with cinnamon sticks and dried apples and mandarin, plus red and silver baubles and jingly bells that ring out as the door is swung open.

'You're here. Thank god.' Jesy grabs my arm and yanks me over the threshold. 'Whose stupid idea was it for me to stay over at my parents' house last night? Because they're all driving me mad.' I'm almost choked with festive cheer as she swings the door shut and I'm blasted with the scents from the wreath.

'They've already started on the fizz. Mum's pissed, Tina's halfway there, Anna's one sip away from texting her ex and Evie's just cried buckets over the Tesco advert. Even Dad's been knocking it back and he isn't even part of the hen weekend. There's only Rosa who's still sober and that's only because she lost *rock, paper, scissors* over who's driving, which means she's sulking big time. Can we run away and celebrate my hen weekend by ourselves? Just you, me and Callum?'

'If we run away to the spa, they'll know where to find us and I'm really looking forward to a massage.' I rub the back of my neck. Being hunched over biscuits for eight hours a day takes its toll.

Jesy whimpers. 'I'm looking forward to the pampering too. I haven't seen my feet for weeks, so I've probably got toes like a Gruffalo. I guess we're spending the weekend with them after all.'

She trudges along the hallway and I follow, passing the framed wedding invitation on the wall, which is now edged with vibrant red tinsel. There's a small tree in the hallway, topped with a star with flashing LED lights, and a four-foot nutcracker standing guard beside the coat rack. But these little touches are just a taster of what is to come when we step into the living room. There's an enormous tree in front of the bay window, its branches stretching out wide as though it's trying to prompt the family into a group hug. Everything has been thrown at the tree: red and gold tinsel, polar bears and robins in woolly hats and scarves, Santas and reindeer and elves, mini felt stockings, glass angels and snowflakes, glittery stars and sequinned hearts and wooden Christmas trees with festive messages – joy, love, peace, believe. There's a rainbow of flashing lights, both on the tree and framing the windowpanes, with a curtain of light-up stars dangling down between the pane and the blinds. Every surface is adorned with festive ornaments and candles and even the ceiling is decked out with foil chains and glittery stars. It's a winter wonderland right in the middle of a drizzly Woodgate street.

'Daisy!' Jesy's mum stumbles towards me, jangling a bottle of prosecco in the air. 'The party's already started. Come and have a tipple. Toast the bribe-to-be.'

'I think you mean *bride*-to-be, Mum.' Jesy wrestles the bottle from Carolina's hand. 'And I think you've had enough to drink. You're driving down with Rosa. You're not puking in my car.'

'Er, no she isn't.' Rosa, who's been slumped in the armchair, pushes herself up to her feet and crosses the living room. 'She isn't puking in my car either. The mum-of-the-bride should be with the bride, surely.'

'But I'm pregnant.' Jesy rubs her belly. 'If she hurls, I hurl too.'

'If she hurls, I boot her out of the car while it's still moving.'

Jesy and her sister gaze at each other intently, almost nose to nose, neither flinching as they wait for the other to break. A knock at the door startles them both from the stare-off.

'Rock, paper, scissors?' Jesy holds out her fist. Rosa does the same. They shake their fists up and down three times before revealing their weapon of choice: scissors for Jesy, paper for Rosa.

'Damn it!' Rosa marches away and throws herself back into the armchair, arms crossed, eyes narrowed, mouth screwed up tight.

Having answered the front door, the eldest Wilson-Jones sister bursts back into the living room, the door thwacking the side table adorned with a lantern filled with glitter sprinkling down on a carol-singing scene. The door bounces off the table and whacks Tina on the arm. Not that she notices.

'The entertainment's here, girls.' Tina's grin is cheek-aching wide as she steps aside. 'Come on, Magic Mike.' She ushers a pink-faced Callum into the room and starts to tug at his jumper while humming stripper music.

'Leave the boy alone.' Jesy steps in to yank her sister away. 'You're in Rosa's car with Mum.'

'What?' Rosa sits upright and shakes her head. 'No way. I'm not having them both.'

'And I'm not having my best mate mauled by Tipsy the Teletubby either.'

Tina gasps. 'Are you calling me fat?'

Jesy shoots me a pleading look. 'How set are you on that massage?'

There's another round of rock, paper, scissors and Rosa ends up with both Carolina and Tina in the back of her car, plus Anna, while Jesy drives me, Callum and Evie to the Cheshire village. We play car games and crank up the radio and sing along to Christmas songs. We particularly rock Cliff Richard's 'Mistletoe and Wine', with Jesy taking on the role of Cliff while Evie and I harmonise, and Callum's high-pitched choir boy solo will go down as a legendary hen weekend story.

'Is this your first hen weekend, Callum?' We've sufficiently recovered from pissing ourselves laughing over Callum's choir-boy performance when Evie asks him the question, and she beams at him when he says that it is. 'Mine too. I've been really looking forward to it.'

Jesy smirks. 'Callum's been looking forward to this weekend for about twenty years.'

'But you only got engaged a couple of years ago.'

Jesy glances over her shoulder, so she can aim the smirk directly at Callum. 'It's not so much my hen weekend he's been fantasising about but spending the weekend with Anna.'

Callum rolls his eyes and shakes his head. He doesn't even bother denying his crush on Jesy's older sister.

'You fancy our Anna?' Evie makes a spluttery laughing sound. 'But she's a lesbian.'

The sound Jesy emits is full-on laughter. 'Like *that's* what would get in the way of Anna fancying him back.'

'What are you trying to say?' Callum leans forward, so his head is almost poking through the gap between the front seats. 'Are you saying I'm too unsightly to be fanciable?'

Jesy shakes her head, and I can see the beginnings of another smirk. 'I was thinking more about your personality.'

There's a moment of silence in which we pass several sheep in the field beside us, and then we all crack up again, including Callum, because he knows Jesy adores him.

Finally, we turn off the last narrow country road into Little Heaton, passing over an iron bridge into the cutest village that could star in its own festive rom-com. There are thatched-roof cottages and pubs festooned with lights, and we pass a barge with a lit-up waving penguin on top. There's the quintessential red pillar box on the corner of the high street with a knitted festive scene placed on top, and a huge lit-up Christmas tree next to a war memorial. All that's missing is a dusting of snow.

We make our way through the village and drive up the hill that leads to Durban Castle, which is even more breathtaking than I was anticipating. The building looms above us, with turrets and huge wooden doors and rows of tall, panelled windows. The gravelled car park is to the right and it's chilly as we step out from the warmth of the car, although it barely registers as I stare up in awe at our home for the next two days.

'Happy hen weekend, Jesy.'

Jesy joins me in gawking at the castle, leaning her head on my shoulder as she emits a sigh. 'She's a beauty, isn't she? Almost as good as a bender in Benidorm.'

'We'll do that when I marry Joshua.' I nudge Jesy, to show that I'm kidding because although I know Joshua and I are about to be mind-blowingly in love, marriage is a way-off-in-the-future concept. We haven't even said 'I love you' yet, never mind 'I do'.

'We'd better. I was looking forward to getting trashed at the beach.' Jesy lifts her head from my shoulder and waves as Rosa's car turns into the car park. The car comes to an abrupt stop and Tina stumbles from the passenger seat, her hands on her knees as she dry-retches over the gravel. One arm is still tethered by the seatbelt.

'Obviously not *that* trashed.' Jesy winces as her sister continues to heave up air. The door on the opposite side of the car swings open violently and Rosa stomps her way across the gravel towards us.

'There's an Aldi bag full of vomit in there.' She thrusts a thumb back towards the car. 'And I'm not dealing with it.'

I place my hand on Jesy's shoulder as we watch Rosa march back to her car, where she wrenches her suit-case from the boot and drags it towards the castle's main entrance. 'Happy hen weekend. It's going to be fun.'

Chapter Thirty-One

We check into the hotel and get settled (or have a nap, in the case of Tina) before meeting on the heated terrace at the back of the castle. Perfectly manicured lawns stretch out ahead of us, bisected with paved pathways lined with low post lights that lead down to a walled fountain. Beyond the fountain is an uninterrupted lawn that leads down to the woods that surround the grounds. The sky has already started to turn inky and the terrace is draped with white fairy lights that twinkle gently. The lights are replicated on the potted Christmas trees that stand guard on either side of the terrace area, giving off a sophisticated festive feel, which is enhanced by the slow piano version of 'I Wish It Could Be Christmas Every Day' that's playing softly from hidden speakers.

Most of us have opted for mulled wine to sip on as we begin our first evening at the castle, but Jesy has chosen a pomegranate martini mocktail to toast her hen weekend while Tina is taking delicate sips of water as she sits with her knees tucked up under her chin on the sofa furthest away from the twinkly Christmas trees. I think she's regretting smashing the fizz so early. Rosa is definitely brimming with regret – among other strong emotions – as she scowls across at her sister, who's left the tang of vomit in her Audi.

'I'd like to propose a toast.' Carolina, who's recovered significantly more than her daughter after their morning prosecco session, lifts her glass goblet. 'She may be my middle daughter, but she's the first to get married and I'm so proud to be the mother-of-the-bride. To Jesy.'

Everyone raises their glasses and joins in the toast, apart from Tina, whose grey pallor suggests she's in danger of violently chucking up if she so much as blinks too hard.

'Thank you, Mum.' Jesy beams at the group gathered on the terrace. 'And thank you to all of you for coming to spend the weekend with me getting pampered.'

'And plastered.' Evie nudges Tina with her foot. Tina whimpers and places a hand over her mouth.

'I've got some catching up to do.' Rosa's scowl smooths out as she leans across the table to fill her glass up with more mulled wine from the jug that's being kept warm over a tealight stand.

'Lucky you.' Jesy takes a sip of her mocktail. 'Whose stupid idea was it to get married while pregnant?'

Rosa sniggers. 'I think that one was down to you and Ant.'

'It'll be worth it when you hold that little one in your arms.' Carolina's eyes are shining as she reaches across to squeeze her daughter's hand.

'I know.' Jesy nods. 'Still sucks a bit though. Do you know I can't have a body wrap while I'm here? Or get in the hot tub?'

Anna sits up straighter. 'There's a hot tub?'

'There's one outside my room.' Jesy pulls a face. 'Not that I can use it.'

'But we can.' Rosa stands up and grabs the jug of mulled wine from its stand. 'Let's take this party to the hot tub.'

'But what about me?'

Rosa shrugs at her sister. 'You can sit on the side and resent your unborn child.'

'I don't think so.' Jesy huffs as she dumps her mocktail down on the table so she can fold her arms across her bump. She looks to her mum and her other sisters for support but they're already vacating their seats. Even Tina is dragging herself from the sofa.

'Come on, Magic Mike.' Evie grabs Callum's hand and pulls him to his feet. 'It's time for all your teenage dreams to come true. Hey, Anna. Did you bring a swimsuit or a bikini?'

'We're not doing this.' Jesy shoves her hands further into her armpits and juts her chin into the air. 'You lot are not getting in my hot tub.'

They're in the hot tub less than ten minutes later.

—

Jesy has a suite on the ground floor of the hotel. We all insisted she should have the luxurious room all to herself as an extra special treat as she's both the bride-to-be and the mum-to-be, but the truth is Ant had warned us about Jesy's snoring, which apparently is off-the-scale now she's heavily pregnant. As well as a massive bed, a huge walk-in shower with built-in sound system, and a seating area with plush sofas and tub chairs, Jesy's room has a set of French doors that lead out onto her own private terrace where you can take in the view while relaxing in the hot tub. Not that there's much relaxing going on as the Wilson-Jones clan submerge themselves. Tina, despite her delicate state, was the first of the sisters to arrive in Jesy's room, shortly followed by Rosa and then Anna, and they're splashing about when Callum and I arrive in our complimentary fluffy robes. The non-alcoholic bubbles have revived Tina, it seems.

'Come on then, Magic Mike.' Tina lounges back against the wall of the hot tub and looks Callum up and down. 'Get your kit off. Slowly.'

Callum shoves his hands in his robe's pockets. 'Maybe I'll just join Jesy for a bit.'

'Spoilsport.' Tina splashes water out of the hot tub towards Callum as he drops into the rattan chair next to Jesy. 'You're getting in, aren't you, Daisy? You're not boring like those two.'

'I'm not boring.' Jesy jabs her index fingers above her bump. 'I'm pregnant. And Callum isn't a piece of meat, so leave him alone.'

Tina mimes a long yawn before she slams her hand down into the water, splashing her sisters. There's a knock at the door, which Jesy goes to answer, and I whip off my robe while everyone's distracted and slip into the water. The Wilson-Joneses are all naturally slim and wearing the bikinis they bought with Benidorm in mind, so I feel dumpy in my plain black swimsuit.

'I hope you haven't finished off the mulled wine.' Carolina steps out onto the terrace and kicks off her flimsy hotel slippers.

'Forget the mulled wine. It tastes like nail polish remover.' Tina stops splashing about and points at the table, where Jesy is joining Callum again. 'I've brought fizz. Open it up now we're all here.'

Jesy eyes the bottle warily while Carolina and Evie join us in the hot tub, but she relents and opens it, pouring it into the plastic cups Tina has thoughtfully provided.

'Do *not* throw up in the hot tub.' Jesy aims this instruction at Tina as she passes her a cup of prosecco. 'I am not spending my hen weekend fishing vomit chunks out of there.'

'Chill out. I'm fine now.' Tina settles back with her cup. 'But maybe not after a drinking game or two. Let's play *never have I ever*.'

'Never have I ever drowned my big sister in a hot tub.' Jesy flops down on the rattan chair. 'But today that may change.'

Never have I ever turns into a game of truth or dare, and Callum finally ends up in the hot tub after being dared to by Tina. I think he got off lightly, to be honest. He's still wearing his shorts for a start.

'Truth.' Despite being banished from the hot tub frivolity and the alcohol-imbibing, Jesy has thrown herself into the drinking games and she's much more relaxed as she lounges on the sideline with her feet up on the low table in front of her and a room-serviced mocktail in hand.

'Are you really going to call your baby Lotus?' Rosa scrunches up her nose. 'Like, for real?'

'I think it's beautiful and unique.' Jesy places a hand on her stomach. 'There aren't going to be any other Lotuses in her class.'

'There aren't going to be any Poo-On-A-Sticks either, but that doesn't make it a good name to impose on a child.' Jesy stares down her sister. 'My child, my choice.'

Evie shrugs. 'It's better than Cricket, I guess.'

Tina snorts. 'And Otter.'

'Moon!' Rosa hoots. 'Do you remember that one?'

'They're all beautiful names.' Carolina smiles at Jesy. 'Apart from Echo. Please don't name my first grandbaby Echo.'

'Don't worry, Mum, I won't.' Jesy moves the little paper umbrella out of the way so she can take a sip from the sparkly straw jutting out of her glass. 'I'm quite taken with Poo-On-A-Stick though.'

Carolina whips around in the hot tub so she can glare at Rosa in a look-what-you've-done kind of way, all flared nostrils and wide eyes.

'She's kidding, Mum.' Rosa rolls her eyes before leaning to look across at Jesy. 'Right?'

Jesy shrugs. 'Maybe. Anyway, it's your turn. Truth or dare?' She raises her eyebrows and takes another slow sip of her drink. She has some dirt on Rosa to deliver so Rosa, unsurprisingly, opts for a dare and ends up showing her most embarrassing pic on her phone, which is a selfie of her left bum cheek after she bruised it while ice skating a couple of weekends ago. Tina is next and she bravely chooses a dare and more bravely carries it out.

'I can't believe you just did that.' Carolina shakes her head at her daughter as Tina fastens the clip on the back of her bikini top. Callum, I notice, is studying the jet of water beside him intently.

'What?' Tina shrugs and slips back into the water. 'They're only boobs, and they're still pretty much pointing up. There was no-one out in the corridor to see me running past anyway.'

'That's nothing compared to what she did in Corfu.'

Carolina's eyes snap to Anna. 'What did she do in Corfu?'

'Nothing.' Tina widens her eyes at Anna. 'It's Magic Mike's turn for truth or dare and we haven't seen any wangs on this trip yet.' She holds her hands up. 'Just saying.'

'Truth.' The word propels itself from Callum's mouth before Tina's last syllable is uttered.

'Ooh, I know.' Evie raises her hand and wiggles it around. 'Who's your most embarrassing crush?' She smiles slyly at Callum as her eyes slide towards Anna.

Callum closes his eyes and sighs. 'I didn't have a crush on her.'

There's a splutter from outside the hot tub. 'You absolutely did.' Jesy turns to Anna, her teeth bared as she grins with pure glee. 'This isn't the first time Callum's seen you in a bikini because he used to shimmy up the tree in his back garden so he could watch you sunbathing.'

Everyone turns to Callum, whose cheeks are lit up like a Christmas tree.

'I did not.' His eyes bore into Anna's. 'I swear, I didn't.' I think at this moment in time, Callum wishes he'd asked for a dare and was standing up with his pants around his ankles while he helicoptered his willy.

Anna shrugs. 'Even if you did, I'm afraid you're not my type. Not even with those girly knees.'

The hot tub occupants – bar Callum – erupt with laughter and Jesy's laughing so hard, she's in danger of sending herself into labour. Callum watches her with narrowed eyes as she bangs her hand down on the table.

'Your turn, Jesy. Truth or dare?'

There's something in Callum's tone. Something playful yet menacing at the same time. The mirth freezes. Jesy stops banging her hand on the table and settles back in her chair. Her eyes are on Callum's, unflinching, and she shrugs.

'Truth. I have nothing to hide.'

Callum is silent for a moment, his eyes still locked with Jesy's.

'Have you ever...' He presses his lips together, savouring the moment before he drops whatever truth-bomb he's holding onto. '...sneezed all over a boy's face when he leaned in to kiss you, snot and everything?'

I close my eyes, but I manage to see Jesy's glare before my lids shut.

'You *told him*? I told you that in confidence! You weren't supposed to tell anyone. You *promised* you wouldn't tell anyone.'

Shame floods me, because Jesy is right. I *had* made that promise, and I'd tried to keep it. I really had, but there were times when we got stupidly drunk on two-for-one drinks in Clementine's back in the day and it had slipped out one night. But Callum had never said a word about it afterwards and I'd assumed – hoped – he'd been too drunk to remember.

Clearly not.

'Wait.' Tina holds up a finger as she looks at her sister over on the seating area. 'You snotted all over a boy?'

Anna scrunches up her nose. 'Did the snot go in his mouth?' She makes a gagging sound while Tina snorts at the suggestion. But Jesy doesn't answer. She isn't even looking at her sisters. She's looking at me. Intently.

'Isn't it your turn for truth or dare?' Jesy tilts her head to one side and smiles but there's no joy to it. She has something up her sleeve and I'm not going to like it. 'Truth, I think.' She pauses, much like Callum did a moment ago, before he asked his question. The knot of dread tightens. I feel a little bit sick. 'Have you ever had a crush... on one of your friends?'

Chapter Thirty-Two

Oh. My. *Crap.* Jesy knows about my silly crush on Callum. I'm not sure how because I've never admitted it out loud and not even God could drag that info out of me. But maybe it was obvious? Maybe I wore it on my face like neon-pink lipstick, there for all to see, hard to miss unless you had your eyes squeezed shut tight. Oh, god. Did Callum notice too? Did I go all heart-eyed whenever I saw him? Did I hang off his every word, practically drooling? Could he hear my heart galloping like a Grand National champion? I glance over at Callum, but he looks intrigued rather than mortified. He doesn't know. Yet.

'I'm hungry.' I push myself up onto the side of the hot tub and reach for my robe. 'Is anyone else hungry? We should get something to eat.'

Jesy shakes her head, the corners of her lips raised slyly. 'Answer the question first.'

I shake my head. I won't. I can't. I'd rather push my face into a switched-on blender and make a Daisy smoothie than confess my most shameful secret.

Jesy leans forward. As much as she can with a massive bump in the way. 'Have you. Ever had a crush. On a friend?'

'She definitely has.' Tina and Anna have stopped giggling and are looking at me. Tina points at me with a smirk. 'Look how red she is.'

My eyes are wide and pleading as I silently beg Jesy not to do this. She shakes her head, dismissing my appeal. I betrayed her confidence and this is payback.

'How did you even know?' I'm not sure I want to hear the embarrassing details of how obvious my crush on Callum was but I'm stalling for time. Hoping something – anything – will happen so I don't have to say the words out loud. The fire alarm piercing our eardrums would be great about now. Or the sudden bright lights of an alien aircraft hovering above the hotel. I'd offer myself up for a different kind of probing.

'You told me.'

I didn't. I couldn't have. The words wouldn't have left my mouth without me combusting with shame on the spot.

'You were drunk.'

Oh. That again. Clementine's two-for-one offer has a lot to answer for.

'It was the night you met Lars.'

I met – and had a holiday fling with – the Belgian back-packer while we were in Amsterdam celebrating Callum's twenty-first birthday, which means Jesy has known about my shameful crush all this time. I want to slip back into the hot tub and drown myself.

'You've never said anything.' I'm still stalling, before I confess or drown myself, I can't decide which is the least awful option to go for yet.

'That's because I'm a better friend than you.' Jesy settles back down against the chair. 'Until now. Now I'm being a terrible friend and making you confess all about your weird crush.'

Drowning, surely, is the way to go.

'Oh my god, who is it?' The intrigue has deepened on Callum's face. His eyes are alight with it, the blue beaming bright across the hot tub at me, and his hand is placed half over his mouth as though he's trying to cover the grin that's clearly itching to spread across his face.

'It was nothing, really. Not even a proper crush. Just a teeny, little thing. A blip. An insanity. I didn't actually fancy you. I think I just missed you while you were away at uni and I got confused. And it was over in, like, a nanosecond.'

I turn to glare at Jesy. There. Happy now? But Jesy doesn't look like she's happy or gloating or even mildly satisfied that's she's wreaked her revenge on me. Her jaw is practically on the tiled floor and her eyes are in danger of popping right out of her skull as they flick from me to Callum and back again.

'You had a crush on *Callum*?' Her eyes flick to Callum again but I don't dare follow them. She laughs, a short, almost hysterical sound. 'What? When? *How?*'

Oh, sod it. Might as well drown myself too at this point. I'd bid my friends goodbye and slip under the water for the sweet release if I wasn't frozen in place.

Jesy didn't know about Callum. She's in utter shock at the revelation right now – and rightly so.

'Hey, Magic Mike isn't so bad. He's cute in his own way.'

I hear Tina's words, but I can't look at her in case I accidentally glimpse Callum. I can never look at him again.

'He's a good-looking lad.'

'*Mum.*'

'What? He is. I'm not saying I fancy him, Evie, calm down. But he is a handsome lad.'

'I'm a lesbian and even I think he's pretty fit.'

'I've seen worse, to be honest.'

Jesy's family is discussing Callum's attractiveness but I'm focusing on Jesy and the impressive range of emotions that are flying across her face: the shock makes way for confusion, which edges away to reveal mortification and then she's giggling, her hand smothering the noise too late.

'I am so sorry.' She doesn't look sorry, not even a little bit. Her hand is hovering in front of her mouth in an attempt to mask her delight, but it isn't working. 'I had no idea. I was talking about McKenzie Nolan.'

'McKenzie Nolan?' There is disgust dripping from Tina's words. 'Wasn't he the kid who lived above the post office? The one with the neon-yellow teeth who could fit his entire fist up his giant nostrils?'

'That's the one.' Jesy drops her hand and openly grins now. 'He used to stuff his pockets with little bags of Haribo and share them with us in the cafeteria at college.'

'His dad went to prison, you know. Got accused of stealing twenty grand from the post office's till.' I can almost feel the buzz of scandal emitting from Carolina as she shares the years-old gossip. 'Turns out he didn't take the money at all, but it's too late for poor Gary. His wife left him while he was inside and shacked up with an electrician. He got out to no wife, no job, no home. Practically lives in the Farthing now, drinking himself stupid.'

'Never mind Gary Nolan.' Tina wades towards me but I still can't look at her as Callum's in that direction and I can't put my eyes on him, accidentally or otherwise. 'I want to know about his son and how Daisy could fancy him.'

'I was seventeen and he had a motorbike.' I look down at my hands, which are clasped on my thighs as I sit on the edge of the hot tub. I'm surprised any words can leave my mouth, but there they are. 'It was the leather jacket that did it.'

'And the helmet, because it covered his face?' Tina sniggers. Carolina tuts.

'Forget about McKenzie.' Jesy bunches her fists up and jiggles them about with pure joy. 'I want to know about Callum.'

'And I want to run away.' Which I do, only stopping to scoop up my robe because the key to my room is in the pocket.

–

Oh, god. Oh, god. Oh, my flipping *god*. I've lost both of my best friends over a stupid hen weekend game because now I'll never be able to face Callum again and I'm going to have to strangle Jesy for tricking me into spilling the most embarrassing secret I had in my possession. The option of drowning myself in the hot tub is gone – there's no way I'm going back to the scene of the crime – and the sink in my en suite is tiny, barely big enough to fit both hands in at the same time, never mind my face, and there's no bath, only a shower. Perhaps I could shove my head down the toilet and bog wash myself to death?

There's a knock at the door. I ignore it. It'll either be Callum, who I am never putting myself in the presence of again, or Jesy, whose neck is going to get squeezed very, very tightly the next time it's within reach.

I sink down onto the bed by the window and drop my face into my hands. I'd weep but the shock has shut off my tear ducts and so I simply whimper. What have I done? Why don't I remember telling Jesy about my crush on McKenzie Nolan? Why did I tell her at all? *And why did I have a crush on him in the first place?* Yes, he had a motorbike and a leather jacket, and he was generous with his Haribo, but he also never brushed his teeth and he used to talk about nothing but Man United and how Liam Gallagher was the greatest poet in the universe.

There's another knock at the door. I flop down on the bed so I'm looking up at the ceiling. I have messed up. Badly. My life has been gathered up, shaken up, and chucked back down again like a pair of dice, landing on the numbers that are going to send me to jail. I'm not going to be physically locked up (unless I really do get my hands on Jesy's neck) but a door has been slammed on my old life and bolted shut, because how do I go back after this? My crush on Callum had been bad enough when I kept it locked up tight, but now it's out in the open and everyone knows that I used to pine for my best friend, that I used to daydream about kissing him, about seeing him naked, and I want to shrivel up and die from the shame of it.

How do I look at Callum again with us both knowing that I would have quite liked to have seen his willy? I simply can't, which means our friendship is over. No more hanging out at Clementine's or Sunday walks with Frankenstein. I don't think I can even face the 'Friends Without Benefits' group chat any more.

Another knock at the door masks the sound of a sob. What have I done? Why am I such an utter *knobhead*? I have sabotaged everything, because this is going to affect my friendship with Jesy too. The tight trio is no more, right when she needs us most. She's about to get married.

About to have a *baby*, and I've taken a wrecking ball to our friendship group. The wedding is going to be beyond awkward and I'll have no choice but to avoid Callum like the plague, and we'll have to meet the baby separately, bonding not as Auntie-Daisy-and-Uncle-Callum but as single entities, and this makes me very, very sad.

There's another knock at the door, louder and sharper this time. A rap that means business.

'Go away, Jesy.' I turn onto my side and tuck my knees up into my body, my hands holding them in place. 'I don't want to talk to you.'

'It's me.'

Callum's voice. Worse than Jesy by a million times. I don't want to talk to him. I want him to forget I ever existed.

'I'm not opening the door.'

'I've got a key.'

I close my eyes and groan. Callum and I are sharing a room. I'm in the bed by the window, he's in the one closest to the door. It seemed like a good, cost-effective idea to share when we made the booking. It seemed like a good idea an hour ago. Two friends sharing a room. No big deal, right?

'Can I come in? I need to get changed. I'm freezing.'

He's out there in the corridor, wet, in a pair of shorts and a robe. I'm embarrassed but I'm not a monster.

'Fine. Come in. But I'm not discussing it.' I turn to face the window as the keycard is slotted into the lock, my back to Callum as he steps into the room.

'Are you okay?'

I want to laugh. *Am I okay? I want to expire from mortification, pal. Does that sound okay to you?* But I don't laugh and I don't get snippy with Callum because none of this is his fault. It's mine, and a little bit of Jesy's for being a trickster.

'Yes, I'm fine.'

'Right. Good.'

I hear a couple of drawers being opened and closed and then the bathroom door closing. I consider making a run for it, but where would I go? I'm still in my swimsuit and robe so I can hardly wander around the hotel. This is a nice place. Posh. Not a cheap place to crash between days on the beach and nights out in Benidorm.

'We're going down into the village to the pub for something to eat.' Callum has emerged from the bathroom. I'm still staring at the wall, determined to never put my eyes on him ever again. 'Carolina looked up the menu for the hotel's restaurant online and nearly died. She said she'd need to take out a second mortgage for a plate of chips. I prefer pub grub anyway.'

'Are you just going to act normal then?' I turn to peek at Callum. He's sitting on the bed, doubled over as he ties his shoelaces, so we don't make eye contact. Relieved, I turn back to the wall.

'How do you want me to act? It's no big deal. People have crushes all the time and it was years ago. It doesn't mean anything. Unless you still have a crush on me now?'

'As if.' I twist around and see Callum grinning at me. 'I've found my dream guy, remember?'

Callum flicks his gaze up to the ceiling and puffs out a little sigh. He still isn't sold on the whole prophecy dream thing, even with all the evidence stacked up in front of him. 'Good. We're fine then. So get up and get changed. I'm starving.'

I sit up slowly. Cautiously. 'You really don't think it's weird?'

Callum shrugs. 'I think you're weird, but I always have.'

'Oi.' I grab a pillow and chuck it at Callum as he stoops to tie his other lace. It thwacks him on the head, which is highly satisfying. 'Seriously though. No weirdness between us?'

Callum chucks the pillow back at me with no real intent to make contact and I catch it. 'Why would it be weird between us? It was a long time ago and it was only the teeniest, weeniest of crushes apparently.'

'It wasn't even a proper crush at all.'

'Right. Good. That's settled then. No real crush. No weirdness.'

I toss the pillow against the headboard and shuffle off the bed, grabbing my suitcase and flipping it open. I'm reaching for the handle of the bathroom door with a pair of jeans, a jumper and clean underwear tucked under my arm when Callum speaks again.

'I'm more concerned that you had a thing for McKenzie Nolan, to be honest.'

I pause for a nanosecond before I push down on the handle and step into the bathroom without retaliating, which I think is extremely big of me. I find there's a smile on my face as I spot myself in the mirror over the tiny sink. I'm still fatally embarrassed by this evening's admission but I'm hopeful our friendship will survive if I can get over the toe-curling shame.

Chapter Thirty-Three

The pub wraps its warm arms around us as we step inside out of the cold. There's a roaring fire to the right of the bar and although the seats closest to it are already taken, we sit near enough to feel its benefit. Tina and Anna head straight to the bar while the rest of us squeeze around a couple of round tables, grabbing extra chairs to accommodate the group. Still feeling the itch of shame, I place myself between Rosa and Evie, with Jesy and Callum on the next table over. I'm sure one day I'll be able to look them in the eye without wanting to shrivel up to dust, but today is not that day.

I peel off my coat and scarf and drape them over the back of my chair, taking in the full festiveness of the pub. There's a large, bedecked tree next to the fire, with smaller trees dotted around, all of them twinkling with soft white lights. The fireplace is dressed in a garland of greenery, with glossy red apples and berries nestled in the foliage, and there's a matching, oversized wreath sitting centre stage above. There's another garland above the bar and glass vases filled with red and gold baubles on the windowsills. It's festive and tasteful and a welcome distraction from my best friends, whose gaze I don't want to accidentally meet.

This Christmas is going to be perfect. I will spend the most magical day of the year with my boyfriend, doing romantic things like wearing matching pyjamas, sipping buck's fizz as we open our presents and giggling over the cheesy jokes from our Christmas crackers. Finally, I get to join in the picture-perfect Christmas that's shoved in our faces on the TV over the festive period.

'Drinks.' Tina dumps three bottles of wine on the tables while Anna sets down a tray of glasses. 'And food.' She grabs the menus she has tucked under her arm and distributes them. 'Order quickly because I really need to line my stomach before I have anything else to drink.'

'How are you still standing?' Evie's brow is creased and I'm not sure if she's baffled, impressed or concerned about her sister's alcohol intake.

'Practice.' Tina plonks herself down next to Rosa and opens her menu. It's warm inside the pub but the chill from outside after being in the hot tub nudges me towards the Polish stew. After the hot tub confession, I'm in need of comfort. I sneak a look at Callum and Jesy. Their heads are together as they gently debate curry versus all-day breakfast and I wonder if I'll ever be able to sit with such ease with them again, because to me at least, my stupid crush has manifested as a massive boulder that's plonked itself slap bang in the middle of our friendship group – and I'm not sure I'll be able to shift it.

Jesy drops into the seat next to me after we've eaten, not seeming to pick up on the unease I'm feeling. We're alone at the table as the others have wandered over to the pool table across the room.

'So, that crush thing. Is that why you didn't want Callum to go out with Gia?'

The dishes are being cleared away by the young waitress and while I bet she hears all sorts working in the pub, I don't want to become another snippet of gossip among the kitchen staff. I convey this to Jesy by widening my eyes and nodding at the girl as she gathers up the plates.

'Because that makes total sense now.' Either Jesy didn't understand my shut-the-heck up signal or she's ignoring it as she ploughs on. 'You were jealous.'

I glance at the waitress. She doesn't appear to be paying attention to Jesy's big gob, but she is taking her sweet time stacking the plates as Jesy blabs about my crush.

'I wasn't jealous. Why would I be jealous?' My words come out in a hiss as I shoot them from the side of my mouth, my eyes lingering on the world's slowest waitress. 'I don't like him. I did once, briefly, when I was much, much younger, and now I don't. I told you why I didn't think him seeing Gia – or anyone else – was a good idea.'

'The Zara thing?' Jesy scrunches up her nose. 'But everyone knows the best way to get over a relationship is to find someone else, even if it's just for a bit of fun. Gia wasn't looking for anything super serious either. She could have helped the healing process.'

I shake my head. 'I don't think that's how Callum works.'

Jesy pulls back her chin. Even the waitress tears her eyes off the plates, which she is still stacking with the utmost care, to flash me a look of utter disdain.

'He's a *man*, Daisy. Of course that's how he works.'

'When has Callum ever had casual sex?' I don't usually bandy the S-word in front of strangers but I need both Jesy and the waitress to know that I'm neither naïve nor in love with my best friend. 'He's more sensitive than that. It's why we love him so much. In the most platonic way.'

'Maybe it wouldn't have ended up being casual sex with Gia? Maybe they'd have ended up having a long and loving relationship. Maybe she'd have got him to walk down the aisle.'

The waitress isn't even pretending to clear the table any more. She's simply standing there with the plates resting on her arm as she awaits my response.

'But he didn't want a relationship with her, long, loving or otherwise. Because he wasn't ready. Like I said he wasn't. I was looking out for him as a friend.' I fold my arms across my chest and tilt my chin. 'And not because I was jealous.'

Jesy and the waitress share a look. Jesy raises her eyebrows and the waitress flicks one corner of her lips upwards.

'You know, it's okay if you were jealous.' Jesy nudges my knee with hers under the table, and I wish there actually was a boulder between us right now. 'It's okay if you like Callum. He's a really great guy. And cute too.' Jesy points him out to the waitress, who turns towards the pool table. 'I think it's quite sweet when two friends get together.'

'My mum and dad were friends before they got together.'

I smile at the waitress in a 'that's nice. Now buzz off' sort of way. She does not buzz off.

'They lived next door to each other for years and went to the same school and everything but they didn't get together until they were in their *thirties*. My mum had even married someone else, and it was only after she'd got divorced that he told her how he felt and they ended up together with three kids. That could be you and him.' She nods towards Callum, who's laughing at something one of Jesy's sisters has said. 'He is pretty cute, if you're into freckles. Are you into freckles?'

'I'm into my boyfriend.' I give Jesy a pointed look. 'Joshua. Remember him?'

'There's a boyfriend?' The waitress dumps the pile of plates back down on the table and drops into the seat next to me. 'This is getting *really* interesting. Do you love him? The boyfriend?'

'Joshua.'

The waitress nods. 'Yes. Do you love Joshua?'

I gape at the waitress. 'That's a really personal question to someone you don't even know.'

She shrugs. 'Sorry. I'm nosy.'

I shake my head. I'm not answering that. I don't even know this girl's name and yet she wants to know everything about me.

'No, you don't love him? But you love that guy?' She nods back towards the pool table. 'The friend?'

'No.' I sigh, short and sharply. 'I don't love Callum. I had the tiniest thing for him years ago, when I was, like, eighteen. How old are you?'

'Seventeen. Eighteen in three months and sixteen days.'

'And how many crushes have you had over the past year?'

The waitress narrows her eyes. 'Three? Maybe four? One of them was an anime character so I don't think she counts.'

'And do you still have a crush on all of them?'

She shakes her head, her nose scrunched up. 'God, no. Except maybe Grell Sutcliff. The anime character. That crush will *never* die.'

'And in eight years' time do you think you'll be *in love* with any of them?'

She snorts. 'No way. Not even Grell because, you know, anime character.'

'There you go then. I had a little crush on Callum and then I didn't and I'm not in love with him now.' I look pointedly at the plates stacked on the table.

'Fair enough.' The waitress stands up and grabs the plates before heading off for the kitchen.

Jesy leans in close. 'You didn't answer that question, did you?' She quirks an eyebrow. '*Do* you love Joshua?'

'Maybe. Maybe not yet. But I will.' I've felt it in my dream. It was there, the most intense, breathtaking realisation I've ever felt in my life, so it doesn't matter if I'm not quite there yet. I will be, on New Year's Eve, and there'll be no questioning, no doubts, no silliness over an old, buried-long-ago crush. I'll be totally, utterly, head-over-heels in love.

'How many times have you messaged him since we got here?'

'How many times have I messaged him since we got here?' I shrug. 'What's that got to do with anything?'

Jesy wriggles her phone free from her pocket, unlocks it and taps on her messages, turning the screen to show me the flood of texts between herself and Ant. She scrolls up to show the extent of their exchange. It's a *lot*.

'I miss him so much, it makes me ache.' She places a hand on her chest, over her heart. 'I know you and Callum are my best friends, but he is too. He's my fiancé – soon to be husband – and I love him more than anything. But, more importantly, I *like* him. I want him to know about every detail of my day and I want to know his.' She jiggles the phone. 'I couldn't go a whole day without talking to him in one way or another.'

I shrug and start to pick at my fingers. 'Joshua and I are built differently. We don't need to be in each other's pockets.'

Jesy nods. 'That's fair enough.'

I don't tell her that I haven't messaged Joshua once since we've been here. I meant to text him to let him know we'd arrived safely, but it had slipped my mind and then the whole hot tub thing happened. He hasn't texted me either. But it's no big deal.

'I just want you to be happy.' Jesy nudges me with her arm. 'Whether that's with Joshua or... someone else.' Her eyes stray towards the pool table, towards Callum.

'Don't.' I cover my face with my hands and groan. 'How am I ever going to live this down?'

Jesy peels my hands away. 'How long have you known Callum?'

'Since college. So, what, ten years?'

'So you know him.' Jesy nudges my arm again. 'He isn't going to let something as silly as this faze him. You might feel a bit awkward for a bit, but it'll pass.'

'You're being oddly calm about this whole Callum thing.' I watch as Jesy taps out a quick message to Ant. I'd have been floored if Jesy revealed she'd once been totally besotted with our best friend.

'It was a bit of a shock, to be honest, but now I just find it really, really funny.' Jesy muffles her giggle with her hand as she taps her thumb against the send button on her screen. 'I am a bit miffed you didn't confide in me. I thought we told each other everything and I never said a word about McKenzie Nolan until I found out you'd blabbed about the snot-kiss thing, did I?'

'Sorry.' I look down at the table in case Jesy twigs that I'm not sorry at all for not confiding in her. I never wanted anyone to know, but now everyone does.

'It's okay. I get it.'

I start to pick at my fingers again. 'What if Joshua finds out and dumps me?'

'How would he find out?'

I give Jesy my best 'duh' look. 'Everyone here knows and word spreads, doesn't it? I'd be surprised if my parents don't know by the time I get home, and once they find out it'll be a matter of nanoseconds before Oscar and Carmen are clued in. Joshua will inevitably find out by accident and how will he feel about the fact I once harboured feelings for Callum?' Rationally, it shouldn't matter as it was way back in the past, but people don't always think rationally in the heat of the moment. What if he breaks up with me before New Year's Eve and the kiss that lights a thousand fires in my belly? There are less than two weeks until the New Year's kiss and I cannot fall at the final hurdle.

Jesy takes my hand in hers, to stop the picking and to give it a squeeze. 'If Joshua dumps you over a crush you had as a teenager, then he really isn't The One for you.'

I nod, relieved. Because I know, despite the Callum-shaped spanner that could hit the works, that Joshua is my happily ever after.

Chapter Thirty-Four

There's a buzz in the air at Brinkley's on Monday morning, a haze of anticipation mingling with restlessness. It's the last few days before the factory shuts down for the festive period, one of the only times the factory completely ceases production and nobody has to rock up to work. And unlike the summer family fun day, the Christmas shutdown is for an extended period, spanning Christmas and New Year. People are in such good moods that piles of sweets and chocolates have been left on the table in the staffroom in a gesture of goodwill, and I select a purple-wrapped chocolate and pull at its sides. The door to the staffroom opens and Melanie bounces in, a bunch of fake mistletoe held in the air. She plants a noisy kiss on my cheek and eyes the table of goodies.

'Are there any orange crunches left?'

I rifle through the rainbow of wrappers on the table, Quality Street and Roses mixed with Fruit-Tella and mini bags of Haribo, and pluck out a foil-wrapped hexagonal chocolate. I hand it to Melanie, who pounces on it as if someone will swoop in and take it, even though we're the only ones currently in the room. I was hoping to see Joshua before my shift started so we could have a quick chat, but he must be out on the floor already. We were going to meet up last night but I was knackered after my weekend away, so we've agreed to meet in the pub later.

'Want me to dangle my mistletoe over you and Joshua later so you can have a smooch?' Melanie asks the question mid-Orange-Crunch-chomp, but I've known the girl so long that I can decipher her muffled words.

'No, you're alright, thank you. PDAs at work are not our thing, mistletoe or no mistletoe.'

Melanie sniggers. 'That's not what Sabina says. She says she saw the two of you *canoodling* in here a few weeks ago.'

'Sabina's full of...' I think of Kath's swear jar, even though it's been absent for months. 'Sprinkles.'

'You said that when she told everyone she'd caught Jeremy and Eileen going at it in the photobooth at the fun day and that was true. There was actual photo evidence.' Melanie's shoulders droop. 'I should have dragged Dougie in there and snogged his face right off.'

'You should have. You've liked him for ages.'

Melanie scrunches up her nose. 'I don't think he likes me, though. Not like that. I've defo been friend-zoned.' She shrugs. 'But never mind. There's plenty more biscuits in the factory. Have you seen the new guy in sales? *Proper* fit and he comes to work on a motorbike. Hey!' She grabs my arm and squeezes hard. 'Maybe I'll get to snog him under my mistletoe!' She winks at me as the door opens and Joshua steps into the room. 'After you and Joshua have had a go, obviously.'

I roll my eyes and hope Joshua didn't hear, because he really hates the teasing at work. It's just a bit of fun but he says it tramples all over his authority.

'Good weekend?' Joshua's smiling, his face open, and I take this to mean he didn't hear Melanie's remark about the mistletoe.

'Really good.' If you forget about the hot tub confession, which I'm trying really hard to. 'It was fun and the massage I had was bliss.' I root through the treats on the table and select a strawberry cream. 'Oh, I need to talk to you about Christmas Day. I know we haven't discussed it yet, but Mum was wondering if you'll be having lunch with us? It's just so she knows how much veg and stuff to get in.'

'Oh. Right.' Joshua grimaces and scratches the back of his neck. 'The thing is, I usually go to Birmingham for Christmas.'

The chocolate freezes between the wrapper and my mouth. 'Birmingham? Why?'

Joshua clears his throat, still scratching at his neck. 'It's where Liv's parents live. We always spend Christmas with them.'

Melanie frowns. 'Who's Liv?'

'Olivia.' I try to sound casual, but the name comes out all squeaky. 'Joshua's ex-wife.'

Melanie's frown deepens. 'You're spending Christmas with your *ex*?'

'Not with my ex. With my daughter.' Joshua snatches a chocolate from the table. It's a Toffee Penny, which I know he doesn't like but he starts to unwrap it anyway.

'*And your ex.*' Melanie flashes me a look that says *and you're okay with this?* I'm not sure, to be honest. This is the first time I've heard of the arrangement.

'Yes, she'll be there, but it's something we've always done. It's tradition.'

'And where's Daisy in this *tradition*? Does she get to tag along too?'

'Well, no.' Joshua fiddles with the toffee but doesn't put it in his mouth. 'Like I said, it's my ex's family. It'd be a bit weird if I went there with my new girlfriend.'

Melanie snorts. 'It's already weird, mate.'

269

My face is growing hot. I should tell her to stop, but I can't. I'm mute with discomfort and disappointment, because Joshua and I were supposed to have the perfect Christmas together. The matching PJs. The buck's fizz. The cheesy cracker jokes. I was finally supposed to have someone to snuggle up to while we watch festive films. Someone to wake up with on Christmas morning. But it looks like I'm going to be alone, yet again.

Melanie, however, is not mute. Quite the opposite, in fact.

'What about when you and Daisy have kids? Do they have to stay at home with her while you go off with your ex and her family to cosplay the life you once had?'

I suck in a breath. Melanie isn't holding back and my whole body is curling up on itself. I really, really should tell her to stop but... what happens if we do have kids? I haven't thought that far into the future, to be honest. I've been trying my hardest to get us to New Year's Eve and the magical kiss.

'I, er, no, I don't...' Joshua is fumbling over his words and although I'm curious about how Joshua sees our future beyond the new year, I also don't want him to feel under attack. I nudge his foot with mine. A little silent act of solidarity. *You don't need to answer that.* Not yet. Not here, with an audience.

'I think it's nice that Joshua has such an amicable relationship with the mother of his child.' I force myself to hold Melanie's gaze, even though I'd quite like to slide under the table and hide from the whole conversation. I nudge Joshua's foot again. *See, I'm cool with you and Olivia spending Christmas together. Please don't break up with me. Please kiss me at midnight on New Year's Eve and make my dream come true.*

270

Melanie shrugs. 'It's your life, I guess.' She turns as the door opens, her eyes widening when she sees who's on their way in. She grabs the plastic mistletoe and rushes to meet him. 'Oi, Dougie! Pucker up!'

I take Joshua's arm as Melanie launches herself at Dougie, steering him further into the room. 'You will be back for New Year's Eve, won't you?'

Joshua nods, finally popping the sweet in his mouth. 'I'll be back the day after Boxing Day.'

I place a hand on my chest and sigh with relief. Crisis averted. There will be plenty of time to iron out all the details about our future once New Year has passed.

By the end of the day, there's a new piece of gossip circulating about a blossoming relationship. Love is in the air, for Melanie and Dougie and for Jesy and Ant as their wedding rapidly approaches, and, fingers firmly crossed, for me and Joshua.

Chapter Thirty-Five

Jesy looks absolutely stunning. The empire line of the faux wrap dress is flattering, cinched above her bump with a crystal-encrusted band, while the bright ivory fabric sweeps down to the ground. The sleeves are long – perfect for a late December wedding – and the narrow, rolled hems give another touch of simple elegance.

I hand a tissue to Carolina, whose mascara is starting to pool under her lashes.

'You look…' The mother of the bride sniffs as she dabs under her eyes. 'You look…'

'Beautiful.' Tina steps forward and pulls her sister into a light but tender hug, expertly dodging the bump and being careful not to crease the dress.

'Gorgeous.' Anna pecks a featherlike kiss onto Jesy's cheek.

'Like a princess.' Evie smiles but it crumples immediately, and I wriggle a tissue from the pack and hand it over.

'She isn't a princess.' Rosa pauses long enough to receive a death glare from Evie. 'She's a *queen*.'

'You guys.' Jesy rolls her eyes and wafts the compliments away with her hand but she's beaming. 'Daisy? What do you think?' She holds her hands out to the side, crossing her feet and dipping into a mini curtsey.

'I think Ant is the luckiest man alive.'

Jesy nods, short and decisive. 'He sure is.' She grins and opens her arms wide, beckoning the bridal party for a group hug. We gather around Jesy in a glamourous huddle.

It's four days before Christmas and today I get to witness my best friend living out her fairy tale. My heart feels heavy in the most fabulous way as I help Jesy sprinkle a few finishing touches to her look. Her hair has been swept into a low, loose bun and I attach a silver comb with crystal embellishments to really make her sparkle.

There's the rumble of engines outside and I push the blinds aside to see the bridal party cars pulling up outside the Wilson-Jones house.

'Are you ready?'

Jesy takes a deep breath and looks down at her dress as she exhales, though she can't see past the bump. 'Physically, yes. Emotionally?' She takes another deep breath. 'Absolutely.' Her lips spread into a grin. 'I can't wait to marry Ant.'

'He really is the luckiest man alive.' I haven't cried today, but now it's just the two of us in the bedroom that Jesy once shared with Rosa and Evie, with the cars waiting to whisk us to the ceremony, a bubble of overwhelming happiness rushes to the surface and I have to swallow it down very hard.

'I'm the lucky one. I'm about to marry the man I adore and in a few weeks we'll have a family of our own.' Jesy runs her hand over the satin fabric covering her bump. 'And I have the best friends a girl could wish for.'

There's that bubble of happiness again, threatening to spill over. 'Are you *trying* to make me cry?'

Jesy huffs out a fake-exasperated breath. 'Babe. Your best friend is about to get married. You *should* be in floods of tears right now. I can't actually believe your eyes are dry.'

'Do you know how long it took me to do my make-up this morning?'

Jesy tilts her head to one side for a moment before nodding. 'Fair enough.'

My phone pings with a message and my stomach drops in case it's something bad to do with the wedding: the cake has been dropped, *You've Been Framed*-style, or the best man has lost the rings, or the wedding venue has burned down. But it's only Joshua. It isn't good news, but it doesn't affect Jesy's big day. Hallie's had an accident at the playground so he's going to be late to the wedding.

'Who's that?'

I start to tap out a reply, glancing up at Jesy as my fingers move. 'It's Callum. He wants a photo of the bride-to-be.'

It's a little fib, but I don't want anything to cause even a flutter of stress for Jesy today. Her day should go as smoothly as possible.

'Are things okay with you two now then?' Jesy smooths down her dress and makes sure the loose tendrils of hair are framing her face.

'Yep. Everything's fine.' Another teeny fib but again, it's crucial to keep Jesy as relaxed as possible. She doesn't need to know that I haven't seen Callum since he dropped me off at home after the hen weekend, that I've been avoiding seeing him with excuses ranging from last-minute Christmas shopping to picking up an extra shift at work to help with the cost of the aforementioned Christmas shopping. I'm still mortified about the hot tub confession, and I need to tread carefully during the next few days, to ensure the dream scenario remains on track.

'Good, because I can't imagine you and Callum not being friends. I'd be devastated if you couldn't get past it.'

'You don't have to worry about that.' I press Jesy's bouquet into her hands. The posy is made up of hand-tied pale pink and lilac roses, sprays of tiny vibrant pink and lavender flowers, and finished off with coppery foliage. It feels wintery and festive without being in-your-face red and green.

Taking a step back, I take a photo of the beaming bride, sending it to Callum even though he hasn't asked for it.

'Shall we go down?'

Jesy nods. I take her bouquet so she can lift her skirt to walk down the stairs without tripping and we find her family squeezed into the hallway. Terence hasn't seen his daughter in bride-mode yet and he covers his mouth as she steps down the final stair. Carolina pats her husband on the back as he fights to contain himself, though she's openly weeping again. I distribute the tissues once again as we head outside for a few photos before the bridesmaids, Carolina and I slide into the waiting car. I blow a kiss to Jesy through the window as she waves us off with her dad.

The bubble of happiness fights to the surface again. Today is going to be perfect and I feel privileged to be a part of it. And one day, maybe it'll be me waving Jesy off with my mum and bridesmaids as they make their way to my wedding. I'm certain I'll finally feel that rush of love on New Year's Eve (just over a week away!) and live happily ever after with Joshua.

–

The ceremony is beautiful and romantic and everything you'd want to mark the beginning of your marriage. Callum has joked that Jesy's waters will break mid-vows, soap-style, but everything runs smoothly and there isn't so much as a twinge as Jesy and Ant say yes to a lifetime together.

Confetti is thrown and photos are taken and I keep myself busy ushering guests into position. I'm itching to pick my camera up from around my neck to snap a few shots myself, but obviously my camera isn't here with me. The bridesmaids' dresses are a shimmery copper chiffon, with a round neck and ruffled sleeves and I'm pretty sure even the most compact of cameras would spoil the effect.

So, I watch the photographer capture the day, hoping that one day that will be me, living the dream by doing something I love for a living instead of icing biscuits all day long. No matter how artistic the design, finishing off the biscuits at Brinkley's doesn't bring me the joy that I know professional photography would. I should have listened to Callum years ago when he insisted that I pursue my aspirations, but I'm there now, about to embark on a new chapter of my life in the new year with my college course. And with Joshua. I can't help smiling as I think of the bright future ahead of me.

'I can't believe our little girl is all grown up.'

I feel Callum beside me, his arm grazing mine, but I don't turn to look at him. My eyes remain fixed on the happy couple as they pose with their parents. Carolina is adjusting Terence's tie while he tries to bat her off.

'Have you ever seen her this happy?' I still refuse to look at Callum because the cringe will be painful. It's been several days since the hot tub but I'm still drowning in shame.

'There *was* that time two bags of Maltesers came out of the vending machine in the college cafeteria.'

'She *was* pretty pleased with her bonus bag of Maltesers, but that's nothing compared to now. Look at her.' I hold my hands out towards my friend as she reaches up to kiss Terence's cheek. 'She's radiant.'

'So are you. You look beautiful.'

My head starts to turn to look at Callum, but I stop before my eyes make contact. 'Even though my dress matches your hair?'

I don't see the look of mock outrage on Callum's face, but I know it's there and my lips flicker up as I picture it.

'*Because* your dress matches my hair, lady.'

I do turn to Callum now and it's okay. It's just my best friend. The boy I've known for a decade. The boy who knows everything about me, including my most embarrassing secret now. It's Callum and nothing can get in the way of our friendship, not even the silly crush of a hormonal teenager.

'Your hair *is* radiant. Brighter than the sun, some might say.'

Callum holds his arms out. 'That's me. A little ray of sunshine, sent to brighten even the gloomiest of days.' He lowers his arms again and nudges me lightly with his elbow. 'I've missed you.'

'I haven't been anywhere.' There's movement from the steps where the photos are being staged. Ant and his parents are moving aside so Jesy can have photos taken with just her parents.

'I haven't seen you in ages.'

I roll my eyes. 'It's been a few days.'

'Which is ages.'

I roll my eyes again and nudge him. 'I've been dead busy.'

'Too busy for the group chat?'

I pull my chin back and frown. 'It's Christmas in a few days. Plus, we've had the last-minute wedding prep. If you want to blame anyone, blame Jesy for getting married four days before Christmas.'

'Is that all it is?'

Jesy makes her way carefully down the steps, holding her skirt out of the way so she doesn't end up in A&E on her wedding day. Ant takes her place, standing between his new in-laws.

'That's all it is.'

'It isn't because of… you know…'

Carolina's reaching across Ant so she can smooth down Terence's jacket. He doesn't bother to bat her fussing away this time.

'I've been a busy bee. That's all.'

'So it isn't because you're still madly in love with me?'

I didn't realise I could roll my eyes so deeply that it hurts, but I do. 'I was never *madly in love* with you. I had a microscopic crush for like, five minutes and then it went away.'

Callum holds his hands up. 'I wouldn't blame you if you were madly in love with me. I'm an extremely lovable guy.'

'You're an extremely annoying guy.'

'Cute though, eh?' Callum nudges me and I try not to smile but it's hard. Damn it.

'You are quite cute. Pity about those girly knees though.'

'Why does it always come back to my knees? My *manly* knees, FYI.'

'I don't think you know what manly means. I should have bought you a dictionary for Christmas.'

'Maybe then you could have looked up the definition of cruel.'

'Or the definition of knobhead, where there'd be a picture of you.'

And just like that, we are back to being Daisy and Callum, BFFs who find great enjoyment in ribbing each other. The way we've always been and the way I hope we remain forever.

Chapter Thirty-Six

'Joshua isn't here?' Callum looks around us as people climb into cars after the photos have been taken. I'll be heading to the reception with Carolina and the bridesmaids, but I've wandered towards Callum's car as we've been chatting.

'There was an accident. Hallie fell off the climbing frame at the park, so he had to go and meet Olivia at the hospital.' Mum's been holding onto my phone for me during the ceremony so I haven't had an update yet. 'He felt guilty for missing the wedding, but his daughter has to come first.'

'Of course.' Callum touches my arm. 'I hope she's okay.'

'Me too.' I crane my neck to find Mum so I can check my phone but there's no sign of her or Dad. I stupidly hoped the A&E trip would be quick and that Joshua would dash over to the church in time for the ceremony but it didn't happen. Guilt gnaws at me because I should be thinking about poor Hallie and not myself, but it really isn't fair. First the spending-Christmas-without-my-boyfriend thing and now I'm without a plus-one for my best friend's wedding. It wasn't supposed to be like this. I was supposed to meet the man of my dreams, and everything was supposed to slot into place, fairy tale-like, yet I'm still alone, as always.

'Does this mean I get to have the first dance with you?' Callum takes my hand and twirls me, and the smile finds itself back on my face. I'm not completely alone, even if it isn't quite the same as having my boyfriend there.

'Only if it's "Gangnam Style".'

Callum cringes and covers his cheeks with his hands, squishing up his mouth. 'Did we really used to do that?'

I nod sagely. 'I'm afraid we did.' I spot Carolina waving me over from the other side of the car park. 'I'll see you at the reception then. Get practising those moves.'

The reception is being held in an old schoolhouse that has been restored and turned into a venue hall. With its original stone walls and exposed beams, the building has retained its centuries-old charm, enhanced with soft lighting and rustic furniture. Complimentary glasses of champagne are handed out as we arrive in the main hall, with a violin instrumental version of Aerosmith's 'I Don't Want To Miss a Thing' playing in the background. Jesy and Ant are welcoming their guests as they arrive, and I head over to help direct people to the cloakroom and to make sure they've got a drink in hand. I'm stashing a couple of gifts at the back of the room when I spot Mum and Dad chatting to Jesy's parents near the bar. Carolina is dabbing under her eyes with a tissue while Mum rubs her arm, nodding in understanding. Mum was a mess during Oscar's wedding, so much so that she made me tinker with the photos to get rid of her puffy eyes and red cheeks before she'd frame them.

I don't want to disturb them, but I would quite like to know if there's an update on Hallie.

'Sorry. Can I just...?' I nod towards my handbag, which is looped onto Mum's forearm, backing away once

I have my phone, leaving Carolina to sob as she recalls Tina's reading during the ceremony.

There isn't a single missed call or message, but then Joshua knows I'm at the wedding and wouldn't want to disrupt an important moment. Equally, I don't want to interrupt anything vital that's happening at the hospital and I'm not entirely sure what the rules are regarding phone use these days, so I send a message instead of calling. The reply comes as I'm directing an elderly guest to the toilets, and I wait until she's inside before reading it. I place a hand on my chest and puff out a breath as I take it in.

'Everything okay?'

I didn't see Callum arrive, but he's by my side now, a hand on my arm.

'Update on Hallie. She's hurt her arm and they're waiting for an X-ray, but it doesn't sound like anything serious.'

Callum gives my arm a squeeze. 'That's good.'

I nod and take another deep, calming breath. I can relax a bit more and celebrate Jesy's special day, and maybe Joshua will make it to the reception later.

'Shall we go to the bar?'

I lock my phone and drop it into my bag. 'Yes please.'

–

The meal is served in the adjoining dining hall, which has been dressed with oversized copper bows on the backs of the chairs and copper vases filled with lilac roses as centrepieces. Jesy and Ant have kept the top table for them and their parents only, so I'm sitting with Callum, the bridesmaids and the best man, with Tina keeping the atmosphere jovial as she works her way through the table's allocated wine.

'What time are you performing, Mike?' She winks theatrically at Callum, and I'm taken back to the hen weekend. To the hot tub and the secrets that were spilled. I push them to the back of my mind, before things get weird between me and Callum again because I feel like we've got past it, and I don't want to ruin things.

'I'm sure Stuart will join you.' Tina pats the best man on the back. 'And you'd have no trouble convincing Gabe to get his kit off.' She bumps her boyfriend with her arm. 'You could put together a little troupe. Magic Mike and The Mechanics.' She splutters out a laugh and bangs the table. 'This has to happen.'

'It absolutely isn't happening.' Callum looks at the best man for back-up, who shakes his head resolutely.

Tina's shoulders slump and she pouts at Callum. 'Spoilsport.'

After the meal, we pour back into the main hall, where more guests have started to arrive. I resume my maid of honour duties, greeting the new guests and directing them to the cloakroom to drop off their coats and accessories. There are more gifts added to the table at the back and mini crises to smooth: children sliding in their socks too close to the cake, the misplacement of Ant's great-aunt's dentures (she'd left them wrapped in a napkin in the dining hall), and a small scuffle between Jesy's cousin and her boyfriend who has been 'ogling every woman in the sodding building'. It turns out being maid of honour is proper knackering, but Jesy's having a stress-free night and that's the important part.

The cake is cut, a million photos are taken and then it's time for the bride and groom's first dance. Jesy looks beautiful, her face serene as Ant twirls her around the dancefloor to Ellie Goulding's 'How Long Will I Love

You'. I take enough photos to recreate the dance in flip-book form until a message pings. It's from Joshua. Hallie's arm, thankfully, isn't broken but she's still upset and clingy and would it be okay if he stayed with her instead of joining me at the reception? I assure him that it's absolutely fine and I'm just glad she's okay, even though I'm gutted that he won't be here to share this moment with me. Weddings are so romantic, their very purpose to showcase love, and it's the perfect opportunity for the two of us to reach the level of adoration and deep affection I felt during the dream.

But it isn't to be, and I won't let it affect my mood and so, after instructing Joshua to give Hallie a massive cuddle from me, I open the camera app and resume my flipbook pics just in time to capture the final dip as the first dance comes to an end.

A DJ is set up in the back corner and Tina grabs Anna and Evie's hands and drags them onto the dancefloor to get the party started. There's another wedding reception mini crisis when Tina's vigorous bout of jumping around threatens to jostle the contents of her stomach (mostly wine) out onto the dancefloor, but she manages to make it to the toilets in time. She's feeling much better after splashing her face with water and is currently doing shots with Evie and the best man at the bar.

My feet are on fire and I'm wondering if anyone would notice if I kicked my shoes under the gift table when John Legend's 'All of Me' makes way for 'Gangnam Style'. I turn towards the dancefloor and there's Callum, grinning as he holds out his hands, inviting me to join him. I hesitate for a second before making a dash across the room. Standing beside Callum, I cross my hands at the wrists and bounce them up and down while galloping, which isn't easy in a floor-length gown.

'Did you request this?' I have to yell over the music, and Callum nods as he starts to lasso his arm. We're doing the 'sexy lady' leg drag when Jesy joins us, one hand supporting her bump as she carries out the moves. It's even harder to dance 'Gangnam Style' when you're in a floor-length wedding gown and quite heavily pregnant, but she gives it a good go and we're all gasping and giggling by the end of it, arms draped over each other for support. The song seems to have warmed the guests up as there's a surge onto the dancefloor as 'Sweet Caroline' follows. There are arms in the air and lots of jumping around and the three of us remain on the dancefloor to join in. The bridesmaids bound over to our little group, Tina singing along at the top of her lungs in her boyfriend's face because she's absolutely tanked already, and even Mum and Dad are bopping along with Carolina and Terence.

Ant finds his bride and they link hands, waving them in the air to the beat of the music until Stuart charges over and jumps onto the groom's back. Jesy throws her head back and laughs as her brand-new husband gallops around the dancefloor with the best man on his back. I want to bottle up this moment of pure joy as we roar along to the chorus, fists punching the air, faces alight and hearts full.

Neil Diamond comes to an end, the song merging into Hall and Oates' 'You Make My Dreams Come True'. Everyone around me starts to pair off and when Callum holds his arms out and tilts his head, I concede, stepping towards him and placing my hand on his shoulder. With his hand on my waist, we link hands and start to jig along to the jaunty beat. It's cheesy but fun and my face is starting to ache as much as my feet from smiling so much, but I don't mind at all. I honestly can't remember the last time I felt this chock-full of happiness and I don't want it to end.

The brisk beat makes way for something softer, but instead of pulling apart, Callum and I remain together, swaying now instead of bouncing around. Unlinking our hands, Callum places his on my waist and I loop my arms around his shoulders, bringing us closer together. The hen weekend and its awkwardness drifts away as we rock gently side to side and I'm simply dancing with my best friend.

We continue to sway as the next song plays and the joy of the evening simmers in the pit of my stomach, almost boiling over as I rest my cheek on Callum's shoulder. I close my eyes to savour the moment and the joy bubbles, spreading up through my chest and down my arms, my fingertips tingling in a way that's either enjoyable or uncomfortable, but I'm not sure which…

Opening my eyes, I smile up at Callum, about to ask if he feels it too, this utter joy, as though we could stay here forever, in this moment and never want to leave. But the words refuse to form as my gaze fixes on Callum's lips as he returns the smile. Heat floods my chest and neck, rushing up to burn my cheeks, and I'm hyper-aware of my heartbeat as it thumps against my ribs. Dragging in a shaky breath, I drag my focus from Callum's lips and place my hands on his chest and take a step back.

'I should call Joshua. Find out what's happening with Hallie.'

I already know what's happening with Hallie, but I push through the couples on the dancefloor, sidestepping Evie as Stuart sends her into my path with a twirl that makes her giggle as she stumbles. The music fades as I step outside, my arms crossing as I instinctively rub them.

It's freezing out here, the sky inky and glittering with stars, the air sharp as I take deep, calming breaths. My heart, I realise, is galloping, as though it's still dancing to 'Gangnam Style'.

My fingers are jittery with cold as I find Joshua in my contacts and press the call button. Tucking my free hand under my armpit for warmth, I press the phone to my ear and wait for Joshua to pick up. I sink back against the wall when I hear his voice.

'Hey. Just calling to see how the patient is.'

Joshua laughs. 'She's absolutely fine. Milking it, if anything. She had ice cream *and* a handful of Roses after tea, and she's up past her bedtime watching *Bluey*. One more episode she said, half an hour ago. But I can't say no. She scared me half to death, so I'd give her pretty much anything right now.'

'I'm glad she's okay. But are you?'

Joshua puffs out a breath. 'I might be over the shock in about a decade. But yeah, I'm good. I'm sorry I missed the wedding. How's it been?'

'So much fun.' I glance back towards the doors to the hall. 'Romantic.' My fingertips tingle again, which is probably because it's so bloody cold out here.

'Everything a wedding should be. Will you bring me a piece of cake home?'

'Of course. I'll sneak a piece for Hallie too.'

Joshua laughs. 'Because she hasn't had enough junk today. But she'd love that. You're amazing. Do you know that?'

I shrug, even though Joshua can't see me. 'I'm okay, I guess.'

Joshua laughs again and I smile at the sound. 'I should go. *Bluey*'s about to finish and I'm going to try to convince Hallie to go to bed.'

'Good luck. Give her a big kiss from me and tell her she's the bravest girl.'

'Will do. Bye, Daisy.'

'Bye.'

The call ends and I push my phone into my bag. I'm zipping it up when the door to the hall opens and Callum steps out into the cold, the sound of Bruno Mars wanting to get married drifting out with him. My heart starts its 'Gangnam Style' gallop again and there's something in the air. Cold, yes, evidenced by the tremble at my core, but there's something else that's making my stomach heavy and my breath shallow. Callum looks across the car park before turning his head left and right. He raises his chin in acknowledgement when he spots me and my lips lift into a smile of greeting, warmth spreading through my body despite the cold. There's that tingly sensation again, making me buzz with anticipation and a giggle bubbles out of my mouth. The smile fades as I shove my hand over my mouth in a bid to capture the sound and my spine jerks, ramrod straight, my whole body rigid, as though it's been filled with concrete as it dawns on me what this heart-galloping, rock-heavy stomach feeling is. I feel, inexplicably and knee-quakingly, nervous.

Chapter Thirty-Seven

What on earth is there to be nervous about? It's only Callum, one of my favourite people in the world, so I force my lips to lift upwards as he approaches.

'I needed to escape.' He leans his shoulder against the wall beside me and lets the bricks take his weight. 'Tina's making eyes at me. I'm sure she's planning on stripping me against my will.'

I laugh, despite the confusion swirling in my brain. 'Pray nobody requests "You Can Leave Your Hat On" from *The Full Monty*.'

Callum tilts his head back and groans. 'I don't even have a hat to leave on. We're going to have to stay out here for the rest of the night, I'm afraid.'

'But it's freezing.'

Callum gapes at me, blinking slowly. 'What's more important? Your comfort or my dignity?'

'My comfort. Sorry, mate.' I pat Callum on the arm and set off towards the warmth of the hall, but he grabs my hand and pulls me back. My whole body flushes with warmth despite the teeth-chattering chill in the air, and I feel the flutter of nerves again, my off-the-scale heartbeat making my chest ache and my body is trembling despite the flush. I rub my arms to ward off the bite of cold and look past Callum towards the safety of the hall. I wish I was in there, bouncing up and down with my hands in the air with Jesy instead of standing out here, freezing and fearful of something I don't understand.

'You cannot leave me, Daisy Grant. I insist you stay here with me. Don't make me play the best friend card.'

There's a smile playing on Callum's lips and his eyes are lit up with amusement. He hasn't had a trim in a while so his curls are longer than usual on top, and there's a couple of strands falling over his brow. My fingers itch to reach up and sweep them away but my hand remains clamped to my chest, pressing against my thumping heart, the other still entwined in Callum's. I shake my head. This is too much. Too close. I take a step back and wriggle my hand free.

'I, er, I need to, um…' I indicate the vague direction of the hall because my eyes are still focused on Callum's half-obscured eye. He really does have beautiful eyes and I'm jolted as I recall the moment it dawned on me during his first visit home from uni, as though I'm realising all over again, seeing Callum not as my best mate but as a beautiful, stunning man.

I realise it isn't nerves that are making my stomach heavy and my heart race. And the knowledge of what I'm actually experiencing makes me want to belly laugh, because it's utterly ridiculous.

'Please don't make me go back in there.' Callum pouts, dipping his chin so he can give me full-on puppy-dog eyes and suddenly I'm not cold any more. Not at all. My cheeks are volcano-hot and surely burning bright out here in the dark like over-sized Rudolph noses. I open my mouth, but no words will form and there's nothing coherent happening in my brain anyway.

'Five minutes? Please?' Callum presses his palms together, his brows pulled down low. 'Tina will hopefully do more shots and be too wasted to pull my pants down by then.'

I nod, because I can't seem to make my legs work. My knees have turned to dessert-dry sand and will crumble if I attempt to move.

'Thank you. Here.' Callum shrugs off his jacket and drapes it over my shoulders, bringing with it the warmth from his body and a trace of his favourite Gucci scent. It's so familiar but strangely intoxicating, and I breathe it in as I pull the jacket tighter around my body. 'Do you need a hug to warm you up a bit more?'

I shake my head and shuffle backwards, my sandy knees somehow withstanding the movement. The last thing I need right now is to be closer to Callum. Dredging up my teenage crush over the hen weekend coupled with too much prosecco is making me go a bit funny and I'm in danger of doing something stupid. Something that would not only jeopardise my friendship with Callum but destroy any chance of my New Year's Eve dream coming true.

'I should have brought a bottle out with me.' Callum looks back towards the doors to the hall. 'Shall I sneak back in and grab one? Take a chance?' He wrinkles his nose. 'Better not. Tina would have my kit off before I'd made it to the bar. She's scarily determined.' He tucks his hands under his armpits and stamps his feet up and down on the ground. 'It really is cold out here. Maybe we should go inside before we turn to icicles. You'll help me fight Tina off, won't you? Defend my honour?'

Callum frowns and places a hand on my shoulder. 'Are you okay? You're being very quiet. Has your mouth frozen shut? God, I'm so sorry. I'm such a selfish plank. Let's go back inside. I'll ask the DJ to put "Gangnam Style" back on. That'll warm you up. Or "Cha Cha Slide"!'

'You hate "Cha Cha Slide".' I finally find my voice, and a tiny smile. 'You're always three steps behind everyone else.'

Callum shrugs. 'That's how long it takes me to process the instructions.'

My smile grows. 'You look like a right wally.'

'I *feel* like a right wally.'

'But you'd ask for it anyway, for me?'

'Daisy Grant.' Callum takes a step towards me and leans in so that his forehead is a whisker from mine. 'I would dance to the *Fast Food Rockers* if you needed me to, and you know how much I *detest* that cheese-fest of a song. I have never felt so passionate about anything in my entire life. My loathing for that song and its ridiculous dance routine knows no bounds and...'

I don't even feel it coming. Not really. There's a surge from deep within my gut, but I barely have the chance to acknowledge it before I'm up on my tiptoes, pressing my lips to Callum's. I don't know what I'm doing. I don't know why I'm doing it, other than the fact I've drunk a lot. I'm very, very drunk and being very, very drunk makes me very, very stupid and very, very reckless.

I expect Callum to pull away, to look at me as though I've completely lost the plot (because, let's face it, the plot is nowhere to be found at this point) but he must be as stupidly drunk as I am because instead of pushing me away, his hand is in my hair at the back of my head, the pressure pushing us closer, not further apart. His other hand is feathery on the side of my neck, his thumb on my jaw, and his tongue is in my mouth. *Callum's tongue is in my mouth*. I should be repulsed by this, but I'm not. Shocked, yes, but not in an unpleasant way. In a way that pushes me further up on my toes, that makes me reach up to hold his face in my hands, holding him in place in case he comes to his senses and tries to flee. In a way that makes my tummy flood with a flurry of butterflies, that turns my insides to liquid, as though I could melt into a puddle on the ground. I'm breathless yet energised, as though there's a massive current surging from my toes to my fingertips.

I'm confused but I can't quite care about the consequences because surely nothing else matters right now but this. This stupid, wonderful thing that shouldn't be happening, but I can't – don't want to – stop.

But I do come to my senses at the jolt of cold as Callum's jacket slips from my shoulders and pools on the ground, bringing me abruptly back to reality. The jacket tangles in my feet as I step backwards and put my fingers to my lips. What the hell are we doing? We don't do this, ever. We're best friends. Totally platonic, apart from that tiny nonsensical blip when I was a hormonal eighteen-year-old. We don't kiss on the lips. Not even a peck. Definitely not with tongues or butterflies or that other stuff that was going on downstairs that I don't want to think too carefully about.

I have a boyfriend. A boyfriend that I like very much and will, in a matter of days, be crazily in love with. Joshua and I are meant to be. It's already written, mapped out before we'd even met. I've seen it. Felt it. And I can't risk that because I'm giddy on prosecco and an overload of wedding romance.

'Sorry.' I stumble my way out of the jacket puddle. 'I shouldn't have… that was…' I shake my head, my eyes not quite reaching Callum's. 'I'm going to go back inside and find Jesy.'

I hold my hand out as I totter away, legs like jelly from too much alcohol and whatever that was just now.

Please don't follow me. Not yet. I lurch at the door and yank it open, throwing myself into the hall. I'm assaulted by Leona Lewis's 'Run', and that's exactly what I do. I run from Callum, throwing myself into maid of honour duties for the rest of the night, rounding up guests for group photos, smiling brightly in the ones I pose for myself even though my insides are in turmoil, dancing with elderly relatives and the best man (when he isn't dancing with Evie) and generally making sure everyone has a good time. I never once look at Callum, even though I know he is there, I *feel* him there, in the background, watching me.

Afterwards, once the bride and groom have headed off to the hotel they've booked for the night, I wave goodbye to guests as they leave in taxis and designated-driver cars before the clear up begins. Callum hangs back to help to tidy the hall, but I avoid looking at him as much as possible, avoid talking to him even more, and I don't think about what happened outside the hall earlier.

But later, as I crawl into bed, I can't help wondering why, if I'm supposed to be utterly in love with Joshua on New Year's Eve, if he's truly The One, have I just kissed my best friend? And why did it feel like the most perfect kiss of my life?

Chapter Thirty-Eight

Christmas Eve is magical enough, but I wake up with the knowledge that there's now only one week until New Year's Eve and my dream coming true. In seven days I will walk into Clementine's with Joshua and feel overwhelmingly in love and I'll start the year the happiest I have ever been. All the pieces are there – the dress hanging in my wardrobe, the Elton John tribute act readying for the New Year's gig, the broken watch on Joshua's wrist, and my dream man waiting to live happily ever after with me.

The Callum thing at the wedding was a blip. A test. A remnant of a teenage crush mixed with too much booze but I'm clear-headed now as I step out of the shower, all the confusion and anxiety draining away with the soap suds. I dress in a pair of jeans and my tackiest Christmas jumper and head downstairs to finish my advent calendar, pushing the chocolate reindeer out of door twenty-four and into my hand before chomping the festive treat. I'm usually a little bit sad to eat the final chocolate from the calendar, the last chocolate-for-breakfast of the year, but I have only good things to look forward to now and this simply brings me one day closer to a blissful future with the man of my dreams.

The house is empty as Mum and Dad have gone off to work but the factory shutdown has given me the opportunity for a lengthy lie-in, and the chocolate-for-breakfast reindeer is verging on a chocolate-for-lunch reindeer. There are a couple of messages on my phone: one from Joshua, letting me know he's arrived at his former in-laws', and one from Callum, letting me know he's finishing work at two o'clock and should be home by three. I feel a flutter in my stomach. Guilt and a dash of relief. It's our tradition to meet up to exchange presents the day before Christmas, because we're busy with family commitments on the actual day, and I secretly prefer Christmas Eve to its flashier kin. We eat takeaway pizza and lounge around watching Christmas films and I'm glad Callum hasn't called it off due to my unforgiveable behaviour the other night. He has every right to be miffed about what happened between us because although he kissed me back, I instigated it and I'm the one with the love-of-my-life boyfriend, so I'm relieved he's gracious enough to forget about it, to brush it off as a momentary act of pure stupidity. Maybe he was even so drunk he's forgotten it happened, which would be, bar time-machining it back and not kissing him, the best-case scenario. And maybe him being super-drunk, and therefore super-hungover, would explain why we haven't spoken since, other than obligatory messages in the group chat.

It's usually the three of us (plus any significant others) who gather for our Christmas Eve lounging about tradition, but Jesy and Ant have gone away to the Lakes for a mini honeymoon and won't be back until the day after Boxing Day, so we'll be spending Christmas Eve as a duo this year. I'm a bit nervous about spending the day with Callum after the thing at the wedding, but it wasn't really 'a thing' at all and if Callum can move past it, so can I.

So with Callum's gift bag in hand and my ear buds in place, I head over to his flat with George Michael lamenting about his heart being given cruelly away the day after he'd offered it to the one he loved, which is a sad but jaunty Christmas playlist staple. It's only a ten-minute walk away, which is quite nice on a crisp but sunny Christmas Eve with festive music playing and decorations to admire on the way.

Callum buzzes me into the building and I make my way up to his first floor flat, my stomach rolling with hesitation as I climb each step, but I'm greeted by a self-deprecating eye-roll when he opens the door and the chatter that ensues has absolutely nothing to do with 'the thing', and I'm almost bulldozed down by Frankenstein, who bashes his tail from side to side as I crouch down to receive his adoration and administer ear scritches.

'Whose dumb idea was it to go to work the day after your best friend's wedding? I should have booked two days off. Rookie mistake! I think I'm still hungover now. Still, at least it wasn't a full day. I think I'd have crumpled at my desk if I'd have stayed a minute longer. I fell asleep on the tram back home. Luckily, I was woken by a couple yelling about turkey – one of them, or both of them, had forgotten to take it out of the freezer so it probably won't be defrosted in time for Crimbo dinner. But their loss is my gain because I was nearly at my stop and I didn't miss it.'

We've moved through the hallway and into the living room during Callum's chatter and I sit carefully on the sofa, as though any sudden movement will remind him about 'the thing'. Frankenstein jumps up next to me, twirling three times before he drops down and flashes his belly at me.

'You're so lucky the factory shuts down over Christmas. What's it like not having to work on Christmas Eve?'

'Quite nice, actually. Restful.' I shrug off my coat and drape it behind me over the back of the sofa before giving Frankenstein the fuss he's demanding by flicking his paws at me. 'I didn't get up until after ten.'

Callum groans. 'Lucky. I was on the seven-thirteen tram. Still, that's me done until second of January, so shall we crack open the beer? Hair of the dog and all that?'

'Can I have a brew instead?' I don't think getting sloshed with Callum is a good idea right now. I clearly can't trust myself to not act like an utter fool.

'Seriously? You want *tea*?' Callum raises his eyebrows, but he shrugs without further comment and heads over to the kitchen. Callum's living space is open plan, so I see him take two mugs out of the cupboard after switching on the kettle, popping a teabag into each of them. So, either he doesn't want to drink alone or he doesn't trust his judgement while inebriated either. I choose to believe it's the former.

'Did you see the photo Jesy sent of the cottage by the lake?' Callum places the mugs of tea on the table and eases himself down on the opposite end of the sofa, wincing and rubbing his forehead once he's seated. He really is still feeling rough. Fingers crossed he drank enough to induce a bit of memory loss for a very specific moment that night.

'It looks like something from a Hallmark movie.' Jesy sent the photo just before I set off, showing off the wooden-beamed cottage with its gigantic Christmas tree and nutcracker-lined fireplace. 'I'm very jealous.' While Jesy has hopped into a cheesy festive film with the love of her life, I'm spending Christmas alone. Again. Because

Joshua is in Birmingham playing happy families with his ex-wife. I'm trying not to resent him for it but it's hard. This was supposed to be the perfect Christmas, and we've buggered it up between us.

'We'll rent a cottage next Christmas. An even bigger, flashier one with tartan rugs and so many festive cushions you can't even sit on the sofa.'

I smile at this thought, pushing away the thoughts of Joshua and Olivia spending the festive period together. 'Can we have fairy-light garlands snaking up the banister?'

'It makes the banister totally unfunctional and poses a safety risk but why not?'

'And the table has to be set even when we're not using it, with gold-plated chargers and a table runner and a candle-lit centrepiece.'

Callum pulls his chin back. 'Obviously.'

'And it'll be snowing so we can make snowmen and have a snowball fight before warming up in front of the roaring fire with hot chocolates.' I'm loving this fantasy. It's so much better than the reality of spending Christmas with my parents.

'Really fancy hot chocolates.' Callum reaches out to fuss Frankenstein, who's sitting between us on the sofa. 'With whipped cream and chocolate sprinkles and enough marshmallows to send us into a sugar-induced coma.'

'And then we'll make gingerbread men and decorate them.' I'm really getting into this now, envisioning the ultimate Christmas experience. I'm so glad any awkwardness I expected after 'the thing' hasn't occurred.

Callum rubs his hands together. 'And it'll be just the two of us, so we can send photos to Jesy and make *her* jealous.'

Just the two of us. In a festive cottage, throwing snow-balls (the flirtiest of winter activities) before snuggling for warmth in front of the fire. The awkwardness has arrived. Slightly late but here all the same. Did we mention snuggling earlier? Okay, now I've made it even more awkward for myself. Thank sweet baby Jesus that Callum can't read my thoughts.

Callum must feel the awkwardness too because his smile falters and he clears his throat before leaning forward to grab his tea, taking a sip even though it must be far too hot. I busy myself by fussing the dog while scrabbling around my brain for something to say to make things fun and breezy and normal again.

'So, um, how's Hallie after her tumble the other day?'

My shoulders drop as the tension eases as we move onto a safer topic. 'She's doing okay. Bandaged up but in good spirits. They've gone to her grandparents for Christmas so she's excited about that.'

'And you're really okay with Joshua spending Christmas with his ex?' Callum quirks an eyebrow. I give Frankenstein an extra-vigorous scritch behind his ears, which makes him close his eyes and tilt his head. If he was a cat, he'd be purring.

'I really am.' I really am lying, but what can I do? I can't kick up a fuss this close to our dreamy New Year's kiss.

Callum nods, though I know he isn't convinced, and he changes the subject. 'We always said we'd go to the parade in town on Christmas Eve. We never did make it.'

'We could never be arsed.'

'That's true. Better to stay in and drink... tea.' He grimaces at the mugs on the table. 'Are you sure you don't want a beer? Or wine, if you're feeling fancy? There's some rum and whisky in the cupboard. I could make Christmas cocktails?'

'What Christmas cocktail has rum and whisky in it?'

Callum shrugs. 'I was just going to throw some in a glass with a Red Bull. We'll call it a Flying Reindeer.'

'No, thanks.' I reach for my tea and take a sip. 'I don't want to spend Christmas Day with my face in the toilet.'

'Can we at least do presents then?'

I plonk my tea back down on the table. 'It's the only reason I'm here, to be honest.' I make grabby hands at him. 'Gimme.'

Callum grabs a flat, square parcel from under the tree. He ushers Frankenstein to the other end of the sofa so he can sit next to me and I tear open the paper to reveal a calendar made up of photos of me, Callum and Jesy over the years, starting with a last-day-of-college snap of the three of us for January, where Callum's hair is still wild and sticking up in every direction and my glasses are small and don't suit my face, and Jesy's grin still displays a double set of braces. I flick through the months, giggling and cringing as each image is revealed. Finally, I land on December. The photo was taken last Christmas Eve, on this sofa. Zara had taken the shot of the three of us raising our glasses in a festive toast, each wearing a garish Christmas jumper.

'The photos aren't as good as yours, obviously. Especially the earlier ones taken on my crappy old phone.'

I close the calendar and press it against my chest. 'The photos are amazing. I love it. Thank you.'

Callum bumps my arm with his. 'You're welcome. Now give me mine.' He mimics my grabby hands, and I hand the gift bag I brought with me over. Inside, there are two packages, containing matching jumpers for Callum and Frankenstein.

'You dork!' Callum holds the man-sized jumper up against his body and drapes the smaller one over Frankenstein. 'We love them, don't we, boy? We love *you*. Thank you.' Callum leans in and kisses me on the cheek and my body stiffens, as though the pause button has been pressed. If Callum notices my unease, he doesn't react to it. 'I'll go and change into mine, you wrestle Frankenstein into his and you can take a photo to send to Jesy to show her what she's missing out on in her stupidly perfect cottage by the lake.' Callum dashes off to his bedroom while I give myself a talking to with stern instructions to pull myself together.

Chapter Thirty-Nine

'Are we going to talk about it?'

The photo of the twin jumpers has been sent, we've worked our way through a large meat feast pizza, and we've watched *Home Alone* one and two and discussed what we'd do if we spent the weekend in New York. (I'd wander around Central Park and go to the top of the Empire State Building and Callum would visit the *Ghostbusters* fire station and FAO Schwarz.) Although Jesy isn't here, I know she'd head straight for the Met and the Museum of Modern Art because, like the pizza and festive films, this conversation is a Christmas Eve tradition. *Arthur Christmas* is on the screen, but Callum has yet to press play.

'Talk about what?'

I suspect I know the answer, but I have everything crossed that I'm wrong.

'The wedding. The kiss.'

'Oh. That.' I swallow hard, even though my mouth is painfully dry. 'It was nothing.'

'It wasn't nothing to me.' Callum drops his gaze as he passes the remote from one hand to the other. 'Do you love Joshua?'

I nod, even though Callum isn't looking at me. I feel a swirl of guilt in my stomach. How could I have kissed Callum when I'm supposed to be head-over-heels in love with Joshua? It's only a week until New Year's Eve, until my perfect dream comes true, and I'm ruining it.

'Do you love Joshua?' This time Callum is looking me dead in the eye as he asks the question, and I squirm under his gaze. 'Because I've realised something. When Zara called off the wedding, she said I wasn't ready to do the whole marriage and babies thing with her, and she was right. It wasn't Zara that I want all that forever stuff with — it's you.'

I pull my chin back. 'Me?'

'Yes, you.' Callum places the remote down on the table and sits down next to me on the sofa. 'Daisy Grant, I'm stupidly head-over-heels in love with you and have been for a very long time. Years. Quite possibly since that first time Jesy dragged you into the cafeteria and forced you to join our gang.'

'She didn't drag me anywhere, and she definitely didn't force me to be your friend.' I'm focusing on the wrong bit here, so I shake my head and start again. 'You were going to marry Zara. You loved Zara.'

'I did, but not in the way I love you. The way I pretend that I don't.'

It doesn't make sense. Callum wasn't in love with me. He showed no signs of feeling anything but friendship towards me. Close, tell-each-other-everything friendship, but nothing that hinted at romantic feelings.

But we didn't tell each other everything. *I* didn't tell Callum about my crush until it was accidentally prised out of me in that hot tub.

'You were my first love, Daisy.'

I shake my head. I can't believe what he's saying. 'You never said anything.'

Callum snorts. 'Why would I?' He grabs the photo calendar and flicks it open to January, to the three of us on the last day of college. 'With my massive ginger curls, I looked like Chucky from the *Rugrats*.'

'It could have been worse.' I try out a small smile and miraculously it works. 'It could have been Chucky from *Child's Play*.'

'I think that would have been cooler. Edgier.'

'Scary as hell though.'

Callum nods. 'True, but then I wouldn't have had as much dinner money nabbed at school.'

'The bullies would have been queuing up to hand over their dinner money to you.'

'I'd have made a killing.'

'Not literally, I hope.' My lips start to smile but I stop and shake my head. 'I still don't understand.'

'I guess I didn't think you'd ever look at me like that, and then you got together with Rhys.' He shrugs. 'And then I met Ellie at uni and I thought that was it, I must be over you if I was with someone else. And then I came home after uni and I knew that I wasn't. But you were with Harvey by then and clearly not into a nerdy ginger with girly knees.' He nudges my knee with his. 'I came to terms with the fact that you'd never be anything more than a friend to me and I thought I'd got you out of my system and that I didn't want anything other than friendship and then the other night…'

The other night, when we kissed. When I took my plan to live happily ever after with Joshua and screwed it up into a ball in a moment of madness. But all isn't lost. I can smooth that ball out again.

'The other night was a mistake because I'd had too much prosecco.' I can't look at Callum directly when I say this, focusing instead on the small gap between us on the sofa. 'I'm sorry Callum, but I'm meant to be with Joshua.'

'Because of a stupid dream?'

I take in a sharp breath. I know Callum hasn't been overly accepting of my quest to find the man of my dreams, even when all the pieces of the puzzle slotted perfectly together, but I'm hurt that he would be so openly disparaging.

'I'm meant to be with Joshua.' My voice is strong even though I'm wobbling inside. It doesn't matter that I felt a flurry of butterflies last night when I don't usually with Joshua, and I know that I'm choosing a slightly more rugged path with Joshua as he navigates parenthood with his ex. It isn't easy or without its flaws, but I know we are going to be so happy together and I have to focus on the way I'll feel on New Year's Eve rather than during an ill-advised drunken snog.

'I'm sorry, Callum.'

Callum shakes his head and offers me the ghost of a smile. 'Don't be. Be happy, Daisy. That's all I want for you.'

I shuffle to the edge of the sofa. 'I should go.'

'You don't have to.'

But I do.

'Merry Christmas. Thank you for the calendar. I really do love it.' I shove my feet into my boots and grab my coat, zipping it up as I make my way to the door. 'Hopefully I'll see you before, but if not, I'll see you at Clementine's on New Year's Eve.'

'I don't think I'll go.' Callum opens the front door, but I don't step out into the hall.

'But you have to.'

Callum shakes his head, a sad smile lifting the corners of his mouth. 'I'll be happy for you and Joshua in time, but right now I can't be there.'

'But you *were* there.' Panic makes my voice sound strangled. 'You and Jesy were at Clementine's and if you don't turn up, the dream won't come true.'

'Daisy.' Callum sighs. 'You feel how you feel about Joshua without the dream. You don't need it, and you don't need me there spoiling your night with this dopey love-sick face.'

'But you have to be there.' My voice is small, barely audible. Callum was there in the dream, and he's wrong. I *do* need the dream. I need all the pieces together to make it come true. I can't take the chance of it all going wrong.

'I can't. I'm sorry.' Callum opens the door wider, and I step over the threshold. 'Have a wonderful Christmas, Daisy. How about a walk in the park on New Year's Day? You can tell me all about your magical New Year's kiss.'

'Would you want to hear about it?'

Callum shrugs. 'Probably not, but you'll be bursting to tell me, and I won't trample on your joy.' He leans towards me and presses a kiss to my cheek. 'Goodbye, Daisy.' He steps back and closes the door and I walk home feeling as though someone has pulled the plug on my optimism for the future.

–

Christmas passes in a blur of wrapping paper, turkey and sprouts, the twins running wild, high on selection box consumption and the fact that a man in a red suit sneaked into their house during the night and left a mountain of new toys. Oscar looks shellshocked when he arrives and by the time they leave that evening, I totally get why.

Joshua spends the day with Hallie and Olivia, though he left me a present under the tree. I open the gift, and I'm delighted with the camera shoulder bag for when I start college in January, but what I really want is for Joshua to be here, with me, watching me open it. And I'd love to see his face when he opens the canvas print of the shot I took of Hallie jumping on the bouncy castle back in the summer, the biggest smile on her face, cheeks rosy with delight and eyes bright, hair *everywhere*.

I message Jesy to wish her the merriest of Christmases, my fingers hovering over my phone as I contemplate reaching out to Callum. Normally I'd leave messages in the group chat for them both to see but I'm not sure I can now as I don't know what's happening with me and Callum. He loves me, and not in the way he usually loves me. Not in a you're-my-best-mate way. He *love* loves me and I don't know what to do with that. How to deal with it. Are we still friends? Do we carry on as normal? I can't imagine my life without Callum in it, and what would that mean for our trio? Everything is a mess and I don't have the tools to fix it.

In the end, Callum messages the group chat in the afternoon, wishing me and Jesy a wonderful Christmas and I reply with a simple 'you too x', which makes me feel both relieved that we've communicated but also cowardly for my lukewarm effort.

On the day after Boxing Day, Joshua and I take Hallie to the pantomime, which I enjoy far more than I was expecting to, and I manage to tidy thoughts of Callum away while we shout out and sing along but the situation plays on my mind over the next few days as we inch closer to New Year's Eve. Jesy returns home from the Lakes and suggests we meet up at Clementine's for a catch up. Part of me wants to make an excuse to avoid it because I know I'll want to shrivel with discomfort when I come face to face with Callum, but another part needs to be there, to convince Callum to show up at Clementine's on New Year's Eve so the dream can play out as it should.

But Callum doesn't join us. He's spending the day with his dad and Carrie, recreating Christmas Day with the siblings he didn't spend the actual day with. As excuses go, it's more plausible than anything I could have come up with.

I don't see Callum during the days in between Christmas and New Year, and when I message him, pleading my case for him to stick to the plan and join us at Clementine's on New Year's Eve, he replies with one word that shatters my heart.

Sorry.

Callum won't be there. He's a small piece of the puzzle, but without the whole picture, will the dream come true at all?

Chapter Forty

When I pictured myself getting ready for my magical New Year's kiss, I didn't think the person looking back at me in the mirror would look so glum. I thought she'd be glowing, barely holding in the elation of knowing what lay ahead. But I'm not glowing and there's no elation to hold in because I'm not sure what lies ahead tonight without Callum being there.

My phone pings with a message from Jesy.

> Where are you??? It's after eleven! You're going to miss the big countdown and the bigger kiss!

I place my phone down without replying and look at the miserable girl in the mirror.

'We don't have to go if you don't want to.'

Joshua's lounging on my bed, feet dangling over the end, his head propped up on one hand.

'I want to.' I unzip my make-up bag and rifle through for my foundation. I'm usually a lipgloss-and-sweep-of-mascara girl but this is a special occasion. If I'm not feeling the glow from within, I need to fake it on the outside at least.

'We won't even make it by midnight at this rate so there isn't much point in going.' Joshua pushes himself up into a sitting position. 'And I'm not sure I'm in the mood for a big crowd tonight. Why don't we stay here and have a few drinks with your mum and dad?'

Because that didn't happen in the dream and if I stand any chance of living the happily ever after I saw in the dream, I have to at least show up.

'I thought you were looking forward to going to the party?'

'I was, but…' Joshua shrugs. 'Maybe we could stay in and chill? Chat about stuff.'

'We *can't* miss the party.' My eyes widen with panic. We *need* to go to Clementine's tonight. Our future happiness depends on it. 'I've been looking forward to it. Plus, we didn't get to spend Christmas together, so it'll be nice to celebrate tonight, won't it?'

'I guess.' Joshua doesn't sound too enthusiastic, but I don't have time to convince him. He'll feel it, once we're there, and we'll leave that party stupidly head-over-heels in love. With a fire lit in my belly, I throw my make-up on and change into the dress. The wrap style is flattering while the silver sequins add a bit of party glitz and I feel more like the part once I'm wearing it. With the camera pendant necklace, the dream look is complete and I'm ready to see my future, now my present, all over again.

–

There's a blast of noise as I push the door to Clementine's open, the music blaring over the chatter and laughter of the customers. The place is packed, the chaotic party atmosphere oozing and permeating every spare nook and cranny. My eyes find the stage, making sure all is as it should be and I'm relieved to see the Elton John tribute act sat in front of the piano, belting out 'Crocodile Rock' as he mimics bashing away at the keys. In front of him, people sing and dance along with him, waving balloons and flags, having the time of their lives as they bring in the new year.

I turn to the bar, straining to see past the throng. There's Jesy, perched on a stool, hand resting on the bump that isn't a shock this time. She raises her hand when she spots me and clambers off the stool, stumbling for a brief second as she lands before righting herself. My hand presses against my chest in relief but something catches on my palm. It's my necklace and I clasp the pendant between my finger and thumb.

I turn to Joshua, who's looking down at his watch. 'It's almost midnight.' His voice is muffled against the roar of the party playing out in front of us so I lean in closer so I can hear him better. 'Nearly a new year. Oh, Daisy. I'm sorry. I'm really sorry, but I'm not sure I should be here for this. I think I should be somewhere else. *With* someone else.' His face looks pained, and my heart starts to drum out a rapid beat in panic, because this doesn't sound like it's leading to a declaration of love. 'I like you, Daisy, I really do, but I think… I think I'm still in love with Olivia. We've been talking over Christmas, and I think there's something still there. I think we can have another go at being the family Hallie deserves. I'm so sorry but I need to do this. For Hallie. For me. I hope you understand?'

I pause, waiting for the grief to hit me. Joshua doesn't love me. He loves Olivia. My dream isn't about to come true, and I won't get to live happily ever after with him.

But it doesn't hit and I realise I am not really surprised. It's been staring me in the face for weeks, even if I've been too focused on this moment in time to properly acknowledge it. I should be devastated but I'm not. I feel... relieved. It's been such hard work trying to make the dream a reality, trying to force us together even though we don't seem to fit, and I didn't realise the toll it was taking until Joshua unshackled me from my self-imposed duty.

I close my eyes and let out a breath, feeling lighter as I finally face up to the facts. Joshua isn't in love with me and I can finally admit that I'm not now, nor will ever be, in love with him either. I like him, but it isn't enough. The dream isn't coming true, no matter how much I want it to, and although I'm disappointed, I can't force either of us to feel something we don't.

'Goodbye, Daisy. I'm so sorry.' Joshua stoops to kiss my cheek, his stubble scratching lightly for a second before he pulls away. As he does so, I spot someone in the crowd.

He's here. Callum is here. For me. He wants me to be happy, even if it isn't with him, and although it would break him to see me so blissfully happy, he's come here to make my dream come true and I feel something stirring in my tummy. Butterflies, but more intense, breathtaking in its force, and as it spreads through my body it makes my knees turn to jelly and my head fuzzy, just like I felt in the dream.

Callum loves me. He would do whatever it takes to make me happy, and my breath catches in my throat when I realise the dream wasn't about Joshua. It was about *Callum*, about his love for me and how he makes me feel. Safe and loved, with butterflies and a racing heart when we kiss. My dream guy wasn't a stranger with a broken watch. He's my best friend and he's been here all along.

As Joshua is swallowed up by the crowd behind us, I surge forward, battling my way towards Callum as the countdown to the new year begins. The numbers roar in my ears as I edge my way between people, my need to get to Callum overriding my manners, and I shove my way through the last few people, reaching him as the crowd erupts in cheers and whoops.

'Happy New Year, Callum.' Reaching up onto my tiptoes, I press my lips to his, the butterflies as chaotic as the partygoers around us as Callum pulls me in close. This is it, I think as I thread my fingers through Callum's curls, my heart heavy but joyful, my fingertips sparking with electricity. This is what being utterly in love feels like.

Epilogue

The New Year

The wind whips at my face, like icy hands slapping at my cheeks. It's a bitter mid-January morning and all the fluffy feelings of Christmas have left, leaving behind the misery of a British winter. But I'm not miserable, not even when it starts to rain, and I have to wrestle my hood up over my hair. Callum helps me, tucking in a few stray strands to keep them dry.

'Shall we head home?'

I shake my head and stoop to pick up the muddy tennis ball at my feet, launching it as far across the field as I can. 'A few more minutes.' We watch as Frankenstein bounds after the ball and my hand finds Callum's, my fingers tingling not from the cold but from his touch. I can't believe I ever thought Callum was *just a friend*, and apart from that teeniest weeniest of crushes when we were eighteen, that I didn't feel this way every time I was around him because it's palpable, this thing between us. The butterflies. The way my face flushes when he kisses the side of my neck. And the fact that I need to kiss him as much as possible and *pine* for him when we're not together, which isn't all that often, to be honest. It's only work, and now my college course, that's keeping us apart.

I started my course a week ago and I'm loving it. I was nervous about heading back into education, but all my fears have been unfounded. I'm getting to know new people and my passion for photography has blown up so all I think about these days is creating art and getting back to Callum and picking up where we left off the last time we were together.

Frankenstein drops his ball on the ground and I crouch beside him, indicating that Callum should do the same. I take a selfie of the three of us and even the image of him on my screen gives me a jittery, I-can't-believe-we're-together feeling. Callum is beautiful, inside and out, and I could kick myself that we wasted so much time messing around with just being friends.

But was it a waste? I got to know Callum over those years, the real Callum, not the version men often present to win you over before breaking your heart. I trust him a million per cent and he's already proven that he will do whatever it takes to make me happy.

'Come on. Let's go.' I hold my hand out and Callum takes it, Frankenstein trotting beside us. We drop him off at Callum's place before we head over to Jesy's flat. We have to side-step the travel system in the tiny hallway before we even make it to the living room, which is a happy chaos of balloons, teddy bears, piles of muslin cloths and blankets. Jesy looks tired but serene as she scoops the baby from the Moses basket in front of the window so she can present her daughter to us.

'Guys, meet Poppy.'

Jesy and Ant's daughter is three days old, and although we met her almost as soon as she was born, she didn't have a name at the hospital as Jesy was adamant that she didn't look like a Lotus. She didn't look like an Otter or a

Cricket or any of the other names Jesy had floated during her pregnancy either.

'Poppy? Isn't that, like, a really popular name?' Callum's face is bemused as he looks at Jesy. 'Didn't you want something unique, so she'd be the only one in her class at school?'

Jesy shrugs. 'That's her name, even if there's a whole reception class of Poppys when she starts school. I look at her and she's a Poppy, it's as simple as that.'

'It's a beautiful name. And you.' He gazes down at the little pink bundle, who's looking back up at him with the biggest, bluest eyes. 'Are a beautiful girl.'

Jesy beams. 'Isn't she gorgeous? I'm not being biased here but I think she is the most beautiful baby ever born.'

'Agreed.' Callum makes grabby hands. 'Now can I have a hold?'

Callum heads over to the window, chatting to the baby about the view, even though there isn't much out there apart from a stretch of motorway and a few trees and bushes.

'How are things going with you two?' Jesy joins me on the sofa while Ant puts the kettle on.

'Amazing. I thought it might be a bit weird kissing my best friend, but it isn't.'

'And the other stuff?' Jesy nudges me and raises her eyebrows. 'Is that weird or toe-curlingly good?'

I shake my head. 'No comment.'

Jesy smiles slyly. 'Toe-curlingly good then.' She isn't wrong. 'Go, Callum. I didn't know he had it in him.'

I nudge Jesy, my eyes wide as they check Callum hasn't heard, but he's oblivious as he counts the cars whizzing by with Poppy.

'And how are things at work with Joshua? Any weirdness there?'

'Not really. We work in different departments, so we rarely see each other, and when we do we say hello and chat for a bit. I guess we've found a nice neutral level as work mates. I did notice that he's wearing his wedding ring.'

'So things must be going well between him and his ex. Or his not-ex.'

I nod. 'I'm glad. I hope it works out for them, for Hallie if nothing else.'

Jesy watches Callum for a moment. Or rather, she watches the baby in his arms. The tiredness around her eyes pales as her eyes shine.

'I don't think I've ever seen you this happy.'

Jesy drags her gaze away from her daughter. 'I don't think I've ever seen *you* this happy. He's your dream man then?' She nods at Callum, who's gently rocking the baby as he murmurs a lullaby.

'Yes. He's definitely my dream man.' And I don't need to see a glimpse into the future to know that this is it, forever.

A Letter from Jennifer

Thank you so much for choosing to read *A Magical New Year's Kiss*. I loved writing Daisy's story, and I hope you enjoyed reading it just as much! If you did and would like to be the first to know about my new releases, you can subscribe to my newsletter or follow me on social media.

I'm a huge fan of romantic comedies with a sprinkling of magic and I loved the idea of having a snapshot of the future, a future that's so much brighter and happier than the life you're currently leading. A snapshot that would give you hope that there are better things within reach. This seed of an idea started to grow and Daisy's story emerged. A twenty-something singleton who has a great family and a supportive friend group but who also feels lonely at times when she sees those around her living their happily-ever-afters while she's stuck in the dating game, experiencing disaster date after disaster date until she's ready to give up.

But what if she sees a glimpse of a future where she is utterly, head-over-heels in love? Would she believe she was seeing her future? Or would she think she's having a funny turn and ignore it? But what if parts of the prophecy start to come true, little details she couldn't have predicted? Would she believe it then? And how could she ensure she gets to live out the life she's had a sneak peek of?

I wanted to write a book that is crammed full of joy, and I hope I've achieved this, not only through Daisy's romantic endeavours but also through her friendship with Jesy and Callum. Daisy deserves a happily ever after in a romantic sense, but she is also surrounded by love whether she finds her dream man or not.

I hope you loved *A Magical New Year's Kiss* and if you did I would be so grateful if you would leave a review. I always love to hear what readers thought, and it helps new readers discover my books too.

Thanks,
Jennifer

Newsletter: https:
//mailchi.mp/310b4ee4365f/jenniferjoycenewsletter
Blog: www.jenniferjoycewrites.co.uk
Instagram & TikTok: @writer_jenn
Facebook: www.facebook.com/jenniferjoycewrites

Acknowledgements

Thank you to the team at Hera, with special thanks to my editor, Jennie Ayres, who helped me to bring Daisy's story to life.

Thank you to my friends and family, who are always so supportive of my writing and books. Extra special thanks to June, Michelle and Janet, and extra *extra* special thanks to my daughters, Rianne and Isobel, and to Luna, who was the best girl.

Thank you to the book community, especially on Instagram where I spend A LOT of time. And finally, thank you to *you* the reader. By choosing my book to read you've made this writer's dream come true.